This Too Shall Burn

Cat Rector

For more information, address: catrector@gmail.com.

First printing September 2023

Edited and Proofread by Ivy L. James
Cover Art by Grace Zhu
Cover Text Design by Cat Rector
Interior Formatting and Design by Cat Rector

Further contact information for contributors can
be found at the back of the book.

ISBN 978-1-7780763-6-7 (paperback)
ISBN 978-1-7780763-8-1 (hardcover)
ISBN 978-1-7780763-7-4 (ebook)

www.catrector.com

Also By Cat Rector

This is the book that grief wrote.

May we all rise anew from the ashes of the flames that devour us.

TRIGGER WARNINGS

This book deals with many topics surrounding bad healthcare, religious trauma, and menstrual health. Trigger Warnings Include:

Endometriosis/Chronic Period Pain
Deep discussion of period health and pain
Discussions of miscarriage and other similar issues
Examination of Religious Indoctrination
Childbirth-related body trauma
Panic Attack Style Symptoms
General Violence
Horror-esque imagery
Witch burning
Human Death
Wild Animal Death
Misogyny
Neglect
Supernatural Suicide
Religious Trauma
Medical Neglect
Sexual content

PREFACE

This book is a work of fantasy fiction that attempts to look at medicine, midwifery, and religion. It draws on and is inspired by the Puritan witch hunt era, but the setting, culture, and religion are not factual in nature.

There are things that this book does aim to draw attention to. One of them is the historical duplicity, control, and fear around the spiritual and medicinal workings of women. The world's past is full of women and queer people who worked as healers and midwives. They were pillars in their communities that used their knowledge of life, plants, and the world around them to heal the sick, deliver babies, and fulfil spiritual needs. In Western Europe and Puritan America, these people were kept on the outskirts of society. Some were branded as witches and became prime targets for the witch hunt movement. While we hear most often about Salem, the witch hunt era actually spans from roughly 1450 to 1750 and resulted in an estimated 40,000 to 50,000 deaths.

Even after the witch hunts ended, the rise of the Western profession of doctors sought to push women and queer people away from healing. Systems were put in place to ensure that no one could practice healing without an education, and only men could acquire that education. The history around this is tangled. It was often considered inappropriate for a doctor to examine a woman, but with no women allowed to practice, patients would often forego asking for help. And considering that early

Western medicine believed that the uterus could migrate to other parts of the body, causing a slew of medical issues, I can see why the average woman was sceptical of doctors.

Frustrating isn't close to the word for what I've learned in the last few years.

Verity's menstrual pain is also inspired by the suffering of real-world people with a uterus. There are several diagnoses that could apply to Verity, or to someone in your life, including yourself. One such condition is endometriosis. It affects as many as 1 in 10 women, but it can take 10 years to diagnose due to a lack of public knowledge and the long history of sexism in the medical world. Symptoms are not always universal, and many are easy to sweep under the rug as normal, unconnected, or all in your head. If your period is making your life complicated or unbearable, believe your body and find a doctor who will listen when you say "I want treatment for my period pain."

Ironically, I started writing this hoping to be a voice for others, and in the process have become convinced that my chronic blistering headaches are connected to my menstrual cycle. And since I'm on the waitlist for a doctor, a list I'll be on for years, I have no one to ask.

Healthcare is rarely fair.

If you find yourself intrigued by the subject matter in the book and would like to learn more, I've included a recommended reading list at the back of the book.

This book has been written and edited in British English. Don't worry, I can spell. Usually.

Only my spellcheck knows for sure.

CHAPTER ONE

Arden

The world was full of spirits. Anyone who wished to see them, who wished to live beside and in service to them, could do so. It took work, however. Patience. Sacrifice. In return, the spirits gave generously. Food, friendship, knowledge, and even magic. But it required a person to live within the expectations of the spirits whom they served, and not everyone was cut out for such a life.

Arden lived and breathed that life, and she couldn't imagine wanting to live any other way.

The early morning sun peeked through the windows of her tiny cabin, casting rays of warm light across her bedsheets. The sunshine made her companion's skin glimmer just slightly where she was curled up on the modestly sized mattress. That sight was a magic she would never take for granted.

Ilyana still slept soundly, her body nestled up against Arden's. Breathing against Ilyana's soft brown hair, Arden recognized the wild scent of an animal's fur and the musk of autumn leaves. As it should

1

be. Ilyana was a spirit of the forest, one who protected the fauna and their balance. Often, she was one of them, prancing among the trees in whichever form she liked.

Of course she smelled like the forest.

Arden loved that about her, and she smiled for no particular reason at all, really. Simply because in that moment, everything was good.

Trailing a finger down Ilyana's arm, Arden dared to wake the spirit from her sleep. As beautiful as she was, her hair spread across the pillow, the blankets loosely draped over her stomach, Arden needed to get up at some point soon. Winter was approaching more quickly than she'd like, and she had things she had to attend to.

A long, languid exhale escaped Ilyana as she woke. Her limbs stretched and adjusted, and she settled back against Arden's body, turning her head to look her in the eyes. "Good morning."

"Good morning." Arden kissed her softly. "I hope I didn't wake you from any exciting dreams."

Ilyana turned to face Arden, entwining their ankles together. She reached up to touch Arden's hair, running her fingers through the witch's long silver tresses, a colour she'd grown into decades too young. "I was in the body of a hare, running through a field. She was very fast and I can still feel the wind on me. Feel my heart."

Placing a hand on Ilyana's breast, Arden felt the quick thump-thump against her hand. But it was Ilyana's eyes that stole her breath, so wide and dark and innocent. She had no choice but to kiss her.

Ilyana fell into the kiss, pressing against Arden and running her hands down to the witch's strong thighs. The gentle touch stole a gasp from Arden, and she felt grateful for such soft, beautiful mornings.

When Arden finally broke away to breathe and gather her wits, she placed another kiss on Ilyana's nose. "Would you like some tea?"

"Mmm, absolutely." Ilyana let Arden loose from the tangle of their limbs and watched her lover get out of bed.

The air outside the blankets was crisp. The fire in her wood stove had gone out overnight, as it usually did. The cabin was modest in size; it had room enough for a bed, a wood stove, a small table with two chairs, a set of cupboards, a working counter, and a washing basin. Everything she needed, but small enough that the fire would soon warm the space.

Arden draped her favourite old shawl over her naked body and set about placing thin strips of wood in the stove. Two on the bottom, two across those, and the middle stuffed with kindling. She carefully set a quartered log on top and pressed her thumb to her forefinger. Where the two met, a tiny flame appeared. It was the handiest magic anyone had ever gifted her, and she used it most mornings to get her stove burning.

When she peeked over, Ilyana was hugging the pillow against her chest, curled up, watching Arden's every move with soft, caring eyes.

"What?" Arden laughed, getting up from her crouch in front of the wood stove.

"Your bum is sticking out of your shawl."

Arden rolled her eyes, smiling. "You never wear clothes."

Ilyana shrugged, a smirk playing on her lips. "It's just an observation."

Warmth was already spilling out from the wood stove, and Arden was grateful for it. While autumn hadn't become unbearably chilly yet, she still found herself eager for the warmth of a fire and a cup of tea.

As Arden filled her kettle with drinking water she kept in a glass jar on her cabinets, Ilyana slipped out from under the covers.

"What do you intend to do today?" Ilyana slid her fingers over Arden's back as she passed. Her pelt was on the back of the chair where she had left it, and Ilyana slung it over her shoulder, back where it belonged. It changed colour all the time, and that day it was a soft, light brown, the same as Ilyana's hair. The spirit sat down at the table, which had been made from the trunk of an eclectically shaped tree.

With the kettle on the stovetop, Arden set to work pulling down jars of herbs and tea leaves, mixing highly personalised concoctions into two clay mugs. "The same thing I do every day, sweet thing. Get ready for winter." She let out a long breath. "And prepare to make the offering."

Ilyana nodded. "It's been some time since the last. Are the others growing restless?"

"The Gloam is always restless," Arden conceded.

The mere mention of the Gloam soured Ilyana's expression.

"I know you don't care for it." Arden really didn't feel like having that particular discussion again, but there it was.

"Even among other spirits, the Gloam is a fearful thing." Ilyana stared into the distance. "I hate that you work with it."

"So do I." Arden put back the jars of herbs one at a time, deliberately not looking Ilyana in the eyes. "If I had any other choice, I wouldn't."

"Isn't there something the others could do?" Ilyana nervously ran her hand over the wood grain patterns of the table. "Dalic, or myself, or a spirit you don't yet have a bond with?"

"The Gloam is protection, Ilyana. You know that." The kettle had started to steam, and Arden used a thick bundle of cloth to take it from the fire. She poured the water into the mugs, then set the kettle on the same burned ring on the counter that she always put it back onto. "If the village ever comes for me, I need more than a respectful relationship with the plants and animals to protect me. My mother needed it as well, and her mother before her. Working with the Gloam is the cost of being a living witch in these woods. If the village ever decided to burn me for their god, I need the power to end them all." When Arden turned to give Ilyana her tea, the spirit was staring at the ground. Setting both mugs on the table, the witch took her lover's chin in her fingers and urged her to look up. "It may never come to that."

Ilyana nodded. "Death of that scale is not in balance."

"I know." Arden kissed her forehead and then sat in the second chair, their toes close enough to touch. "It's a precaution, nothing else. Fear is a useful deterrent."

Picking up her mug, Ilyana blew on the tea for a moment. "I wish I understood these people better. Your people from away are not the same as the people of this land."

Arden nodded in solemn agreement. "Their values are far removed from each other."

"They don't understand what it means to live in balance with the world around them." Ilyana took a long drink. "They take and take. The people of *this* land know better."

That too was a conversation the two of them had had over and over and over, often at length, and so Arden let it die. They agreed with each other, and to talk further was to mourn what neither of them could do anything about. Instead, they sat in the quickly warming cabin, their ankles entangled, and drank their tea in each other's quiet company.

When both their cups were empty, Ilyana stood to leave. She leaned down to kiss Arden. The brush of her lips made the witch's heart skip a beat. The gratitude she held in those moments was more than she could ever put words to.

"I'll see you soon, yes?" Arden breathed against her lips.

"Of course." Ilyana brushed Arden's cheek with her finger, adjusted the pelt hanging over her shoulder, and turned toward the cabin door. As she walked, that morning's animal manifestation made itself known: a hare's tail had grown just above her bum, a soft, fluffy brown point that twitched as she moved.

Arden grinned as her lover left. She never knew which beast the spirit would take on the traits of, and a hare was always preferable to a snapping turtle.

The cool fall morning air was proving good for Arden. She'd thrown on a pair of loose trousers and gone out bare-chested to face the chill of the forest. The cold on her skin had woken her up right away.

After gobbling down a breakfast of fresh fruit and deer jerky, she got right to work. She hoped the movement would drive the chill out of her body until the sun warmed even the underbrush. Among other things, wood needed chopping. Her cabin wouldn't heat itself through the winter.

She'd gotten through almost half the pile and was mid-swing when a young woman stumbled into view from between the trees. Arden put down her axe and waited for whatever would happen next. Visitors were few and far between, and when they did show up, it usually meant trouble.

At first glance, the young woman looked about sixteen. Twenty at most. A girl to Arden, but a woman to most. If she was from the village, she'd probably be married with a child or two. Clothed in a long-sleeved grey dress and lacking a cloak, she was arguably underdressed for the weather. As she stumbled closer, Arden saw the blood.

The stranger's hand was clasped on her upper arm, red dripping liberally from between her fingers. She had nothing with her; no weapon, no pack, and clearly no sense. The woman's dark brown hair had fallen over her eyes. She pressed forward, bumping into a tree and veering away. Dizzy, by the look of it. Perhaps from loss of blood, by how dark her sleeve was. The fool hadn't tied off the wound.

Arden wiped the sweat of hard labour from her brow and cleaned her hands on her trousers. She had a choice to make: save her as she had saved so many of the women from that village, or give the woman's body to the Gloam. It was nearly time to make a sacrifice anyway, and that *would* save her the efforts of going hunting.

Arden consistently walked a fine line between her spite and her duty. Her mother had been vastly more generous than Arden had ever been. Both of them had pledged to use their magics and their knowledge to care for the people who came to them looking for help, and yet Arden's heart had blackened. The village had done damage to them both, and to everyone inside it. How generous was she expected to feel?

Arrothburg burned witches, and someday, they'd burn her.

The thought curdled the kindness in Arden's heart. If this woman had stumbled onto Arden's land with a determination to die, she might as well take advantage of it.

Arden approached the young woman slowly. It wouldn't do any good to spook her, and she barely seemed aware of where she was. A snap sounded, a stick breaking under Arden's boot. The other woman looked up, lethargic fear spreading across her face. The woman's weary eyes wandered down, trained directly on Arden's bare breasts. The villager paused. Stilled. Her hand stopped cupping the wound and fell against her side. Wobbling a bit, the woman's knees turned to jelly and she promptly passed out on the forest floor.

Sighing in frustration, Arden walked over to her. "You could have at least come closer to the house." She knelt to take a look. A person had to make sure the woman wasn't infected with anything. Rabies. One never knew when the locals would come down with rabies. But there didn't seem to be anything wrong with her apart from the nasty gash on her arm. She was still bleeding enough to be worrisome, but that hardly mattered if Arden intended to let her die one way or the other.

Arden's back cracked as she straightened out. If she summoned the Gloam to dinner where the woman was already lying, there'd be gore all across her camp until she had the stomach to clean it up. The Gloam was a very messy eater. It was best that she moved the body, which meant she'd have to drag her by the ankles. Already tired from cutting wood, Arden slowly bent over and grabbed the woman by her bare calf.

Pain lanced up Arden's arm the moment she made contact with the woman's skin. She hissed and drew her hand back. The skin on her fingertips was charred and when she looked down, the villager's leg was glowing white.

"Well, aren't you special," Arden hissed, curious but in more pain than she wanted to admit.

"What is she?" The voice came from over her shoulder.

Arden looked up. Dalic had crept up behind her, which seemed a near-impossible feat, given that she was made of thick, creaking wood.

The tree spirit bent over the woman from the village, curious. Willow leaves framed Dalic's face, dripping down over her shoulders instead of hair. An entire ecosystem of creatures lived in the spirit's hair, including a field mouse named Mouse, who was perched on the crown of Dalic's head. The tree spirit seemed small that day. Person-sized and somewhat person-shaped. Each of her limbs was made of tangled roots and branches that creaked when she moved. The scent of wet earth and apple blossoms wafted off her.

"She looks human." Arden stretched her fingers, ripped a piece from her own well-worn trousers, and—carefully avoiding touching the woman—wrapped it around her arm above the wound. She pulled it tight. The woman moaned but didn't wake.

Dalic squatted down and peered close to the woman's face. "She smells strange."

"It's soap, Dalic. We talked about this."

"Why are you being so careful with her?"

Arden held up her scorched fingers. "Because most people don't burn me when I touch them."

Arden pulled the stranger by her boots toward the cabin. She never roused, all dead weight from start to finish. Once she was through the door, Arden took a moment to wipe the sweat from her brow and glare at Dalic. "At least help me get her onto the bed."

Dalic nodded and grabbed the woman by her shoulders, the two of them heaving her up onto the covers.

Without needing to be asked, Dalic started gathering some of the forest herbs that Arden kept in pouches above the washbasin. Arden dragged a chair and side table to the bed and set to work mixing and grinding the right combination of herbs. Dalic offered up a drop of water from the pitcher, and Arden mixed it in, everything coming to a sticky poultice.

"And one last thing." Arden reached for a long silver tool that she kept tucked into her hair. It was almost like a needle, if one squinted. She pressed it into the tip of her finger and a drop of blood welled up. It dripped into the poultice and she gave the mixture another stir. A drop of life to keep the girl living.

Leaning over her, Arden scooped out the sticky brown poultice. Trying not to touch her, Arden flicked a glob of the poultice onto her skin and just hoped it stuck. It landed near the wound and she spread it with the pestle.

The herbs began to smoke.

"Arden, that's not—"

"I know it's not normal, Dalic. What am I, a fledgling?" Though she didn't want to admit it, Arden was growing flustered. She was good at what she did, but that was a matter of practice. *This* she had never seen before.

The poultice caught fire.

Panicked, Arden smothered the flame with the pestle and pushed the poultice off the woman's skin. Some lingered, sizzling, but the wound was closed tight, as if it had cauterised the wound, which had *not* been the point of the poultice *at all*. What was the woman made of?

"Do you think she's evil?" Dalic took a step away from the bed, her wood-scaley hands clasped over her chest.

"That depends on your definition of evil. She's likely just a girl." But there was no denying she was *something* more than that. Arden reflexively put her hand out to check the woman's pulse but stopped herself. "If I could touch her, I could get a better idea of her condition…"

Dalic tilted her head, something in her neck cracking like a twig. Mouse clambered down to her ear and let out a series of squeaks. Dalic nodded, seeming to understand Mouse's meaning. She extended her hand and Mouse crept down, hopping onto the strangely dangerous body of the villager. It scrambled to her chest and pressed its ear to her heart, then ran to pry open the woman's lips. The woman's breath ruffled Mouse's fur, and it squeaked again, scampering down to the wound on the woman's arm. Pushing the still-smoking scraps of poultice off the skin, Mouse took a closer look at the wound itself. The flesh seemed closed.

Mouse sat up and let out a singsong series of peeps.

Dalic reached out and Mouse hopped back onto her arm, then up to her ear. She listened as the mouse chirped on further, then turned to Arden. "Mouse says the cut doesn't smell like infection and her heart sounds like a human heart."

"That's something," Arden sighed. "Have you heard of anything like this? From the other spirits maybe?"

Dalic shook her head. "Never. Perhaps she can tell you when she wakes up."

Joy of all joys.

Once the woman woke up, the real trouble would begin. Forget that Arden didn't know why the woman's skin burnt hers. This unconscious thing would wake up with a very pious attitude about being under the care of a witch, and the burning threats would begin.

This was not Arden's first time.

Someone desperate was one thing. They were willing to go against their community and their god and their religion to save their own life, or someone else's.

They were rarely so generous when they were treated against their will.

The people who lived on the other side of the trees had burned a lot of people they called witches. They had tried to burn her mother once, and they'd been trying to force Arden's family out of the woods since her great-grandmother arrived from across the ocean.

Yes, this woman waking up was going to be *wonderful*. A nice, scared, pious holy woman for company.

CHAPTER TWO

Verity

Verity was used to waking up with pain. She was used to her body betraying her, harming her, keeping her up at night. But this time, when she woke, it was different from the myriad other ways she normally felt like death.

Deep, groggy sleep numbed every one of her muscles. Underneath throbbed a subtle pain that grew more urgent by the second. Her arm felt raw and sore on the inside, the way it normally did after churning butter all day, but much, much worse. All that, and her mind was shrivelled like a piece of dried fruit.

Verity's vision was hazy and she couldn't quite recall what had happened before she was sleeping. The mattress beneath her was softer than her own. It felt strange and foreign. The ceiling wasn't her ceiling. The bed wasn't her bed.

Something moved and her eyes darted toward it. A blurred shape—a person. She moved to rub her eye and hissed in pain. The muscles in her arm were angry and biting, forcing her to lay it back down.

A chair scraped as someone got up and came closer. Verity blinked away the sleep and the shape became horrifically clear. Long, silver-white hair framing a sharp face and silver, evil eyes.

"Witch!" Verity threw herself out of bed and onto the floor. God help her, she was going to die. Her heart pounded against her ribs as she scrabbled across the old wood floor. Her head spun and she could only use one arm but she had to get up. The witch—she was going to eat her alive—

The witch groaned. "If you don't stop that, you're going to rip your arm open again. Will you please lie the fuck down?"

No! No, she would not lie down—she was not just going to give up, just *agree* to stop living. She scrambled toward the door on all fours, her arm screaming with the movement. The witch was going to peel off Verity's skin and boil it in a stew and use her insides to decorate the rafters, that wasn't how she was going to die; she had been a good, God-fearing woman and this was not how she ended; she just needed to get a little closer to the door—

The witch blew a fine powder into Verity's face and the world went black.

Verity's head hurt twice as much the second time she woke up. She let out a low groan.

"Serves you right," the witch said. "I save your life and you act like I'm some kind of deadly harpy. Ungrateful shit. Is that what they teach you in that church of yours? To serve your god by loving and cherishing and being an asshole?"

Verity's mouth was so dry she could barely speak. The witch rolled her eyes and held out a cup of water. Verity tilted her head and took a drink. She didn't trust it, but her mouth tasted like copper and she was so very thirsty. Not to mention the dull pulse in her skull. She just wanted to feel better, and surely some water would help with that.

After the witch took the cup and set it on the table beside the bed, Verity cleared her throat. "Are you going to kill me?"

The witch had her back turned to her, working on something she couldn't see. She turned her head to give Verity a sidelong stare. "I was going to *let* you die on my land, but then you got interesting." She walked over to the bed with a mortar in one hand and bandages in the other. "Remove the cloth on your arm."

Verity glared at her for a minute, but the witch just glared back, so she used her good hand to peel away the cream-white linen bandage. Underneath was a messy, burned patch of skin surrounding a scarred line that had seared shut. It was ghastly. "What did you do to me?"

"What did I do?" the witch asked incredulously. "You wandered onto my land, bleeding out, and you want to know what *I* did? What about you? How the fuck did you end up here half-dead?"

Verity swallowed hard. It was bad enough she'd gotten turned around in the forest, but the rest was so much more embarrassing. "I was hunting. I'm not that good at it, but I sometimes have to be. There was a fox in a snare and when I tried to release the snare wire, it whipped up and I fell on my knife and…then I got turned around, I suppose."

The witch looked like she was a moment away from bursting into laughter, her lips pursed and her eyes wide.

"That's not very friendly," Verity mumbled.

The witch smirked. "An astute observation. Now put this fresh poultice on the wound, spread it out, and bandage it back up. It'll help with the burn. I hope."

Despite being put off by the phrase *I hope,* Verity did as she was told, her eyes darting back to the witch every few seconds. She couldn't shake the feeling that the woman was going to do something. Even though the village wasn't that far a walk from the witch's land, Verity had never seen the woman before. She'd heard about her though. How she drank the blood of toads and flew with the ravens and gave her body to dark forces in return for their evil blessings. The pastor talked about it every third day at church, usually when he ran out of things to chide the village for.

When Verity was finished applying the poultice, the witch tapped a finger on the table. Verity set the empty bowl and old bandage down. Without thinking, she tried to put weight on both her hands to help her sit up, and her injured arm flashed pain down to her palm. She hissed and took the weight off it, managing to sit up against the wood wall. And then they were looking at each other, the witch leaning her elbows on her knees.

"What are you?" The witch narrowed her eyes, looking Verity over.

"I'm…a woman?" Verity wasn't sure what she wanted to know, but the witch was looking at her expectantly, so she kept going. "I'm Verity and I live in the village. Seventeen years old. Still unmarried. Umm…bad at hunting? Can I please go home?"

"Maybe. But that's not what I meant and you know it. *What* are you?" Her expression seemed impatient.

Verity was tripping over herself for the right answer. She just wanted to leave before she *really* made the witch angry. "I'm nothing. I don't have a trade or a husband. My mother is dead and my father is tired and I just look after my siblings. I go to the market and to church and I shouldn't *be* here. I'm not a wife or a doctor or a merchant. I'm nothing important to you, I promise. I'm just scared." She shrugged, her confidence wilting. "I don't know what you want me to say."

The witch held a hand out and the sudden movement made Verity jump. The tips of the witch's fingers were scorched black.

"When I touched you, this happened. Got a shock through my whole arm. I've spent a lot of time touching some otherworldly shit but this is a first. Why do you burn my skin?"

Clearly, the witch was out of her mind. "You're mistaken, I'm sorry—"

"Oh, for fuck's sake—" She touched the skin on Verity's ankle and it sparked like flint on wood. They both jumped, and heat burned up Verity's leg, the skin glowing white. The witch was holding her wrist, staring daggers at her. "So. Try again."

Verity's eyes widened, terror rushing through her. "What was that? What was—? I swear I've never—I'm not a demon or something evil. I'm a good, honest girl. I don't have any magic. Please, don't hurt me again."

The witch stretched her neck, breathing deeply and clearly very annoyed. "You're telling me you've never, ever noticed something unusual about yourself. Not once?"

"No, ma'am, not until just now." Verity stilled the quiver of her lip. "It can't be me. I can't be possessed."

The witch got up, taking the chair with her and placing it back at the table. "If a spirit had possessed you, I'd know. All my best friends are spirits. You're something else."

"I don't want to be something else." Verity wriggled herself forward until her booted feet touched the floor. "Are you sure you didn't make that happen?"

"Who's the professional here? Me, I am. And I'm sure." She tapped her fingers on her chin. "Well, short of cutting you open and taking a look around, I'm not sure what else I can do. I can consult someone, but not now. And when you don't show up for supper, your gaggle of God-fearers will think of me first and foremost. I don't need them on my doorstep looking for you." She kept tapping, like she was thinking.

"Shouldn't I stay though? How much blood did I lose? It was a long walk here…"

She waved a hand, still staring into space. "You'll be fine. The first poultice has life restoration properties—"

Verity's breath caught. "You used witchcraft on me?"

The witch groaned. "It was a drop of blood and a bunch of herbs. Please remain calm, Dandelion."

Blood. She had witch blood on her. In her. What in the name of the Lord—? Verity dropped to her knees. "Heavenly Father, protect me from the blasphemous rites of this witch and the things she has done to taint me—"

"Nope, that's it." The witch snapped out of her bored gaze and grabbed Verity by the shirt sleeve. "You're going home before you *really* need your heavenly father to step in."

As she was hauled bodily across the cabin, Verity wobbled on her feet. Oddly, her body held up well enough for someone who had *deeply* sliced herself open with her own knife. Witchcraft must truly be powerful.

The witch hurried her to the door and pushed her out. "Don't come back unless you have answers for me."

Verity turned to look at the witch, her hand over her bandaged wound. "Aren't you afraid I'll tell the others?"

"Tell them what? That you came into contact with the devilish witch of the woods? I think your sense of self-preservation is better than that. They'd burn you right next to me just for fun. And believe me, if you bring an army of them back here, you'll have started a war I'll win. Everyone you love will die and I'll finally be left in peace."

The witch's speech turned Verity's blood cold. After all the stories she'd heard, Verity didn't doubt the woman could do everything she'd said. As for the rest…people had gone to the witch for help in the past and been caught by the town. Every one of them had burned.

Accomplices were witches too, in the eyes of the church.

The witch put her arms over her chest and took a breath. "*You* may need an excuse though."

"What do I tell them?"

The witch sighed, as if she was dealing with a toddler and not a fully capable woman of God. She bent down and pressed her palm to the earth, humming low and rhythmic. Verity didn't say anything, didn't dare interrupt her. She wasn't even sure she wanted to know what the witch was doing.

After a few minutes, a beady-eyed rabbit hopped out from around the back side of the witch's cabin and bounced toward them.

The witch stopped humming and held out her hand to the rabbit. It came close and she crouched down, lifting it into her lap, patting its head and hushing it. She whispered into its skin, just loud enough for Verity to hear.

"I take what is freely given and thank you for your sacrifice."

The rabbit trembled under her, but didn't try to get away. A spell. It had to have been. The witch held tight, reaching behind her for something. A large wooden bowl.

Quicker than Verity could react, the witch had drawn a knife across the rabbit's throat. She held its writhing body with one arm, the bowl in her other hand. The blood gushed into the bowl, filling up quickly, and the rabbit stopped fighting, slumping over in her grasp.

Verity felt sick to her stomach. It wasn't the blood; she'd killed plenty of animals to feed her family, and she dealt with her own bleeding each month. Blood was a part of life. No, it was the magic, the ritual of it. She swallowed the bile that had come up, not willing to risk any ire from the witch. Her mind raced with questions. Why keep the blood? Was she going to curse Verity? Set her on fire? Make her forget her name and her family and wander the woods forever? She couldn't control her heart, her breathing quickening, the fear washing over her completely.

The witch put the bowl down carefully and stood, the rabbit cradled in her arms. She stepped toward Verity.

Verity gasped and backed away. "I don't want to die or become a frog or—or—" Her voice was more of a whimper than she wanted to admit.

"Shockingly I am *still* not planning to kill you. Anymore." The witch held the rabbit out to Verity, who eventually reached out with shaking hands to take it. "Now you have something to show for your hunting. You bring home food and no one asks a single question other than *how could you, a clumsy little girl of all people, actually catch a rabbit?*" She paused. "You know what? Maybe this is too much to believe after all."

"I've caught things before," Verity protested, the rabbit cradled in her arms. She stared at the witch, feeling a little odd. This horrific woman of legend had taken her in, healed her wounds, and given her a story to protect herself with, when she should probably just be dead.

It was a lot to contend with.

"Thank you, I guess. For all of that."

The witch rolled her eyes. "Thank me by getting the fuck off my land."

CHAPTER THREE

Verity

Verity clutched the body of the rabbit tight to her chest as she walked between the trees on her way back to Arrothburg. The guilt was running rampant through every inch of her body. She had sinned, she had spoken with the witch, and something deeply ungodly was happening under her skin.

Verity's lungs felt tight. Every breath she drew was laboured. She was approaching the edge of the village, and she was sure anyone who looked at her would know what she had done. Any good soul would run to tell the pastor and she would surely burn. Verity knew all too well how small an offence could lead to being branded a witch, and though she hoped she was a godly enough woman, she'd harboured doubts in her heart since she was a girl.

Perhaps they would see that on her face as well.

When the trees ended, Verity bade herself to take a deep breath. She drew a thin smile on her face and stepped back into the village.

Arrothburg was a fairly large town, or so Verity had heard it told. She'd never been anywhere else, so she didn't really know for sure how large it was. It housed people she knew well and people she'd never spoken to beyond a passing hello. It was large enough to have a town centre, and for it to take time to walk from one side to the other. Where she was, far from the middle of town, most of the homes were quaint and surrounded by land for cattle or farming. The people she knew well were in those homes, as was her family. The ones with money and luck—and perhaps God's favour—lived closer to the church and the market, and Verity had no business with them.

She passed several homes, drawing shallow, frightened breaths. Each one was as familiar to her as the palm of her hand. Built of wood and will, some had one floor and others had two. Many had a barn or a shed to go with them, because even if there were no cattle or tools, every home with a woman in it needed a place to keep them for a week every month.

A shape rounded the corner as Verity walked down the trodden dirt road. She started. The shape was only Mrs Fairweather, but she was a gossip and something to fear indeed. Verity kept walking, keeping her head bowed in deference and giving the woman a friendly greeting as she passed.

Mrs Fairweather said nothing, which was well enough. Normal, in fact. Verity sometimes bristled at the way some of the village looked down on her family, but she was thankful for it at that moment. She didn't want anyone looking too closely at her.

Verity followed the path where Mrs Fairweather had just come from, and her family home came into view. It was a small home on a large plot of farmland, and she was grateful for it, most of all because anything larger would be hard for her to keep tidy, a job that seemed already to take up all her time. The house itself had a living space and a kitchen downstairs, with three tiny rooms above it, and that was plenty.

A small wooden fence circled the property, a second barrier of defence for the half-dozen goats they kept for milk and occasionally for meat. The goats lived in the barn when they weren't outside, and Verity had spent enough nights sleeping in the barn loft to know them all by every speck of their colouring. They were in the small pasture as she approached, gnawing away at the grass. Behind them was the deep, seemingly endless sea of barley. Her father's harvesting had removed several feet of it, but three times as much waited for him to finish. He was still out there, a tiny speck in the distance, his scythe glinting in the sun as he swung it.

And thank God he *was* still out there. Perhaps Verity could still get through this evening unscathed.

A high-pitched squeal sounded the moment Verity rounded the fence outside her family's house. Clarabel had spotted her and was bounding toward her with the strides of a bolting doe.

Her younger sister was a compact little thing, with all her looks from their father's side of the family: hair so blonde it was nearly straw and a strong-framed, stout body. She was only seven years old but she could already beat her brother at every game he challenged her to. This was partly due to her strong stature, and partly because Clarabel wanted it more.

"Careful, careful!" Verity came to a halt just as Clarabel ran into her, wrapping her arms around Verity's waist. Verity was steadier on her feet than when she had first left the witch's cabin, but she wouldn't be able to stand up to any roughhousing.

"You were gone too long! I'm hungry!" Clarabel eyed the rabbit in Verity's arms.

Verity laughed. "Well, there's no eating until the work is done!"

Clarabel released her, bouncing on the balls of her feet. "Can I help?"

"Of course." In all honesty, Verity would be glad for the help. She was tired down to the bone and trying not to show it. "Do you remember what you did last time?"

"I think so," she answered, and began rattling off the steps of preparing a rabbit.

The two of them started toward the back of the house. Verity only had the one good arm to hold the rabbit, and it had started to go numb. A small, out-of-the-way work shed sat in the back, needing about a half-dozen repairs that no one ever seemed to have time for.

Clarabel held the door open and Verity ducked inside, setting the rabbit on the work table. Drops of blood had soaked through her clothing and dried. Both her arms ached, and she felt altogether grimy, including her witch-tainted soul.

Verity was going to need a hot wash later.

Clarabel pushed a tall wooden stool over to the shelves with a scrape and climbed it, selecting a pair of sharp skinning knives. She climbed back down and handed one to Verity, handle first.

"Where's your brother?" Verity waited as her sister repositioned her stool next to the table.

"He went to the market. The travelling merchant was in town again."

"Did he leave the chores for me again?"

She laughed. "Does a bear shit in the woods?"

Verity hushed her. "Clarabel! Don't let God hear you speaking like that, or anyone else. Just because Father can say it doesn't mean you can." But Verity was smiling too broadly for Clarabel to take the scolding seriously. *She* found it amusing, even if no one else did.

Verity let her sister guide her through the steps of skinning and carving up the rabbit. Naturally, Clarabel made a misstep or two, but she was still young and that was to be expected. Verity herself was a lousy hunter, but she was good at what came after, mostly because a carcass didn't move around when she used a knife on it.

They'd just finished up when their brother came strutting into the yard. Asher had a large canvas sack of something slung over his shoulder, and Verity shuddered at the thought of how much it must have cost.

Asher took after their mother, the same as Verity did. At thirteen, Asher had been growing like a beanstalk. Stubble dotted his face and his brown hair was short-cropped. Some of the girls his age had started to gawk at him, and though Verity hated to imagine him in that light, he was speedily becoming a handsome young man.

Verity wiped her bloody hands on a rag and walked out to meet him. "Good day at the market?"

Asher gave a sly nod and set the sack down beside him. "I think I'm getting very good at this bartering thing. I got us an entire sack of apples in exchange for a little coin and an introduction to the widow Madeline."

"Asher, that's hardly appropriate, messing in the affairs of others." Verity had enough trouble on her hands without the town thinking Asher a sinful wretch. She couldn't keep both her siblings godly all the time.

Asher shrugged. "The merchant mentioned being keen on the woman for years and now she's a widow. Who knows, they could be married by this time next year, travelling the world on his little wagon!"

Sighing, Verity gave up. She did wish he'd save his meddling for later in life, *after* he was married and living elsewhere.

"What's this talk of marriage?" a voice called from behind her.

Jona, their father, had come in from the field. He was a mess of sweat and straw, as ready for a wash as anyone she'd ever seen. His face, lined with wrinkles and dark from a summer in the field, looked tired. God's honest truth was that he'd spent the last six years looking tired, and all his worry lines had deepened in that time. It was a hard lot, trying to carry the house alone, and no matter how much Verity took on her own shoulders, her father still walked around with bags under his eyes and a false smile on his face.

When she looked at him, she wondered if anything she did would ever be enough.

She had been enough for her mother, but her mother was dead

and burned and no one spoke of those times anymore.

"Asher was meddling again and—"

"What happened to your dress?" Her father was scowling, reaching up to touch Verity's closed wound.

"It's nothing." She did her best not to flinch. Verity had learned a little about lying. She was a woman, after all, and being a woman meant a great deal of hiding. "I tore it while I was hunting and managed to get it dirty. I can sew it closed."

"You'd best," Jona grumbled. "We don't have coin to replace it until after harvest."

"I know." Verity gestured to the shed where Clarabel had removed the hide of the rabbit and had started on the meat. "We have dinner, though."

Jona moved past Verity and turned his attention to Clarabel. "I don't like you using those knives. They're sharp, child. Give them here."

Clarabel did as she was told, pouting. "I wanted to help."

"And you have, but you're still young. You're going to be hurt." Jona's expression was hard to read. "Asher, take your sister inside and start a fire for soup. Verity and I will finish up here. We need to talk first."

Verity waited, fingers interlaced in front of her as Clarabel and Asher made their way to the house. She watched in silence as her father started cutting away at the meat. She knew better than to push her father to do anything.

After the others were tucked inside the house, he finally spoke. "You just finished with this? You came home late, then." His father set to work picking away the undesirable pieces of the hide.

"It took longer than I'd anticipated."

"It was nearly all day. If I'd gone myself, I'd have been home before noon."

"Father, please. Animals don't just come when they're called." The irony of the statement hit Verity and she changed her tactic. "I'm not the best trapper, but I can do it."

"I'm not saying you can't. But things need to be efficient around here. I can't work alone in the fields six days a week if you can't handle this share of things."

Verity sighed. She'd been over this a thousand times, and she was more than a little tired of swallowing the words *it was never my share to handle.* "I can work the fields instead, if that's what you want."

Jona shook his head. "You know that's not possible. You're lying about for nearly a week a month and things still need doing in that time, including the fields. I just need you to promise me you can take care of this. Your brother is trying to make a better life than this one and get away from this family curse, and your sister is too young to take on as much as she does. You can't rely on her—"

"I don't." Verity took a deep breath, trying not to get angry. She knew her father's impatience wasn't about her; it was about a hundred other things and the hardship of those things. "Clarabel wants to learn, Father. Should I tell her no? She'll be expected to do these things someday for her husband."

"She's seven. She's not married yet," her father snapped. "Clarabel shouldn't be burdened with that already."

"It takes time, Father." Verity's voice turned sombre. "I was four years older than her when you asked me to be responsible for this home and my siblings. Thank God I had known how."

Jona's hand stilled. His chest moved with the slow in and out of breath, and he stared at the table for a long moment. Verity knew what it was like, getting caught in the past. Having it wash over you and leave you struggling to return.

At last, he tapped his knuckles on the table, leaning on it like it was the only thing keeping him up. "You're right. I cannot protect Clarabel from her responsibilities." He looked up, his brow furrowed. "But you must learn to mind your tongue. Your husband will not tolerate your large opinions the way I do."

A bitter smile quirked up Verity's lips. "By the time Clarabel is married, I will be too old for a husband. I'll have other worries." She didn't let him reply to that, but moved to take the knife from his hand. "Why don't you go out to the barn and pretend you're working. A few minutes' sleep would do you good."

"After this," her father said, his voice distant, his hand refusing to give up the knife.

She knew he wouldn't.

Verity woke early the next day, like she did nearly every day. It was the only time the house was quiet. She stole out to the space behind the shed with a bowl and a cloth, and set to work washing herself. It was a small thing, a little ritual, but she liked it. The crisp morning air caressing the drips of water still on her skin, the trill of birds waking up, the small sounds of the town coming alive. She would soon lose it to the cold of winter, and she wanted to savour the last days of it.

Besides, it was the time of day she felt closest to God.

She did her best to love Him. And sometimes it was hard. Sometimes she was so very sure God was right beside her, hand on her shoulder, guiding her way. She felt Him when she provided for her family, when she knew her siblings had food and shelter and a future. And other times Verity was desperately sure God abandoned them. If not all of her family, certainly her. What God would place such a burden on her shoulders?

Verity had had plans for her life, once.

Now her family was her plan.

Her mother had burned as a witch only six years before, but it felt like a lifetime. Rather than remarry, her father had asked Verity to be of service to the house. It would only be a few short years, he had said. Clarabel had been a baby, and someone had needed to raise her while Jona kept a roof over their heads. Asher was too young and a boy besides, and things would get better in time. Except they hadn't. She hadn't realised what it would cost her, and Verity was so tired.

Tired of the work, and the children who were not hers, and the sleepless nights, and of the pain. Every single month, the pain.

It had started before their mother had died. In bittersweet memories, she saw herself curling up in the loft of the barn with her mother, crying into her mother's skirts. Verity had had her bleeding for uncomfortable years before the pain started. It had come suddenly and violently, two days before her moon cycle, and it kept on, roiling in her stomach until she couldn't bear to be awake.

Seven years, and every month was the same.

She knew by the fading sliver of moon in the dawn sky that it was nearly time again.

It had never been easy to bear, but it was harder now, with her mother gone. There was no one left to believe her. Her father wouldn't speak of it, and was loath to believe it could harm her the way she claimed. The bleeding was a sin, a time when women were made dirty, and so she was exiled to the barn loft and no one spoke of it. Aside from the meals her sister brought, no one so much as set foot near her until it was over.

Everything was worse after her mother had died. Everything.

And yet, the church said a living witch only poisons the flock.

It said they were better without her.

Verity tried to believe that. She did. But it was so *hard* to do.

As she got dressed again, Verity took a deep breath. She looked to the sky and watched a cloud float past, edged in pink and purple. God had a plan for her; He must. All this suffering, all this labour, it was for something.

It wasn't God's fault her plan had been different from His.

A bird landed on the back corner of the shed. It sang, shaking out its wings, its forest-green breast feathers shimmering a metallic blue when they caught the light. Verity watched, breathing deep, savouring the moment. The sun was creeping up further into the sky and there wouldn't be much—

"Boo!"

Verity startled, toppling the bowl of water over as she fell from her perch on a log. Someone was cackling, and when she looked up from the grass, Asher was bent over, laughing so hard he could barely breathe.

"You—should see—" he wheezed. "You were so scared!"

Verity scrambled to her hands and knees and sprung at Asher, grabbing him by the ankles. Asher squealed and toppled into the dirt, kicking to free his legs.

"How do you like that, huh?" Verity pulled her brother close enough to pin Asher down. "You think it's funny to scare your big sister? I bet you're gonna find this funny too!" She started tickling him.

Asher squirmed, laughing breathlessly under the merciless dance of Verity's hands. Years of sibling rivalry had taught her exactly what Asher's weaknesses were, and she was ready for him. She tickled the boy until he could hardly breathe.

"I'm sorry!" Asher managed between gasps for air.

He wasn't really; Verity knew that much. "What's that? I couldn't hear you over the sound of your devilish habits."

"I'm sorry! I swear! I'll—muck out the barn!"

Verity stopped. That was exactly the kind of thing she loved to hear. "That's my favourite kind of surrender."

As she caught her breath, Verity helped her brother up, the two of them brushing the grass and dirt off themselves. Asher's face was still pink from all the laughing, and Verity couldn't help but smile. In another year or two, Asher would be finished with his apprenticeship and old enough to look for a life outside their little house, and there'd be no more morning scares or tussles in the grass. He wouldn't be her responsibility anymore, which left a bittersweet pang in her heart.

They went together to the barn and hauled the doors open. As usual, the stale barn air wafted out, bringing with it the smell of hay, goats, and goat shit. Ten of the little beasts were already staring at them, screaming to be let out.

Verity vaulted over the front of the pen, walked to the other side, and opened the latch on the door that led to the goat enclosure at the back of the barn. They pushed past her, knocking into her legs, and then into one another, all vying to be the first outside. Asher was close behind, a pitchfork of hay with him. He tossed it outside and came back in, leaving the goats to eat.

Verity passed Asher a shovel and took up one of her own. She could get out of the chore if she wanted to—she'd won that right, and her arm still hurt more than she'd like—but she was reluctant to go off on her own. If she left, she'd inevitably start thinking more about God and work and the witch, and that had already kept her awake long into the night. It was more satisfying to be with company.

"Are things going well with your apprenticeship?"

Asher didn't look up, already mid-scoop. "It's fine."

"Just fine?"

"It'll be good work. Father said I've got steady hands and Seamus thinks so too." He heaved the goat shit out the open window that led to the manure pile on the other side of the wall.

"Sure, but that's how *they* feel about it. How do you feel?" Verity brought her own shovel to the window, passing Asher on her way back.

"There's always going to be work for a carpenter, and I'll be able to provide for my own family someday, and for you and Father and Clarabel."

Verity smiled at the generous thought, but nothing was convincing about the way Asher spoke. She stopped him as he returned from the window, putting her hand on his arm. "Is there something you want to tell me?"

"No," Asher said, and Verity heard it, but clear as day, she also heard something else.

I don't want to be a carpenter.

Verity blinked. Her vision was blurry, as if she were seeing double. "Sorry, what did you say?"

"I said no, there's nothing I want to tell you."

Her sight filled with another image, a dream layered over her eyes. Asher saying goodbye to his family and setting out with the iron wares merchant that sometimes came to town. A life on the road. A life of adventure.

And then the image was gone.

Asher was staring at her.

Verity had no idea what had just happened. It was unlike anything she'd ever experienced before. The pictures in her eyes had felt real, and something in her gut told her they were, but not exactly. Maybe not real, but true.

Verity moved her hand away from Asher, flexing her fingers. A dull burning rose in her veins, all the way up to the scar of her wound. Her brother was staring at her like she'd gone mad.

"Are you all right?"

Verity gave her head a shake. "I'm fine."

She was not fine at all. She'd seen something that hadn't been there. That did not bode well. The pastor had spoken at length about visions in the past. Some had been given to men by God, and others were signs of evil. She'd never really known the difference between the two, and in a town that burned witches, she knew better than to let on that anything was amiss.

"Just dizzy, I think," Verity continued. "It's...well, it's nearly time for me to start living up there." She pointed up to the loft and Asher's face paled. As apt an excuse as it was, that single comment was already more than anyone wanted to hear on the subject, so she knew it would be the end of any further questions. She changed the subject. "Just know you can tell me anything. About your life, or your work. If something were wrong," she hinted, "I'd help you."

"I know. You're a good sister." Apparently not getting the hint, Asher gave her a light smirk. "I'll make sure there's fresh hay in here, and up there."

It was a small thing, but as close as anyone came to caring, and it warmed Verity's heart to bursting. Tears welled in her eyes.

"Don't get sentimental on me, Verity. Don't forget you still have to make me breakfast." Asher gave her an evil laugh, propped his shovel against the wall and vaulted himself over the pen. Then he was gone, back toward the house.

But Verity was rooted to the spot. Whatever had happened just then, it had to have a reasonable explanation. If she were hungry or ill, that could make a person confused. Her moon cycle had progressively gotten worse over the years. Perhaps this was a new, horrible part of her condition. Maybe other people suffered from it as well but never spoke of it.

She always felt there was so much about life that she didn't understand. That she couldn't ask about, because questions could be deadly, and she never knew which questions were not.

Maybe she had made the whole thing up.

Dreamt it.

The idea wrestled in her mind, waging war against what she was *sure* she had just experienced. She could feel a headache coming on. Verity was used to questioning what she knew against what God or the village told her. Even Doctor Raam had told her that her excruciating pain was in her head, but declaring it so had never made the pain any less.

Verity tried to sort out her thoughts. She had seen the wood witch's burned fingers, seen the glow on her own skin. And as surely as the sky was blue, Verity knew that Asher had been lying when he spoke, and that the boy had been keeping that secret.

She had no words to explain it, and it was battling with everything Verity knew of the world. The things she had been taught were true.

She *had* seen something, but ungodly power was for witches and she was not a witch. Never had been. She knew the Good Book inside and out and she went to church service as many times a week as her life allowed for, and she prayed, and she was a good, honest woman. She gave. God asked her to give of herself and damnit, she *gave*.

Panic welled in her, and she needed to calm it.

Everything is fine, she thought. *Your life is fine. You are content. Any doubts are simply mistakes. God is good. You were mistaken.*

She breathed deep, once, and again, and again, and the panic ebbed. Everything would be fine. It had to be. Because if something was wrong with her, then she was not a good, godly person, and she was. She had worked very hard to remain one, in spite of all that hardship. In spite of the shunning and the death and the backbreaking labour and the pain. This vision had been a moment of daylight dreaming, because if it was not, she was very much in trouble.

Her father's worrisome nature was rubbing off on her.

Asher was fine.

She. Was. Mistaken.

CHAPTER FOUR

Arden

Arden sat down next to the crackling fire. The sun had set long ago, and evening had melted into night. A chill had settled on her back, but her front was searingly warm, just a little too close to the fire. She reached into a jar of ointment and slathered the pine-scented mixture on her to keep away the bugs, sliding her hands across every inch of her bare skin, toes to knees to hips to head. Closing the jar, she reached for the bowl beside her. It held a few pieces of mushroom. She took a bite of the hallucinogenic fungus, something Dalic had brought her earlier, and then another. And when that was done, she rolled her shoulders, closed her eyes, and breathed in.

The seasons would change soon. Autumn was ending and the air was growing colder, the sun falling earlier each day. She owed the forest her time and devotion; it had been too long. She waited for it to begin, for the forest to carry her away. And it did, gradually. Her heart slowed. Her pulse quieted. And everything around her grew just a little louder.

Crickets in the grass.

Breeze twisting twigs in the trees.

Skittering animals in the underbrush.

The world hummed and buzzed, and she was patient while waiting for the forest to come to her.

After a while, the bushes rustled and out stepped Dalic, her long birch-root legs taking deep strides. Dalic's shape was fluid and ever-changing. She always looked so much taller, so much more frightening at night. The fire illuminated her until it seemed like she stretched all the way to the sky. She sat down next to the fire.

The two of them sat in amicable silence, waiting for the next arrival.

At length, a shadow appeared between the branches of the trees. It darted from one bough to the next. It climbed and skittered, and the sight of it itched at something in the back of Arden's mind, something ancient and instinctual that knew to be afraid. The spirit leapt down next to the fire. It was made of dripping shadow, its head like a wolf's, with round white voids for eyes. The shape of it flowed between human and wolf, its fingers long and clawed, its teeth sharp, black pouring from its maw like mist.

The shadow crooked its head and sat down, its eyes boring into her. It didn't speak, but she had learned to read its mannerisms, learned to know when it was happy or displeased. Her mother had called it the Gloam, but so far as Arden knew, it had no true name.

She would have named it Death.

From behind her came the light sound of deer hooves in the grass. Ilyana passed her, the soft brown of her skin and hair shimmering in the firelight. That night, her calves were arched back like a deer, but the rest of her was human. Sadly, the tiny hare tail from their last meeting had disappeared. She wore a deer pelt fastened over her shoulder and nothing else, the curves of her figure peeking out from under it.

Ilyana sat, and the circle was complete.

Arden stood, but her body did not. She was the shape of herself, but she was translucent, ghostly. Outside of her flesh, the world felt more liquid, hazy. Cold. She had done this once a season since she was young, but she never truly got used to the feeling of leaving her body.

She tiptoed over to Dalic, who looked up at her warmly. She placed her hands on her friend's shoulders. "To the forest that grows and flourishes, I offer protection from those who would take too much and give nothing in return. I pledge to use what I need and no more, and to offer my thanks for what is given. To honour our bond, our friendship, and to give freely of myself."

Arden dug her fingers into her chest and pulled at a small piece of the translucent grey of herself. It wanted to stay, and she had to pull hard, stretching it away from her form until it snapped off. A tiny shudder ran through her, losing a piece of herself like that. She knelt beside Dalic to place the piece in the tree's cupped hands.

Dalic accepted it graciously, smiling up at her as she placed it in her mouth and swallowed.

The next in the circle was the Gloam, staring at her with its head tilted, white void eyes piercing through her. Arden put her hands near it, knowing there was no touching its liquid shape. Normally, the Gloam scared her to her core. It was the mushrooms fogging her mind that kept her calm each time she made an offering to it, its roiling shape twisting and writhing near her. Being close to it reminded her of lying alone in bed at night as things crept outside her windows and in the dark corners of the room. In the crevices of her heart.

She swallowed hard. "To the dark places, I offer devotion. To fear and be feared in equal measure, to be still and quiet and foreboding. To be an agent of death and revenge when it's asked of me. To occupy the unpredictable night and respect its power. When the time comes, I will be unforgiving."

Its writhing became calm and contained in a way that she knew was as content as the Gloam ever got. She tore the piece of herself away and tossed it into the air. The Gloam's head snapped up and it opened its maw, teeth gnashing at it.

The Gloam would eat her whole someday and never think twice about it.

Finally, Arden walked over to Ilyana. She was leaning to one side, legs stretched out beside her, relaxed and majestic. She watched the witch as she approached. When Arden knelt next to her, Ilyana offered her hand, which she took.

"To the creatures of the forest, I offer my gratitude. I pledge to ask permission and forgiveness, to use all of what I take and return the rest to the earth so they can feed the small things. Your life sustains me and I am in your service. Call, and I will come."

The witch tore off another piece of herself and offered it to Ilyana. The spirit blinked coyly and opened her dainty lips. Arden placed the piece in her mouth and cupped the spirit's cheek in her hand for a moment before she withdrew.

Arden went back to stand next to her body. "Is there anything else I can give of myself? Something more you want to ask of me?"

The Gloam stirred, standing and padding at the ground for attention. Its face changed, the black flowing away to reveal a bleached white skull. That cold dread that spilled off it rushed into her again and she knew what it wanted.

Death.

"More sacrifices?" Arden asked.

It snapped its teeth and the mist that made up its body flowed back into place, becoming vaguely wolf-like again. It sat, hollow white eyes unblinking.

She nodded. "You'll have it, beginning with the next nightfall. But you must understand they won't all be human."

The Gloam gnashed its teeth and spun in an excited circle before settling back in.

Dalic moved restlessly, not looking Arden in the eyes. "Winter is coming and the village creeps closer. They're taking as much wood as they can carry, day after day, removing everything from the soil and letting nothing grow but grass. They don't know how to live *with* nature. I'm afraid of what happens when the trees are gone."

Arden nodded. "I know. Talking to them hasn't done any good. If they won't do the work of replenishing the forest, I will. We'll keep planting more trees. I'll continue to burn the underbrush and keep the forest floor from getting too dense. We'll spread our domain in other directions. I'll do my best."

"I know you will." Dalic looked down at her hands, cupping Mouse as it nibbled on a stray seed.

Arden gave Ilyana her attention. The spirit flicked her hair back from her shoulder. "Our arrangement suits me. I wish for nothing else."

The comment was enough to bring a mischievous smile to Arden's face. "If everyone has been heard, I remain grateful for your time and your power. I wish you safe passage through the night. Thank you." She looked up. The sky was already getting lighter and the fire had died down to a shadow of what it had been. The night was over. It had been but a moment in her eyes.

"We are agreed." Dalic stood, her wooden joints creaking with the movement.

Arden watched, hands clasped before her in respect, as the spirits got up from the fireside. Ilyana slid her hand against Arden's arm before she disappeared into the bushes. Dalic gave a solemn nod and walked back into the forest, blending in with the trees. And the Gloam, after staring far too intensely at her, leapt past Arden in one swift movement, up onto the cabin roof, and then was gone, all without making a sound.

Arden let out her breath.

Slipping back into her body was easily done; however, feeling everything again was vastly overwhelming: the chilled dew on her bare skin, the ants crawling across her toes, the moss under her bottom. Her muscles were stiff and upset, having sat so perfectly still all night. And hungry. She was so fucking hungry.

The day after was always hard. A night of fasting and tearing bits off your soul would do that. She came away from each sacrifice a little less herself. Arden's mother had taught her that the soul grows back when nourished with good food, good friends, and good experience, but over the last several years, Arden had found herself with very few friends or nourishing experiences. When she allowed herself to think about it, she worried over how long she could carve off pieces of a stagnant soul, but never sat with it for too long.

She could do very little about it.

Though she desperately wanted to, she couldn't sleep, not yet. She had learned the hard way that ignoring what her body needed usually resulted in fitful dreaming and a headache when she awoke.

As if someone had read her mind, a nearby bush rustled and out waddled a modestly sized turkey. It came toward her, fearless, and stopped in front of her to peck at the ground.

Scooping the enormous bird up in her arms, she ran her hand down its thin neck. "Thank you, Ilyana." She kissed its head and its feathers ruffled, but it didn't try to free itself. "I take what is freely given and thank you for your sacrifice."

Her grip tightened.

When breakfast was ready—grilled turkey and a collection of foraged roots and berries—Arden sat back down to eat. She was licking the last of the berry juice from her fingers when the trees around her began to creak and groan, their leaves tossing as if in a storm, despite the lack of wind.

Arden jumped up, letting her empty plate fall off her lap. She quickly pulled a cloak over her dress and ran into the forest, off in the direction the trees seemed to sway toward.

She ran through the underbrush barefoot, over fallen logs,

through a creek, watching the distance for a sign. Once she rounded a collection of boulders, she almost ran headlong into Dalic, who was face to face with a band of axe-brandishing villagers.

"You know you can't be here!" Arden's voice caught the attention of the band of idiots, their petrified stares peeling one by one away from the menacing tree beast in front of them. An axe was buried in an old oak tree not far away.

"You can't keep us from getting wood," one of the younger— and apparently stupider—villagers barked. "We need it for winter or we'll die!"

Dalic looked at her, irritation written on her wooden face. "Why don't they understand?"

Arden pushed toward them. She slapped the back of one hand into the palm of the other, furious. "You can have wood if you *replace* what you take! You get nothing if you can't learn to respect the forest spirits! It's not a difficult concept! Pay your respect to the trees. Replace what you take. Then life moves on instead of being destroyed. You don't *need* to deforest the area to live."

One of the burlier men braced himself like he was getting ready to attack—which would be a very stupid move. "We don't pray to demons."

Arden sighed, head tipping back. She was so tired of these conversations. "If any of you could tell the difference between a demon and a spirit, I'd eat my own foot. Dalic—" she gestured to her enormous tree friend. "—is a spirit of the forest. She takes care of the things that grow here. She understands you need wood. Taking wood is good for the forest too. But she won't put up with your reckless abuse of the life cycle."

"Life cycle?" The brute laughed. "What does that even mean? Besides, if it's so smart, why can't it talk?"

Dalic's fingers tightened, creaking, pieces of her moving and growing. "I hate these humans, Arden."

"She can talk," the witch said. "You just don't know how to listen."

"That's it. I'm going to kill it." The idiot shifted his axe and stepped forward, and the rest followed. "Maybe it burns extra warm."

"You were warned." Arden took a deep breath and blew. The air shifted, mist rising out of nowhere. It clouded the air until the villagers nearly disappeared in it, their screams dull and drowned out.

The men were scrambling, looking in all directions as if something were coming for them. Arden and Dalic simply stood and watched.

Arden could kill them. They wouldn't leave a scratch on her. Tearing the heads from those villagers wouldn't even keep her awake at night. The Gloam would appreciate the tribute. But if five men disappeared into the forest, the village would rally and come looking for her. She didn't need that kind of trouble.

Dalic stomped her foot on the mossy forest floor, putting all her weight behind it. It sounded like a tree falling, and the screams changed, moving in the mist as the villagers scattered, running back the way they'd come. When the noise died out, Arden sucked in a long mouthful of air and the mist began to clear.

With a sigh, Dalic slumped her shoulders. The dissipation of all that anger changed her stature. She became human-sized and approachable once more. "Thank you, Arden."

"It's nothing. I know it feels hopeless but maybe someday we'll get through to them."

She nodded. "We have to try. The forest would be better without them, but I will not destroy life. That is not my way."

Arden put her hand on Dalic's shoulder. "I know. You're kinder than I am. I like that about you."

Dalic looked up, giving Arden a tired smile. "You're kind as well, Arden. You just choose your kindnesses carefully."

CHAPTER FIVE

Verity

The clamour came through the kitchen window, pulling Verity from the drudgery of kneading bread. She wiped her flour-covered hands on the apron she'd tied around her waist and went to look outside. Men were running past the house, axes in hand; some of them were panting and frantic. She tore the apron off and ran to the door, bread be damned. Even from the back, she knew one was her brother.

The chaos had already passed the house, so she broke into a jog to catch up. They were headed toward the middle of the village, and she did her best to keep pace.

The centre of Arrothburg was a large enough place, all things considered. They had a doctor and a trading post and a population of 738 people, and young Hope Harkness was about to make it 739. The closer a person came to the centre, the tighter the buildings were packed, and so with all the commotion, the streets were full of homemakers and children too young for school, and anyone else who wasn't busy in the fields or homes.

The group of men had come to a halt outside the town hall. One had already gone in, leaving the rest on the steps to catch their breath. As she got closer, Verity scanned the faces. Jeremiah Skinner. Tough ol' Josiah Guthrow. Bartholomew Vanderveld.

And Asher.

Verity pushed through the others, apologising as she did, and bounded up the stairs to Asher. Her brother was leaning against the railing, hands on his knees.

"Are you all right?" Verity squatted down to Asher's eye level, looking for wounds. He seemed to have all his parts. "What happened out there?"

Asher took a deep breath. "We went to cut the wood for the stockpile. Seamus says I need to learn about wood, so I went with the woodsmen. But that tree demon came and the wood witch too." He had to stop to take another breath. "She used her powers to make everything foggy and she had a tree demon, so we ran."

Verity swallowed hard. She knew what the Good Book said about witches, and what the pastor taught, but the witch had healed Verity and sent her home. She'd heard a lot of stories about the witch doing horrible things, but after escaping alive, a tiny bit of doubt niggled at her mind.

She looked quickly over all the young men. "Anyone hurt?"

They all shook their heads.

The town hall door opened and Verity stood. Mayor Hart came out. Tall, thick, and with short, greying hair, he was an intimidating man. No one—or mostly no one—ever felt compelled to second-guess him, because if he couldn't put you right in the eyes of the law, he could just as likely put you right with a swift blow to the gut. Verity had heard him say more than once that he didn't like to resort to violence, but he wouldn't hesitate to do the Lord's work either.

"What's this I hear about the wood witch?" Mayor Hart crossed his arms over his barrel chest and stared down at the band of tired boys. Someone recounted what Asher had told Verity, and the mayor huffed. "That woman is always getting in the way. But you also know better than to go anywhere near those creatures."

The young man looked affronted. "We didn't see it! It's a tree. It just looked like any tree until it started screaming."

The mayor ran his palm over his face. "No one killed?"

"No, sir."

"Sir," one of the other young men spoke up. "I don't understand why we don't kill her and end all these troubles."

Mayor Hart scowled at him. "If you don't understand that, you have not been paying attention. She is God's ultimate test for us, and we are not yet prepared. I have seen what she is capable of, and a bit of fog is the least of it. Do you think you can slay her? With your axe and those tiny arms of yours?"

The young man shook his head.

"Precisely," Mayor Hart snapped. "For now she is a trial we must endure. When we have the opportunity to burn her as we have her fledgling kin, we will. Now, go to the church and speak to the pastor. Cleanse yourselves. We'll try again tomorrow in another part of the forest." The mayor stomped back inside the town hall and slammed the door behind him.

The worn young men looked at each other, clearly not sure what to make of that, and gradually moved toward the stairs.

Verity stepped in beside Asher. "Are you sure you're all right?"

"Yes. It's nothing." But Asher's face was still white as a sheet.

"Did she threaten you? The wood witch?"

"In a way, yes." Asher kept his eyes forward, following the others across the town square, toward the church. "It's hard to know. We were all about to fight her and then the fog came and it's like…it's like all the bravery ran out of us. Like we knew we were going to die. So we ran."

"And the demon?"

Asher shuddered. "Huge. It was as tall as the other trees and it made the worst noise, like standing in the forest in a hurricane. I never want to see that thing again."

They were almost at the church and Verity still had so many questions. She grabbed Asher's hand and kept him from following the others. "Why wouldn't she let you take the wood?"

"Because she's evil, I suppose."

And even as the words came out of Asher's mouth, Verity saw a vision, faint and quick, of the witch standing next to the enormous living tree. *It's not a difficult concept! Pay your respect to the trees. Replace what you take.*

And it was gone.

"Verity? What's wrong?" Asher was watching her, a frown carved into his face.

Her veins were burning again, all the way up to that scar.

She had the presence of mind to blink it away. "Nothing. I have a headache suddenly. I haven't eaten enough today. Sorry."

A chorus of voices rose from inside the church and it caught Asher's attention. "Go home. I'm fine." Asher gave Verity a pat on the shoulder and trudged up the steps of the church.

"Go with God," Verity whispered under her breath.

Visions. Voices. Not just one, not anymore. These things were not of the Good Book. Had the witch poisoned her? Put a demon in her? What sins had she committed to deserve such a thing? Verity could not follow in her mother's footsteps.

The witch would know what was wrong. She would confess to having done something to her.

She had to.

45

It was hard to be patient. Verity had gone home and finished making the bread. Had waited for her father to come in from the field and eat and leave again. She had a few hours now before anyone would come home and miss her. Long enough to go into the woods and speak to the witch.

She didn't *want* to. The church taught her that sin could spread just by being in the presence of something as evil as a witch or a demon, but she also knew this *thing* she was experiencing was too strange to bring to the pastor. If the rumours were true, some women had burned just for asking a question about witchcraft. If she took this to the pastor, she'd have to admit to having been in the witch's cabin, and to being unconscious in her presence, asleep in her bed. She'd have to tell him the witch's blood ran in her veins now and maybe, just maybe, her magic as well.

Verity knew what would happen to her, just like it happened to all witches.

When she finally made it into the part of the forest that held the witch's cabin, the clearing was empty. Cold coals from yesterday's fire sat abandoned, an empty plate on the ground next to it. Barely even a stir in the tree branches.

Maybe she wasn't home. Verity felt quite prepared to turn around as if she'd never been there at all.

A sound came from around the side of the cabin, too low to hear properly. Then she heard it again: a low, throaty moan. Verity tensed and crept forward, careful not to step on anything that might give her away, not until she knew what was happening. The woman was a witch and she could be doing any number of evil, magic things just out of sight. She could be *killing* someone.

When she rounded the side of the cabin, she saw the woman's hair first. She was perched on top of a barrel, hands braced on its edges. Between her oddly jointed legs was the witch, kneeling before this deer-woman like she was praying at an altar. Except the witch's face was tucked out of sight between the woman's thighs and she wasn't using her mouth to pray.

Verity jumped back, mortified by her discovery, and her foot caught on something. She was tumbling backwards, no time to catch herself. The ground rushed up to meet her and stole a pained groan from her. And just like that, the witch was above her with a knife to her throat.

"I'm sorry!" Verity held out her empty hands. "I didn't mean to—to interrupt. I have questions—"

The witch snarled and put the slightest pressure on Verity's throat.

Verity covered her face and squeaked, "I have magic now!"

She waited for the stab of metal, but it never came. She peeked through her fingers. The witch had backed away, glaring down at her. Then she went back to the deer-woman. Verity couldn't hear what they were saying, but after a few long moments, the deer-woman bent her neck and kissed the witch.

Though Verity blushed to see it, the kiss was a tender thing to witness. The witch took the deer-woman's cheeks gently in her hands, and after their lips parted, they stayed a moment to look at one another. The deer-woman kissed the witch's palm and turned to depart, stepping gracefully into the trees.

Verity looked away, trying to ascertain whether she should get up or not, and when she looked back, the woman was gone, and only a regal deer was left, darting off into the distance.

The witch went to a basin outside the cabin and splashed water onto her face. She looked at Verity, her skin dripping wet. Her eyes had dark circles beneath them. Her shoulders sagged, and Verity knew the look too well. She knew how bone-tired sat on a person.

"This had better be good," the witch sighed.

Certain that lying on the ground was a bad idea, Verity scrambled to her feet and followed the witch into her house. "I'm so sorry. I didn't mean to interrupt your time with your wife. That—"

"She's not my wife." The witch opened the wood stove and snapped her fingers, which sparked an immediate fire.

Verity tried not to look like her heart was about to jump from her chest, which it most certainly was. What the witch had just done *and* what she had just said were both equally terrifying. Creating fire from nothing. Relations with someone out of wedlock, let alone with a woman—which was perhaps the most confusing part. Verity had blushed at the beauty of ladies before but she hadn't realised such a relationship was *possible*.

Verity was trying very hard to breathe. "I—I don't understand any of this."

"And you don't need to, but I do love seeing you simpletons pee your pantaloons with fear." The witch's smirk was quite unsettling. "Ilyana is the animal spirit of this forest and sometimes we commit very sinful acts together. I also protect her animals from being hunted to nothing by idiots like you, but one of these things is more fun than the other."

The witch was speaking like all of this was so *normal*. Verity was sure she'd somehow crossed the threshold into hell on her way through the woods.

The witch sighed. "Are you going to tell me what you want?" She poured water into a tea kettle and set it on the stove.

Right. Verity shook her head and tried to ground herself in the moment. She could still clearly envision what had happened and it was stirring something in her blood. *Don't think about the deer-woman and the witch. Ask the question.*

"Miss Witch—"

"Seven hells, I have a *name*. Arden, my name is Arden, *please*."

48

Verity's cheeks burned. "Apologies, Arden. I—Something is the matter with me."

Arden scoffed. "I'll say."

"I'm serious. Ever since I've been home, strange things have happened. I've always had good instincts for people's intentions, but now..." She sat down at the table, per Arden's indication, trying to find the words. "I think I hear people's thoughts now. Or I have visions, or—I don't know."

That got Arden's attention. "Really? Tell me."

Verity ran through both of the moments with her. How it had sounded. How it had felt when her brother's words had built pictures in her mind when he said something false. A tremor shook her voice as she spoke, and more than once she reminded herself not to break down in frightened tears.

"That *is* interesting." Arden poured them each a cup of tea. "I did run into those imbeciles, and I said those things. You're sure they didn't just...tell you that with their mouths?"

"I'm sure." Verity stared down at the table, too ashamed to look up. "I think they were trying to look brave for Mayor Hart. They don't want to admit they ran away from a bunch of fog."

The comment made Arden chuckle. "And these visions, they only happened twice?"

Verity nodded. "Am I a witch now?"

Arden cackled, throwing her head back. "Absolutely not! Do you know how hard I work to be what I am? How *intentional* all my actions are? This takes practice and dedication. You don't get to be me by accident."

"Well, that's good. But how do I make this stop?" Verity tapped nervously on the side of her cup.

"Why would you want to?" Arden took a long sip of tea. "You have something no one else has. You have a power you can learn to use, that you can better your life with. You'd be a fool to give it up."

"This is not what God wants. It can't be. The Good Book says—"

"I know what the Good Book says."

Verity blinked. "You've read it?"

"Of course I've read it." Arden took a drink of her tea, still piping hot. "You think the rabbit doesn't study the ways of the wolf? If I'm going to be hunted, I want to know exactly how."

Swallowing hard, Verity attempted to say something intelligent, though very little came to mind. "Reading it didn't hurt you? You're unholy. Shouldn't it burn you just to touch it?"

Arden got up and went to a small shelf that hung over her bed. She pulled down a book Verity recognized immediately and tossed it on the table with disdain. A worn old copy of the Good Book. "The only thing that hurts me is your ignorance. Your pastor tells you lies and you eat them up like a raven gobbling a week-old carcass."

Verity's gut twisted. These things, they were all too much for her. She was just a simple girl from a simple town. She'd been wrong to think bad things of God and her place in the world. She could swallow her pride and take joy in caring for her family and her inconvenient body, if only God would help her escape all this blasphemy.

Trying to be brave, Verity sat tall with as much authority as she could muster. "This thing you've done to me, I can't keep it. If someone finds out, I'll be burned as a witch." She stared down into her teacup. "My family needs me."

Arden rubbed her eye with the back of her hand, a yawn escaping her. "You're right. If your pastor finds out, you'll be burned. But some secrets are worth keeping, even if they're dangerous." She sat back down and put her hands on the table. "I don't know the extent of it, girl—"

"Verity."

The witch paused. "There is something wrong in your town, Verity. *True* witches are rare in the world. Hard to come by. I've known six my whole life, most of them from other places. Meanwhile, your people claim to have burned one every month or two. That's an impossible number. None of the spirits I work with have admitted to having anything to do with witches from your village. The number of unmarked graves near the swamp, where you throw away the burned…I don't have a truth for you, but, Verity, you need to start opening your eyes. Things are not as simple as they seem."

A chill ran through Verity as she tried to make sense of everything Arden was saying. The numbers roiled in her head, these new things combatting what she knew… "I don't think I understand."

Arden took a deep breath and her shoulders slumped on the exhale. "That doesn't surprise me. Just…don't believe everything you hear."

Verity nodded. "So now what do I do?"

Pulling her hair back, elbows above her head, Arden yawned again. "I have someone I can ask. I have a suspicion about where your power came from, but I want to confirm it. Can you come back in two days? That should be enough time."

Verity sighed in relief. She could wait two days. "Thank you. You have no reason to help me, but I appreciate it. I want to be right with God again and do right by my family. Being aided by a witch just seems a strange way to get there."

Arden blinked slowly, impatiently, and finally gave Verity a strained smile. "Just drink your tea. Your God will wait."

CHAPTER SIX

Arden

Arden was *not* going to do *anything else* that day. It was only by pure
force of will she was still awake, what with the fire ceremony from
last night, the encounter with the woodcutting villagers, and yet
another visit from Verity, all before nightfall. She spared a passing
thought for Ilyana, who would definitely be back at some point to get
her due, and who Arden now had to probe for answers.

Once Arden had sent the pious little Verity home, she stuffed her
belly with whatever was in the cabin to eat, stripped off her clothing,
and crawled into bed. The thick sheets, the down pillow, the soft
mattress…it was all so welcoming. Like lying on clouds. Arden was
asleep so quickly her mind didn't have a chance to toss and turn.

She dreamed of her mother. Of being 12 years old and sitting at the
fire with her, learning to embroider the material they had bought from
the merchant passing through the village. *This is good, honest work,* her
mother had told her. *It makes you close to the world around you, being still*

52

and focused. And when you're done, you have something special. A piece of your soul you can wear on the outside. And as they sat, pushing the needle in and out, her mother sewing daisies and Arden sewing stars, the spirits came. One by one, they sat by the fire, no younger or older than they had ever been. Some that Arden's mother had worked with and that Arden herself would not, and everyone was content.

That was the whole dream, sitting and sewing. When Arden woke in the early hours, she did so with a smile on her face. She still loved being visited by her mother.

It didn't hurt as much anymore.

Some signs were easy to read, and so Arden stretched, pulled on her clothes, and boiled water for tea. She put her woven basket on the table and gathered breakfast—bread, jerky, nuts—and a pair of teacups. She wiped the sleep from her eyes with the back of her hand and left the cabin, basket in one hand, the warm handle of the kettle in the other. The sun was still barely visible on the horizon. Barefoot, Arden followed the flat stones she had laid out for a path years ago, taking in the chirping quiet of early morning, the crisp air chilly on her skin.

Before long, she arrived at the tree. It was still small as far as trees went, but that was because it was young. Arden sat down near it, close to the carefully placed rock that bore her mother's name. Birch trees had been her mother's favourite, and when death had claimed her, Dalic had helped Arden find a sapling to plant over her mother's body.

Burying her mother had been hard. She'd done it alone. Washed her and prepared her, alone. Carried the body, alone. Dug the hole, alone. Placed her inside, alone. Dalic had offered to help. Her mother had served the tree spirit long before Arden was born. But alone was the right way to do it. Arden would have no blood family to rely on ever again, and she needed to know what it would feel like.

She had been a family one moment, and a person the next.

When it was her turn to be laid to rest, Arden hoped the spirits would honour her body in the absence of anyone else. She planned to walk into the woods and simply never be heard from again.

Arden set the kettle in the grass and laid out breakfast, one cup for her, and one for her mother. She set her mother's cup of steaming tea next to the makeshift gravestone and sat back to eat. She had nothing to say; she'd already said it all a hundred times. *I love you. I miss you. Why aren't you here? I'll be all right.* Why bother repeating herself?

Instead, she listened.

As they often did, her mother's lessons came back to her as Arden sat in attentive peace. She imagined what her mother might say to her about the village and about Verity.

You swore to protect the sick and dying, even when it was hard. You swore to heal the people of that village, knowing they do not understand the harm they do to themselves. That girl needs a guide, sweet pea. No matter how frustrating she might be.

Her mother had always been more generous and forgiving than Arden had been. Sometimes it felt as if all of her mother's bad experiences had hardened and crystallised into Arden when she was born. If the witch had a baby, would that child be harder still? She'd never know.

"All right, Mother," Arden whispered to the breeze. "I hear you."

Arden felt better. Rested. The dream had demanded she pay attention to her roots, and so she had. She sat in silence a while longer. After she finished her own cup of tea, she poured her mother's into the grass. Let it become part of the ground, part of the tree that her mother was still becoming. Then she blew the tree a kiss, packed up her basket, and went back home.

She still had things to do, after all.

Calling on a spirit was a very individual thing. Each spirit was unique, and anyone working with them needed to learn their ways. Some things were simply not done. Never call for the Gloam in the day. Never speak to Dalic in anger. Never disrespect Ilyana.

The Gloam could be called in an instant, so long as there was food involved. Dalic came and went as she pleased, and calling her might result in nothing at all. Getting Ilyana's attention was a matter of time.

Arden sat, legs crossed beneath her, and waited. She'd cast her intention out into the world, asked the wind to bring Ilyana her way. As she waited, Arden kept still and quiet. Noise and movement kept most animals away, and it was the same for the spirit that watched over them. Ilyana acted more like prey than predator, and she appreciated calm when she arrived.

It was difficult to say how long Arden had been there when the bushes rustled. She opened her eyes to find Ilyana stepping into the clearing, a hard line on her face in place of a smile. The pelt across her shoulder was covered in spines, like a porcupine.

"Having a bad day?" Arden stood and held out a hand to the spirit.

Ilyana gave a moaning confirmation and pressed herself against the witch's chest. "A bad day indeed. The deer are shedding their velvet and are so upset. It's part of the cycle of things, and it makes me grumpy. So many big emotions."

Arden ran a hand through Ilyana's hair, careful to avoid skewering herself on the spines. "Would it make your day better if I fed you and gave you gossip? I have a rather strange question for you."

"You know I love hearing your strange human stories." Ilyana allowed herself to be pulled along to the cabin, and followed Arden inside. Waiting on the table was an enormous bowl of raw greens and vegetables. The spirit's face lit up. She sat down and rummaged in the bowl with her hands. She chose a carrot and began to gnaw at it like a rabbit might.

Arden found it endearing every single time.

"I have a puzzle for you."

"I love puzzles," Ilyana said, her cheeks starting to resemble a chipmunk's.

"That young woman who barged in on us yesterday. She reads minds. Or maybe just truths. A pious girl." Arden reached across to steal a piece of lettuce from the bowl. "I need to figure out why."

"Is she a spirit worker, like you?"

Arden shook her head. "Not at all. She's a scared little church mouse and she thinks this gift of hers will get her killed. I healed a wound for her a few days ago and used my blood for the poultice. She claims that since then, she's been hearing things. Only twice, and only under very specific circumstances. Her brother, two different times, and both times he said something untrue and she had a vision of the truth."

"That's strange indeed." Ilyana had worked her way up to the greens of the carrot top and kept eating. "If she never had that before she met you, I think you're the one who started it."

"It's not as if I gave her magic. I couldn't do that. I've used the same poultice on a hundred other villagers and no one has come back claiming they had new abilities. Besides, she burned me before the poultice."

Finished with the carrot greens, Ilyana searched through the bowl and came up with a chunk of hard turnip. "Then she has an ingredient the rest don't. Magic in the blood, maybe. Hibernating."

"You think I awoke something in her?" Arden sat back in her chair, letting the idea settle over her.

"Some spirits are braggarts and I've listened to a lot of water spirits talk about how many humans they've charmed into lying with them." Mischief flashed in Ilyana's eyes. "Though none have found a better human than I have."

Arden couldn't help but smile. "So there have to be babies out there, somewhere?"

"There have to be."

Arden let out a long breath. "Just what I want to do, tell a godly young woman that her father is probably a river whore."

Ilyana pursed her lips. "Seems like a bad thing to say."

"Agreed." Arden toyed with the untouched lettuce in her hand. "Perhaps I'll wait until the time is right. Give her some room to grow into this idea first. She's too full of her god to believe in anything else."

"So strange, those people," Ilyana said. "Creating one large someone to worship when there are so many real spirits to serve."

Arden went to pour herself a cup of water from the pitcher. She drank it down in one long gulp. "I do hope I can help her. I think she needs it."

"You will. It's part of what makes you beautiful."

When Arden turned back, Ilyana's spines were gone, the pelt covered in vibrant blue plumage. Ilyana stood and made her way around the table to take Arden's hands.

"You are so beautiful." Ilyana traced a finger over Arden's lips, sending a shiver down the witch's spine. "Inside and out."

And after that, Arden spent no more time thinking of saving young women. Only the delicate thrill of lips on skin, and the warmth of two bodies coming together.

CHAPTER SEVEN

Verity

Verity's estimation of being home before everyone else had been severely incorrect. When she opened the door to her home, her stomach curdled to see her family at the supper table, staring back at her.

"Where have you been?" Jona stood, his chair scraping back against the floor. "Your sister came home to find you gone. All of us came home—" He gestured toward her siblings. "—to a cold hearth and no food and no hint as to what happened to you. When Asher arrived, Clarabel was preparing supper in your place."

"I made myself bread and jam first." Clarabel stood proudly, hands in her tiny apron pockets. "And I would've made the whole supper but Asher stopped me."

"As he should have," Father snapped. "It's your sister's work, not yours. Not yet."

"I'm sorry, Father." Verity's guilt coiled in her, tightening her breath. It was her weakness, guilt. She'd always wanted to make her father proud, but too often she wound up angering him instead.

Jona shook his head. Verity could hardly stand to look at him. The disappointment ran so deep in the lines of his face. "Don't you think I have enough to worry about? You're supposed to make it so I can do my work without wondering what I'm going to do about everything at home. This was selfish, Verity. Very selfish. What would God say if He knew you weren't of service today?"

Verity scratched her wrist with her thumbnail, trying to keep herself from crying. If Father knew what she was really doing, where she had *really* been, she'd likely be killed. "He would find me unworthy until I repent my slothful ways."

"That's right. And now you'll need to do just that. I thought you were a God-fearing, family-loving young woman, but today you prove me wrong. Again."

Verity was brave enough to look up for a moment. Her siblings were the same as her, staring at their shoes and not daring to say a word.

"Was it Mary Beth you were with? Or that other girl from down the road? You need better taste in friends, girl."

The question baffled Verity. How had he not noticed? She hadn't had time for friends in years. After she became a stand-in mother, each of the girls had disappeared, one by one. Verity was too busy or the girls were married off to their new husbands. Or the most likely culprit, that Verity was the daughter of a witch. Shaking her head, Verity began to answer, "I wasn't with anyo—"

Jona pushed his chair in so hard that it crashed against the table. "I don't care. Go wash the sins off you and figure out how you're going to make it up to your family tomorrow."

His boots thumped away from the table, deep, resounding thuds making their way up the stairs. Only when Verity heard his bedroom door slam did she finally look up.

Asher and Clarabel looked at her with pity in their eyes. It was the way of things, but she was glad to know they didn't hate her as much as their father seemed to.

"I'm sorry," Verity choked out, her eyes beginning to water.

Clarabel moved quickly to hug Verity's legs. "It's all right. I liked being home alone."

Verity swept her fingers through her sister's hair. "You'll be a good mum someday."

"Just like you are to us." Clarabel squeezed hard, then let go and bounded up the stairs to her room.

Despite knowing that Clarabel meant it as a kindness, Verity wasn't sure how she felt about that comment. Getting married and having children was part of God's plan for women, but Verity had already done that for her siblings. Shouldn't that be enough? As young as she was, she felt she had already lived two lifetimes. She didn't want anyone else to raise.

She *wanted* the luxury of disappearing for a few hours without being scolded.

Asher still stood awkwardly across from her, like he wasn't sure if he was allowed to leave, so Verity made the choice for him. She turned on her heel, shame and embarrassment washing over her, and rushed out into the dark of night to wash up.

Marching from the house to the shed in the back, she pushed all her feelings down as far as they could go. This washing up was a punishment, and she wanted to get it over with. The moonlight was bright enough to see by, so she fetched a bowl of water and stripped down. The temperature hadn't dipped low enough to freeze the barrel yet, but it felt close enough. As she dipped the washcloth into the bitter-cold water and pressed it against her skin, she bit back the rage and pain.

She didn't deserve this. She hadn't wanted *any of it*.

Chill seeped into her skin, down to her bones. The faster she washed, the faster it would be over, but if she was too fast, she wouldn't appear repentant enough for her father's liking. But it was so cold it *hurt*. It was too much to bear.

So she focused on God and tried to ask forgiveness for all she had done. She spoke to Him in whispers and begged for leniency. She begged to understand the challenges He'd put in front of her. And she scrubbed as she spoke, her skin becoming raw and cold-numb.

No matter how hard she scrubbed, Verity still felt like she could smell the witch's cabin on her skin. Like there was no way to get it out.

It smelled like sin.

Dawn woke Verity with a horrible intensity. The light burned her eyes as it streamed in through the window. Her head throbbed, her joints were sore, and her body felt like the slow pour of cold molasses. She cracked open her eyes and strained to see around the room. Her siblings were gone, which meant she had overslept.

Verity sat up and pressed the heels of her palms into her eyes. She couldn't be sure how long she had slept, but was certain it wasn't long enough. Everything already felt like too much. How was she going to face the day, as tired as she was?

Verity pulled on her slippers and made her way groggily out to the hall and down the plain wooden staircase. She couldn't hear Clarabel chirping her way around the house, which likely meant she had already gone off to school. Guilt filled Verity's gut. Guilt, guilt, always guilt. She knew her family would've woken her if she had truly been needed, but there was always need. They were one mother short of a household.

And if experience told her anything, she'd be scolded later for oversleeping. Especially after yesterday.

The leftovers of breakfast were on the table; someone had baked the bread that had been rising since yesterday, but no one had bothered to make this evening's bread. It would need to sit for hours and she was late getting started, so it would interfere with all of the other chores. Irritation swelled on top of the guilt. She wasn't feeling well and there had been three other people in that house and *no one* else could just make the bread? It was her duty, yes, and she was to be *of service,* yes, but could she have absolutely no reprieve from it?

The table was littered with crumbs, not to mention a bowl of sticky eggshells and a dirty pan where they'd cooked their eggs. Every surface was littered with scraps and dirty plates and she couldn't start on anything else until she'd cleaned up everyone else's mess. God help her, she was not in the mood.

Verity tidied begrudgingly, making a small place for herself to work, then set to pouring ingredients into her wooden mixing bowl. Flour and water and foraged seeds and kneading. So much kneading. She worked at the dough spitefully, squelching it between her fingers. Her siblings always complained on the days she made bread that didn't rise well. It was perfectly good bread; it was just *different* bread and she was in no mood to hear it. Though she knew she wasn't supposed to have opinions like those, she felt it was rather unfair to criticise someone's work when you weren't willing to do better yourself.

Once it was kneaded properly, Verity covered the bowl with a clean baking cloth and set it near the fire to keep warm. She gave the coals a stir with her poker and added a small piece of wood to them. Cold would also keep the dough from rising, and she didn't need anything else conspiring against her.

For the first time, it occurred to Verity that perhaps when someone paid a witch to curse their spouse, it wasn't because of any single large wrong that had been done. Perhaps it was because of a thousand small wrongs over a thousand days that had festered past the point of healing.

The morning's work woke her by degrees and her temperament wavered. As she took care of the homestead and the animals, her muscles loosened and gave respite from the pounding in her head. She did her best to focus on the work, not on the things that threatened to ruin her improving mood, such as witches and impending moon cycles and untidy siblings.

Chore after chore, her mind spun in every possible direction. Her body was busy, but she would have traded all her possessions to have something to occupy her mind.

The distant ring of the town bell filled the air. Her father would come in for lunch soon, then back out again. Verity tucked away all her lingering sour thoughts so her father wouldn't see them on her face.

When he left, she let her shoulders sag again, free to feel everything in her solitude.

The sun was setting earlier and earlier in the day, and as the afternoon flowed into evening, her family came home one at a time, taking their place at the table and chattering on about the minutiae of their day.

"And not one of them complained today about splitting logs." Asher tore a piece of bread in two, spilling crumbs across the table. "I'd much rather be doing that than going back into the woods to get eaten by the witch."

Verity stared at the pile of crumbs, waiting for Asher to wipe them away. He did not, and her patience started to simmer once more. "Surely it can't be so bad. The witch can't be everywhere, can she?"

"How am I to know? If she can summon up fog, she might be able to run quickly or be in more than one place. I don't know the limits of devil magic." Asher took a bite of bread, crumb dust falling from his mouth. "I'm not getting eaten; I know that much."

"Is the rest of your apprenticeship going well?" their father asked.

Verity braced for what might come next. She knew Asher would always lie to protect their father's feelings, and if he did, Verity would have to conceal whatever happened to her as a result.

"We worked on hinges today, for things like wardrobes and

63

doors." Asher's demeanour cooled, his gaze going down to his bowl.

"That's a good skill to have." Their father drank the last of his stew from his bowl and set it back on the table. He got up and gave Asher a pat on the shoulder. "I'm proud of you, son."

Asher's face turned scarlet, a little smile in the corners of his mouth.

Verity took a breath. Her brother hadn't lied. He'd just omitted. He had still told enough truth, it seemed, to spare her. That was well enough for her. She didn't want to have visions at the dinner table in front of her family so they could tie her to a burning post just like their mother.

Clarabel wiped her face with her old cloth napkin, bounced from her seat, and tossed the napkin on the chair she'd just been sitting in. "I'm all finished. May I go see the baby goat before bedtime?"

"Off you go," Father answered. "Back in when the light is gone, eh? Asher, go with her, will you?"

Asher got up from his seat without protest and followed Clarabel out of the house, leaving the table ravaged.

Verity's patience went from a simmer to a boil.

"Every night it's the same thing," Verity grumbled. She got up and started tossing empty bowls into one another. "You'd think they could at least set everything in one place to make the washing easier on me."

Father looked her way, his brow furrowed. "Verity, it's unbecoming for a young woman to be angry."

"Then why did God wake me today with a temper?" Verity snapped, not thinking before she spoke. "I am happy to help this house as best I can, but must each of you place obstacles in my way at every opportunity?"

As she dropped the collection of spoons carelessly into the wash basin, her stomach twinged, stopping her in her tracks. She winced and put a hand on her belly.

Father sighed and went to look out the window. The sun was just barely still in the sky, but she knew he was checking for the moon. He couldn't even look at her as he asked, "It's time, isn't it?"

Verity's face flushed. She hated that. She hated that he knew about this private thing about her body, and that he kept track of it by the moon just as she did. She hated that it *mattered* at all to him, because he saw it as such a dramatic inconvenience. He barely understood the half of it.

"You can't be angry with everyone because this thing is upon you, girl." Jona set to work pouring himself a cup of water so he didn't have to look her in the eye when he spoke.

Verity's jaw dropped. "I'm not angry because of the moon cycle. I'm angry because these things happen every day and I'm the one who takes responsibility for it."

"And I suppose the timing is simply a coincidence?" Father took a long drink.

"It is! Or perhaps it's the reason I can't hold my tongue today, but I feel this every evening. People can leave whatever work they want for me, and I'm supposed to be grateful to have it." Verity saw her words weren't swaying him, and the anger abated enough to feel the hot water she had been wading into. "Please, Father. I am simply tired of it."

When Jona spoke, it was with a calm impatience. "When you're finished with this, ensure your loft is ready. I love you, Verity, but God would not look kindly on this behaviour. Do you believe this conversation embodies the tenets? *Honour those who gave you life.* Do you feel this embodies the spirit of how God built you?"

Exasperated, Verity swung her arm out to show him the house. "I give of myself to this family from dawn to dusk! I took Mother's place and have done the best I can to be of service! Would she also be so dissatisfied with me?"

Father's face fell. "Your mother does not rest with God. I pray every day that she did not poison your heart before she died. Do not look for approval in the eyes of a witch."

The vision came before Verity could brace for it. It was so close to her own memory that it was difficult to see the differences. Hot red flame eating the flesh of a woman bound to a pole. Verity's mother, her hair disappearing in the heat, her clothes turning black and charring away until the shame of her bare body was exposed, cracking and cooking. Her mother hadn't even tried to escape. She had no power to. She screamed as she burned, and the crowd cheered.

And then the vision was gone.

Verity leaned forward, hands on her knees, trying to catch her breath.

"Are you all right?" Her father had come closer, but not close enough to touch her, not with her moon cycle so close to fruition.

She couldn't speak for a moment. Verity drew in breath after breath, the sight of her mother's death making her stomach churn. It was only the third vision, but the other two had been about lies. If they were *all* showing her the truth to a lie, which part of her mother's death was false? Father had called her a witch and—

Was it possible she was not?

It was rare for Verity to think of the day her mother had died. It was too painful and had caused too many ripples in her life. She had been angry for *years* that her mother had chosen witchcraft over her family, and Verity had pushed those things into the back of her mind in order to survive.

What was the lie? Where did the falsehood begin and stop?

"Verity?"

Snapping back to the present moment, Verity realised how much danger she was in. Her father had let his wife burn, and surely a wife was more precious than a child. What would stop him from taking her straight to the pyre if he knew about the visions?

Deciphering what they meant could wait.

"Perhaps you're right," she said. "Perhaps my moon cycle is getting the better of me. I'll stay in the loft tonight to be sure." It was better he thought her unclean than possessed.

Her father backed up a step or two, looking relieved. "Yes, that seems prudent. You have enough work ahead, getting the loft ready after dark. I'll tidy this tonight and your siblings can take up their share while you're gone."

His words soured her stomach further. He was so eager to believe she was made a monster by some blood and pain during each moon. That was what the church taught, and it was what she was supposed to believe, and yet she knew it not to be true.

"Thank you, Father." Verity steadied herself and rose. She would need things from her room if she was to start sleeping in the barn for a week. She knew the collection by heart and habit, and even with the ghastly images of her mother still swimming behind her eyes, she would gather them as swiftly as she could.

She was on the second step upstairs before her father's words stopped her.

"It hasn't begun yet, correct?"

"Correct, Father." She kept looking at the knots in the wooden stairs ahead of her.

"Then I'll expect you in church with us tomorrow. Provided that you are still unsullied."

"Yes, Father." She waited a moment, and when he said nothing else, she made her way upstairs. She prayed her bleeding *would* start in the night. In the past, she had always been afraid to miss church. It might make the town suspicious of her ways. But as she rummaged for her things, her hands shook. Not in fear of what God would think of her blasphemy or of forgoing a sermon, but in fear of what she was unaware of. This power in her heart, whatever it was, had something to tell her about her mother, and she needed to know more.

Tomorrow. She was meant to see Arden tomorrow. The witch *had* to know something about these visions.

If the pain held off long enough for her to visit the woods.

Only time would tell.

She bundled all her belongings into the thick pile of loft blankets she kept under her bed, pulled the corners together, and went down the stairs to face the cold.

As was proper, the entire town was on its way to church when Verity stepped out her front door with her family. Her bleeding had *not* come, and it was the first time Verity found this to be unfortunate. As a child, going to church had been her favourite parts of the week; every single person was wearing their best outfit, which for some meant the clothing with the least holes, and for others meant fur stoles and soft leather gloves. It had once been a joy to see people at their best, but the thought had soured in Verity's mind with age. Especially after her mother had died and she found herself wishing she too had hired help to look after the household with her. It was a sin to covet other people's wealth, so Verity had learned to keep her nose down and be content with her practical garb and her tired, weathered hands.

That day, the looming shadow of the church spire in the early morning sun was menacing. Large and wooden and sun-bleached from decades without fresh paint, it was the core of their town. Though in practice the building was just a building, she felt as if it had a soul, and that soul was looking down on her with judgement. Even in her most trying moments—even after her mother died—she had always been right with God. She had questioned Him just a little, and had baulked at His choices for her, but she had never felt as distant from Him as she did that day.

Verity trembled as she walked through the open doors, her family chattering all around her, excited for the day's sermon. The air was thick with the scent of pine; each week new boughs were brought in to decorate the pews and hide the scent of bog that seeped in from somewhere. They'd built on rough ground, the pastor had said, but God conquers all, and sometimes so does pine.

She followed her family without thinking, taking their place in their usual pew, fifth from the back on the left-hand side. The space echoed the jovial greetings of friends and neighbours. The small talk of a town at rest after six days of hard labour. It created a wall of noise that drowned out Verity's thoughts for one sweet, dear moment. She kept to herself, staring at her shoes and waiting for it all to begin.

Asher whispered in Verity's ear, "What do you think Father's saying to the pastor?"

Verity's head shot up, her eyes wide. Sure enough, her father was standing at the front of the room, leaning in close to Pastor Woolfe in order to have a quiet word with him. After a moment, her father took a step back. Pastor Woolfe put a hand on her father's shoulder and nodded, saying something she couldn't hear.

It was not entirely uncommon for a man of the village to make a request. To ask for a topic that fit the needs of a household or would quell a particular problem. Sermons were for the people, after all, and if the people needed reminding of God's ways, Pastor Woolfe was often happy to do so.

Seven hells, thought Verity.

Father made his way back to their pew and sat at the far end. At least that was a mercy, having him sit anywhere but near Verity.

Pastor Woolfe, dressed in a long, spotless white gown, walked slowly up the steps to the pulpit. The front of his gown had been embroidered with finely detailed black and gold, covering much of his torso in imagery from the Good Book that his wife's hired help had painstakingly made for the benefit of the town. He had several such gowns, and not for the first time, Verity wondered how much just one of them might cost.

The pastor took a moment as the room settled down, flipping through his copy of the Good Book and sliding his fingers across a page. He looked up, scanning the crowd with a gentle, patient smile. Pastor Woolfe had been pastor since long before Verity was born, but that day it was like she was seeing him for the first time. He was different, somehow. His skin was too white, nearly translucent from too many days spent indoors. His age showed in the lines of his face and the grey prominent in his cropped black hair. Just a week ago he had seemed thinner, stronger. As the donation plate circled the room, he seemed to have his eyes on it, and Verity couldn't help but get the impression of a greedy raccoon. God knew most of her neighbours could hardly afford that donation plate, while the pastor looked as well-fed as a lord.

The edges of Pastor Woolfe shook and blurred.

Verity shut her eyes tightly, trying to convince herself she was simply tired. But when she opened them, the pastor was still an amalgamation of two things: the man she had known for all the years of her life, and the stranger in front of her now.

Despite all the differences, all the oddities of his dual selves, he stood like a man who knew God was on his side.

The church had gone silent, and Pastor Woolfe put his hands on the outer edges of his pulpit.

"Good morning, friends. I am so pleased to see you here, once again in the house of God. He is overjoyed to see you; this I know." He paused a moment to let the heads in the church bob in agreement. "This is a hard time for us, isn't it? A trying time. Summer is over and the harvest season will soon come to an end. Our labours are coming to fruition, but that does not mean the end of hard work. No, the season of rest isn't upon us yet. And in trying times, isn't it good to be reminded of the core tenets of God's plan for us?"

Heads nodded around the room once again.

Verity braced herself to sink low into the pew.

"Let us speak today of the body and the spirit. It is beautiful as well to fulfil the purpose you were born to. To lead as man, and to serve as woman."

A sense of deep dread fell over Verity. She swallowed hard, staring forward and refusing to move a muscle, as if any twitch would draw the pastor's eyes like a predator to prey. She'd never been the focus of a sermon before, though she'd known people who had. Asher had been, once, when he'd taken to terrorising the town's chickens and the neighbours had had enough. It had been deeply uncomfortable, even just to watch.

The pastor pointed into the first row. "Debora Smith, have you ever felt unhappy with your lot in life?"

Debora was obscured from Verity's view by the crowd, but she saw the woman's hat shift in the distance. "Why no, Pastor."

That was rich. Debora's husband had enough wealth to employ others to work in their fields. Of course she was happy.

"Sam Wilder, are you unhappy with your lot?"

Sam shook his head. He was a respectable carpenter, one who had repaired more than half the homes in town.

"Beverly Samson?"

"Of course not, Pastor."

But the whole thing seemed off somehow. Pastor Woolfe wasn't asking the people whose lives were hard. He was asking people who had some measure of control over things.

Had he always skewed things so deeply? Or was this simply a thing she was seeing because her moods were making her exceptionally sour?

In fact, as Verity sat and endured, an uneasiness about the place crept over her, one she had never noticed before.

Something about the church felt *wrong*.

"It is normal to struggle," continued Pastor Woolfe, his voice carrying through the high-ceilinged room. "*The vessel of your body is*

71

as God wills it. And is the mind not of your vessel? Is struggle not of the mind and body? We have challenges because we are meant to, and because we can overcome them. God does not give us more than we can handle."

Something pushed at Verity's consciousness. That last line had her thinking of her mother. Of the vision she'd seen of her mother's body on the pyre. Was her mother's death something God felt Verity could handle?

Verity's stomach churned as she delved into her thoughts, ignoring Pastor Woolfe's impassioned speech. The thought crushed her and it took every bit of her willpower to sit and pretend to listen, to stare attentively at the pastor and nod when others nodded. His eyes would be on her, but she…she was in the past, grieving her mother as silently as she could.

That grief had always been silent, because no one would hear of grieving a witch.

Of course not, Verity's inner voice chided. *She was a woman of the devil and she could not be suffered to live. This is what God asks of us, to endure the pain to keep ourselves pure.*

God did not give more than a person could handle.

And those were the thoughts that warred in her mind as the sermon carried on, none of it falling on Verity's consciousness.

At long last, the pews began to stir and Verity knew she'd be expected to leave soon. To get up and stand in line and pay her respects to the pastor in the form of a curtsy. She could pretend. She had to. But as she stood from the pew, she felt a burn in her abdomen. A warm discomfort signalled the beginning of her moon cycle. How long had she sat there, bleeding in the church?

Verity flushed and grabbed Asher by the shoulder, panic in her throat. "I have to go—I—Tell Father I'm sorry." She was unclean and no longer allowed to be near the others, and frankly, it suited her well.

Asher looked confused for a moment, but he quickly understood, making room for her silent escape from the pew.

Pushing past each member of her family, Verity made her way into the sea of bodies, swimming backward against the tide. Her father called after her, but she heard Asher's voice a moment later. The crowd was displeased with her, that much was clear, but they made room all the same.

Once Verity was outside, the cool air enveloped her. It was all too much, and now this bleeding besides. She wouldn't be able to do anything once the cramping set in as heavily as she knew it would and these mysteries—the witch. She would have to wait to meet Arden. Pain was coming. Pain that would stop her doubts of the church and her anger and—everything. That pain always stopped *everything*.

An invisible knife tore her abdomen, the kind that would continue to stab her day in and day out until this thing was done, and sometimes in between. The witch would have to wait. For now, it would be Verity, the four walls of the barn, and the curse God had given her.

CHAPTER EIGHT

Verity

The barn loft was a living nightmare. Each month it came back to haunt her, over and over. It was lonely and chilly and smelled of goat and goat shit. While she was trapped inside, it was her job to shovel the barn out, and whatever she couldn't manage to shovel, she had to live with. In the summer, it stank and sweltered, and in the winter it was a miracle when she didn't freeze to death. It would've been a horrible place to spend the night on a good day, but while she was in agony, she imagined that it must be what Hell felt like.

Curled up under three heavy blankets and sitting on a bed of two-day-old hay, Verity shivered. The sun had set hours ago, and the loft was sparsely illuminated with a tiny oil lamp. She wished the flame would give off more heat.

Though the barn wasn't as drafty as it could have been, it wasn't warm by any means. The days were still sunny enough to bring heat into the space, but a few hours after dark, all that heat was gone again. In the summer it was worse; Verity would wake drenched in sweat and so warm it felt like a fever.

While she was technically allowed to leave and take in some air, God said it was unclean to be near other people while on a moon cycle. If she was well, she sometimes went outside to walk the fields behind the house, but mostly she was confined inside. During the first days, she always bled enough to keep her in one place, wishing to God she had something to stop it. And that was to say nothing of the pain. It kept her rooted, curled up on her rag and spoiled hay and enduring the stabbing ache of her insides.

Verity picked up the small block of wood and the chisel next to the lantern. It was one of the only things a person could do with so little light and so little opportunity to move. She'd started carving a sparrow, but it was slow work with little room for error. One careful movement at a time, she tried to free the bird from its wooden confinement, slivers of wood peeling away under her tool.

She'd had two days with nothing but time to think. She hadn't seen most of her family since church and couldn't be sure how cross her father was with her. Clarabel was allowed to bring food to her since she was also a girl, and small moments were permitted for necessities, but for the rest, she would see no one until it was done. She could only hope they had attributed all her strangeness to her womanly curse. People seemed quick to blame things on it any other day, at least.

If her mother had been alive, and if they'd been on the same cycle, at least she'd have had company.

Verity was already two days in the loft, which meant two days overdue at Arden's. If she were to explain herself, surely the witch would understand. *Surely* the witch was also prone to such curses and she knew what the Good Book said. But Arden lived alone. No one could tell her what to do, or whom she had to separate herself from. Would she be forced to go elsewhere for her moon? Verity thought longingly about what it would be like to live in the solitude of Arden's cabin, with no one to chase her out of her own bed. She could sip on tea and lie next to the fire and read the Good Book for company.

The thought brought tears to her eyes.

A shiver wracked through her again, sparking a wave of excruciating pain in her abdomen. Verity cried out, dropping the wood and chisel. Doubled over, she fell to her side into the hay and curled into a ball, trying to breathe through the wave of pain. It didn't help. It wouldn't cease. Sometimes the waves were quick and shallow, but this one…this one was not.

As she lay there, she did the only thing she could think to do. "God, please. I know you do not give us more than we can handle, but I know this is too much. Every time, it's too much. My burden is so heavy. Please. It cannot be my fate that I am torn apart so often. It feels like something is eating me from the inside. It is unbearable." Verity sobbed, her palms pressed against her face. "Please help me."

No one came.

Verity cried for a long time. She cried for the frustration of it. For the pain that wracked her body. For the isolation. For knowing that no one understood her. Tired and full of despair, she faded in and out of the world, sleeping and dreaming and conscious again, until she was hardly sure what was waking and what was not.

When Verity finally did wake, it was to the sound of Clarabel clambering up the ladder. She knew it would be her little sister because no one else was permitted to come near her.

Verity spread the blankets out around her to cover the hay she'd been lying on, in case she had bled through her clothing in the night. It was likely she had. Her head was pounding and her back protested the horrific makeshift bed.

After a moment, Clarabel poked her head out from over the edge of the loft, her hair in messy, unbrushed tufts. "Good morning!" Her gaze went back to something out of sight—likely a travel bag, the strap of which was hung over her shoulder—and she began to place things on the loft floor. First, a wooden bowl, followed by a thick slice of bread, a beeswax wrap with butter inside, and two hardboiled eggs. "Did you sleep all right?"

Verity groaned in response, making no move to get up.

The happiness leaked from Clarabel's face.

Guilt gnawed at Verity.

"I'm sorry," her little sister said. "I wish I could do something."

"I know," Verity croaked. "Is there water?"

Clarabel disappeared down the ladder. The sound of clinking metal came from below, followed by a little grunt and boots on the rungs of the ladder. When she returned, Clarabel hefted a bucket of fresh water over the side of the loft and set it next to the breakfast plate. She fished a cup out from the bag slung over her shoulder, dunked it into the bucket, and pushed it toward Verity.

The water was enough to make Verity move. She drank it down all at once, hoping it would quell her headache as well as her thirst. "Thank you."

Clarabel put her arms over the loft's edge and rested her head on them. "Does it hurt much?"

Verity nodded. She didn't want to fill the girl with fear, but it didn't seem right to lie. Their mother was gone, and when Clarabel's moon cycle arrived, it would fall to Verity to teach her how to live with it.

"Is it always that bad?"

"Yes. It wasn't at first. Not for a year or two. It's gotten worse since I was a girl. I wish it hadn't." Verity gestured toward the breakfast bowl and her sister pushed it closer to her.

"Will...will it be like this for me?" Clarabel's voice was quiet, worry in every word.

Verity stared down at the bread as she broke it into smaller chunks. "I hope not. I don't know. Mother was worried when it got worse for me, but she never spoke about her moon cycle. I don't know how it was for her. And it's not appropriate to ask—"

"I'm sorry!" Clarabel looked stricken. "I didn't mean—"

"No, no." Verity gestured for Clarabel to stop. "I'll be the one to teach you. It's all right to ask me, but it's also a private thing and not something that God wants us to speak openly about. It's a dirty thing. Do you understand that?"

Clarabel's face scrunched up as she thought. "If it's dirty, why did God give it to us?"

"It keeps us humble." Verity opened the beeswax wrapper and dipped a piece of bread in the soft butter. "It reminds us to stay in God's good graces and to be of service."

"Do men have a moon cycle?"

Verity tilted her head, thinking about it for the first time. "No, I don't think so." No one had said anything either way, so they very well could have, and she just didn't know.

"That doesn't seem fair," said Clarabel.

"Everyone carries their own burden. Being a man must surely have its own challenges and its own curses." Verity made an attempt to sound contrite, but Clarabel's question had awoken yet another doubt in her.

"I wonder if Asher would tell me. I could—"

"No, sweetheart. It's not appropriate to ask anyone. A person's body is between themselves and God."

Clarabel pouted. "I just want to understand—"

Pain struck Verity, another stab in the gut, and she groaned, cutting off Clarabel's words. She tried to breathe through it, slow and deep. Sometimes it felt like the only thing she could do was relax into the pain and will it away.

When she looked up, Clarabel had tears in her eyes. "It's not fair. I want to take your pain away."

There were ways. Verity knew that. She had heard talk in the village of people of poor repute who had broken the laws of God by addling their bodies with plant and poultice and alcohol when they were in pain. "*The vessel of your body is as God wills it*, Clarabel. We can't dilute ourselves with things from the outside. How would we learn from our suffering if we don't learn to endure pain? Our bodies are perfect as they are."

Even as she spoke the words, repeating back the things she had heard over and over in church, they felt hollow. She was so tired of the pain.

A sigh escaped Clarabel. "It seems cruel of God to make you hurt this way."

"I know, but we mustn't think that way."

"I would hug you if I could," Clarabel said.

"I know."

A silence passed over them, interrupted only by the impatient goats below, waiting to be let out. After what felt like forever, Clarabel shifted and made to leave. "I'll come back with supper."

"Have a good day at school, darling." Verity looked away as Clarabel climbed down the ladder. Clarabel let the goats outside, filling the barn with cold air once more. Verity patiently waited for the girl to be done. Once the door of the barn opened and shut again, she allowed herself a few tears. It was so hard to be strong. It was so hard to lie to her sister and repeat the things she was no longer sure were true. Guilt flooded her, knowing that soon, Clarabel would also endure this cold loft and these impossible days. Verity didn't want that for her. She didn't want that for anyone.

And yet, she also knew it would do Clarabel no good to question God and the church. The road Verity was walking was one that led nowhere safe. Questions led to doubt, and doubt was something the church did not abide. When a question could lead straight to the pyre, the safest thing was to lock up your heart and wonder about nothing.

CHAPTER NINE

Arden

When Verity appeared between the trees near Arden's cabin, the witch had already ruled her off as either dead or done with looking for answers. The girl was five days late. Arden had simply gotten on with her life. Sure, the magical mystery of it was compelling. She wanted to know how a person could suddenly begin seeing truths. The voice of Arden's mother had also told her to take care of the girl. But if Verity didn't want to be bothered with it, Arden wasn't going to force her. It wasn't her choice to make, especially when doing so would mean putting them both at risk in a town of people who hated witches. If Verity wanted answers, she could come and get them herself.

And apparently, she had. Five days off schedule.

With a mix of irritation and curiosity, Arden stopped plucking leaves from her bundle of dried herbs. Arden had a long litany of things to say to the young woman about being inconvenienced and missing appointments, but something in Verity's manner stilled her tongue. Arden stood, taking in the girl as she drew closer.

It wasn't that different from the day Verity first stumbled into Arden's camp. Verity walked slowly, bent over herself, and bundled in more than one cloak. What little of her face was visible under her hood gave the distinct impression of weariness. She looked almost like a lumbering bear on two legs, dressed as if it were the dead of winter, not the start of fall.

All the things Arden had been ready to say flitted to the back of her mind. She knew illness when she saw it. She would have time to scold the girl later.

She gestured toward the cabin. "Come inside. There's a fire going and you look like you're already half dead."

"I feel half dead," Verity groaned, making her way to the front door and letting herself in.

Arden closed the door behind them and set a kettle of water on the stove. She was mildly surprised that the poor girl had already made herself comfortably at home, sitting down at the table and slumping across it. Gone was the rigid, worried piousness. That said more to Arden than anything else could have.

Verity was too bad off to keep up her guard.

"I'm late. I'm sorry," Verity mumbled.

"Are you ill?" Arden examined her glass jars for the right mixture of herbs, sprinkling dashes of things into a piece of cheesecloth. A little tea was good for everyone.

"Not ill, no." Verity paused, letting out a long, tired breath. "It's my moon cycle. I couldn't meet you until now, and I know I shouldn't be here because God says no one should be near me when I'm unclean, but you don't believe in God, so maybe you don't care. I still need to know what's wrong with my mind and I didn't want to make you so angry you wouldn't tell me."

Arden stopped what she was doing and looked at Verity. It was a lot to take in, but godly ramblings aside, something she'd said had caught Arden's attention. As someone who had assisted many women in her short life, she knew a few things about the bleeding, but she'd rarely seen anyone look as if they'd caught the plague.

"What are you feeling?" Arden snatched up a few jars of ingredients that helped with things like cramping, nausea, and pain, all pieces of what she would normally brew for her own bleeding.

"I'm feeling ashamed," Verity groaned. "I'm feeling desperate. I'm feeling like God is going to be angry with me for leaving the loft, but I said I'd meet you and I'm already late and I'm just so tired." The girl started sobbing into her elbow, her voice muffled in her clothing.

Arden added a pinch more pain relief to the mixture.

"How much do you bleed?"

"That's...that's not something you're allowed to ask me."

Arden pushed down the frustration that welled in her throat. "Among your people, perhaps, but we're in the woods now. Their rules don't apply out here. You have a right to your secrets, and you can keep them if you want, but I can't help you if you don't talk to me."

Verity sniffed, wiping her eyes with her hand and pushing her face back into the crook of her arm. "What good will talking do?"

It wasn't the first time Arden had heard that from one of the villagers. It spoke volumes about how the so-called doctor was practising his medicine.

"Your body is telling us a story," Arden said, as patiently as she could manage. "The things you feel and experience tell me about what's happening on the inside." She struggled to think of something Verity would be able to relate to. "Like how the colour of the morning sky can tell you about the coming storm."

Verity didn't say anything.

"So, how much do you bleed?" Arden asked again.

"I...if I tell you this, and they..." Verity's voice quivered. "I am afraid of burning."

That struck a dagger into Arden's heart. "It seems to me you're already burning, a little at a time. You're here. You're already taking the risk to sit across from me. You could walk away now, with all the risk and no answers in return. But shouldn't you be rewarded with the care you deserve?"

Verity let out a deep sob, and Arden waited for the girl to run or stay.

It took a while before the words dropped out of Verity's mouth. "I bleed enough that it scares me. It's constant for days and it hurts more than anything else I've felt. It—" Verity took a composing breath, choking down the tears. "This is disgusting to speak of. I'm sorry."

Arden tied off the cheesecloth with a string and put it in a mug, fighting the impatience that ran under her skin. It shouldn't be her job to teach every person in that town one by one what it meant to have a body, and yet, if she didn't, who would? "I asked because it's important."

The look that Verity gave Arden was one of confusion. "Why is it important?"

Arden poured the now-steaming water over the cheesecloth of herbs. A mix of earthy and floral scents filled the room. She put the mug in front of Verity and sat down on the chair nearest to her. Arden hoped the girl wouldn't suspect the cup was more than *just* tea. "Because I have a feeling you're in more pain than you ought to be over something as simple as a bleeding."

Verity sat up a little, pulling the mug under her face and cupping her hands around it for warmth. A look of incredulity settled in on her features. She was *angry*. "There's nothing simple about this. Not for me."

Arden gave a nod, trying to lean into the qualities of the healer, not of the bitter person she was at her core. "When it's my time to bleed, I have some pain. Some discomfort. I get very tired for a day or two, and I bleed, but I can still go about my day if I take the right precautions. Does that sound like your life?"

"No," Verity choked out. "Never."

"I believe you. Tell me about the pain."

Arden listened as Verity sipped her medicinal tea and told her about the loft. About the unbearable stabbing pain and the headaches that lasted for days. The way she felt faint and powerless. About the endless hunger and the cold. Arden listened intently, using every ounce of her strength not to lash out in a rage for every wronged woman who had come before her. She had sat across from so many women who suffered needlessly, and Verity would not be the last. There had been so many that Arden could hardly stomach it.

When Verity was done telling her story, she looked at Arden as if examining her for something. "You're the first person who ever let me talk about this."

"I'm sorry. People should have been listening." Keeping her rage in check was taking every ounce of her discipline. She *hated* that town. "Please tell me you use something for the pain."

Verity looked away. "No."

"Because the Good Book tells you not to."

Verity nodded.

"And your village doctor. Doctor Raam. What does he do when you go to him?"

"It depends. When I accidentally opened my arm on a kitchen knife two years ago, he stitched it up and washed the wound. But if I ask him questions about my private body, he talks over me until I'm quiet. He's told me before that it can't be nearly as bad as I say, and to focus on *not* feeling pain. He got angry when I tried to ask him a second time and told me to ask God why I deserved it."

Very intentionally, Arden numbed herself to the words coming out of Verity's mouth. Short of enacting revenge, it was the only thing left for Arden to do. She tapped her fingers on the table in frustration, thinking about her options instead of her feelings. She knew this young woman needed help. Verity's threshold for pain was high. It had to be. She had endured the pain for years and was only now beginning to seek out help against the word of their god. Sitting at that table, Arden knew the moment they were in was important.

Verity was in too much pain to worry about sin, and it could be a turning point for how she looked at her own body.

Verity *needed* to understand what was happening to her. Arden knew the risks to issues with the womb. They could lead to terrible things. To babies born early or dead or unhealthy. To lethargy and painful sex and infertility. Some things Arden knew how to fix and some things she didn't. She was deeply aware that no matter how much she understood about the body, she would never know enough. What she could do had limits, even with her magic.

The real question was, if Arden taught her things, would Verity listen?

She had to try. It was what Arden had been raised to do. As frustrating and dangerous as that village could be, Verity could only live as she'd been taught to live. She didn't know about any other way.

Arden would *try*.

She'd just need a little help.

"I'd like to take you somewhere." Arden rose from her chair and went to pour herself a non-medicinal cup of tea. The scent of black tea and spices filled the air around her.

"Where?" It seemed as if the fight had left Verity. Gone were the pious rejections of Arden's help, and the leagues of worry in her eyes. All that was left was exhaustion.

Perhaps the young woman truly was ready.

"I want you to meet someone special to me. She taught me everything I know, and she would have had so much to say to you right now, because she was better at this than I am. Would you come with me?"

Verity nodded and took another drink. "I just want this to stop. I can't live like this."

"I'll take that as a yes."

"Yes," Verity confirmed. "Are you taking me to one of your spirit ladies?"

Arden smirked. How many ladies did this girl imagine she had? "No, I'm not. Drink your tea first." She paused, breathing deep, holding in the scent of the spices in her cup. Breath was so important to the body, especially when one was trying not to let their harsh feelings get the better of them. "How do you feel?"

Verity sighed. "Tired. Somewhat better, but not by much."

"It takes time, but that tea will lessen your pain."

Verity straightened like someone had cracked a whip next to her ear. "The tea?"

Arden couldn't help smirking. "Yes, Dandelion, the tea."

"What did you put in it?" Verity lifted the mug, prodding the cheesecloth of herbs as if they would reveal their secrets.

"Herbs that would reduce your pain, soothe your muscles, and calm your mind. They're what I use for myself, when I need them."

Verity was appalled. "But God doesn't want us addling our bodies with herbs and liquor and smoke!"

That statement challenged Arden to her core. She quite enjoyed all three. "By the teachings of your own book, your god created this world and everything in it. That means these herbs are also by your god's design. He meant for you to use them for your pain, or else they would do nothing to alleviate it. Or did your god make a mistake in the creation of the plants around us?"

Staring at the wall of the cabin, Verity's eyes darted back and forth, puzzling out what Arden had said. This went on for a while. Arden watched, amused, until Verity slumped back over her tea and groaned.

"It doesn't make sense! How can one thing God wants from us also go against something else?"

"The Good Book is full of contradictions, Dandelion. People create flawed things all the time." Arden took her own cheesecloth out of her cup and set it in a tiny dish at the centre of the table, sure that her drink was finally strong enough for her liking. "They're there, when you open your eyes to them."

"You just don't want me to believe in God," Verity snapped, venom in her voice. "You want me tempted by your demons and spirits instead."

"Your faith doesn't matter to me one bit." Arden blew on her tea and took a sip. "I want you to be smart enough to see the difference between gods and men. Your book reeks of men pretending to be gods."

Verity fell into silence again, a catatonic expression on her face as she continued to weigh the sins she had just committed.

Self-work was hard. It tore the mind apart and put it back anew. Arden had had plenty of those kinds of headaches in her life and she didn't envy Verity one bit.

"Finish your tea," she said. "We'll leave when you're done."

When they reached the tree where Arden's mother was buried and Arden sat down in the grass, Verity seemed confused.

"Sit down." Arden patted the grass beside her and waited until Verity had settled in. She gestured up to the tree, whose leaves were changing from reds and russets to a flaking, falling brown. "This is my mother. She's buried here, along with all her knowledge. When I'm tired or when I miss her, I come here. Today I need to be near her, so she can guide my hand in supporting you."

Verity gazed up at the tree. "You planted this for her?"
Arden nodded.

"That's beautiful." Verity kept looking, and after a moment, a tear rushed down her cheek. "I miss my mother. I'm not supposed to, because she was a witch too. They burned her and I had to take up her work at home. It's hard, and I know she would understand my worries if she were here, but I'm not allowed to speak to her. I can't even visit her. There's no tree for her. No grave. They tossed her body in the swamp with the other witches."

As cold and unmovable as Arden often felt, her heart broke for the girl. "A mother is irreplaceable. I'm sorry yours was taken from you."

Verity nodded and wiped away the tears, her face hardening as she closed off that door to her heart. "Why are we here?"

"Because I need support." Arden took the leather tie looped around her wrist and pulled her white hair into a loose bun at the back of her head. "There are things you need to learn, whether you're ready to or not, and I need my mother's knowledge for that." Arden had carried her bottle of whiskey with her. She opened it and took a drink. It burned her throat in that old familiar way, and she poured a drink into the ground.

"My family came here long before I was born," Arden started. "The women in my family have always been witches. Some have been more devoted to the craft and the spirits than others, but each of them understood they were from a long line of healers whose duty it was to keep others alive and well, when at all possible. In their homeland, back across the ocean, they knew the plants and animals as if they were their siblings. They understood how the forests lived and breathed, and what could be used in service of humanity.

"When my grandmother came over on the ship to settle here, she hadn't picked her ship wisely. She didn't understand that the people were especially religious until she was in the middle of the ocean. By the time they docked in the new world, she knew she wasn't welcome. She needed a community to survive, so she kept to the woods around the settlement, and she worked in secret with the women of the village, just like I do now. She learned quickly about the ways of your god and how unforgiving he could be. She also knew women in the village would die without her, because god or no, childbirth is a dangerous thing, and your doctors should be hanged for saying they practise medicine—" Arden forced down her rage and took a breath. "I'm sorry.

That's not helpful. In either case, my grandmother put herself at great risk to help your ancestors. So did my mother, and so do I."

Arden took another drink of whiskey and found the bottle empty. "This land isn't like the land from home, or so I was told by my mother. My grandmother learned how to live in reciprocity with the spirits here. You've heard of the people who lived here before us, yes?"

Verity's mouth was hanging open. "I know of them. We're told to stay away from them. They kill people and they have no god, and—"

Arden held up a hand, her patience floundering. "Think for a moment. Your people have lied to you about other things. Is it possible they've lied about that as well?"

Verity pursed her lips, a war raging behind her eyes. She nodded. "It's possible."

"I understand your hesitation. It's hard to learn that what you believe might be wrong." Arden reached out and touched one of the round leaves of her mother's tree, looking for strength. "The people who lived on this land before us are kind and generous. They taught my grandmother how the plants here live and thrive. What heals sickness and what causes it. She was able to give some small bits of knowledge in return, and she was friends with many community members until she died. Grandmother introduced them to the spirits she brought with her across the water, and was introduced to the ones here in turn. So much of what they taught my grandmother has saved people in your village. You live on their land and profit from their knowledge and kill their people."

Having at least the sense of self to be ashamed, Verity looked away, red in her cheeks.

"This land and the spirits who live here, they have so much to offer to the people who live in balance with them. Your people seek to use them until they're gone. They cut trees and refuse to plant them. They kill animals faster than they can reproduce. And what then? When everything has died out and been cut away, what then?"

90

Arden adjusted herself, sitting to face Verity. "We can't change the past, but it's our responsibility to learn from it. To do better than the ones who came before us. Does that make sense?"

Verity stared out into the woods, and Arden could see the calculations running in her mind. "Yes. God teaches kindness as well. He wanted us to love the world as we would love the people in our homes."

It was not what Arden would have preferred to hear, but it was a start. "Now you understand where this all comes from. I'm going to teach you about the herbs that can lessen your pain, and the things you can do for your body that will help you. We're going to talk and you're welcome to ask any question you wish, but I'm asking you to *try* to believe me. Can you do that?"

Verity sat up straight, resolve in her eyes. "I can. Even if it's hard."

"Good." Arden smiled.

And so Arden talked and Verity listened. The witch told her about the connection of the body to the moon and tides, the shape and make of her organs, and what happened inside her body each cycle, to the best of the knowledge Arden possessed. She was allowed to touch Verity's stomach—with her skin covered, lest the contact burn them—to examine what hurt and what didn't. She showed her the shape of the herbs that would help with pain and nausea and taught her where to find them. And she told Verity it might still not be enough, for some things in the body could not be healed with a plant and a prayer.

By the time the shadows had grown long, Arden could see Verity's mind was full to bursting. It wasn't fair to pile more onto her before she had time to sleep on things.

"That's enough for now." Arden picked up the things she'd brought with her for Verity's use. "How do you feel?"

Verity laughed sourly, but she wore a glimmer of a smile. "Tired. It's not that I don't believe you…"

When Verity didn't finish the sentence, Arden took a guess. "It creates holes in the fabric of your life."

Verity nodded. "It means people have lied to me since I was a baby. It means I didn't need to be in all this pain for all these years, and someone else decided that for me. And for what? For what?" Her voice cracked and Verity was crying again.

A small part of Arden wanted to hold the young woman, but only a small part. She'd been generous enough that day, giving all this information and time to Verity, and trusting it was the right thing to do. Instead, she let the girl cry until the tears tapered off. Crying was good for the soul, even if it was quite inconvenient.

"Do you feel more lost than before, or less?" Arden asked.

"Both." Verity laughed as she wiped the tears from her face. "Most definitely both."

Arden pulled a small bundle of herbs from her bag, the same mixture she'd made for Verity's tea. "Keep this hidden and use it only when you're alone. Use it no more than twice a day, until the pain subsides. If you use more, or you drink it too close together, you'll end up shitting your skirts and you'll only have yourself to blame."

The last of Verity's composure broke and she burst into full-hearted laughter. Arden felt a small pang of appreciation for her in that moment. A girl with a laugh like that was someone she could be friends with, if it weren't for all the hand-wringing and godliness.

"Shitting my skirts," Verity echoed, wiping away a tear. "Now that's exactly what I'd like to add to this horrible week."

CHAPTER TEN

Verity

Verity's mind felt like sun-dried fruit. When she'd snuck out of the barn that morning, she'd already felt like half a person, and the avalanche of information she'd been given only clouded her mind further. She had understood the words Arden had said, and she remembered the instructions, but it all felt so foreign to her. So far outside her life. She had gone to Arden to—

Cursing, Verity ground to a stop and leaned on the tree closest to her. She had *gone* to Arden to get answers about her visions. With everything else, she had forgotten to ask. The witch had brought it up when she first arrived, and they hadn't spoken of it again. Verity had also meant to ask about the vision of her mother, and what that might have been alluding to.

Forehead pressed against the tree, she weighed her options.

Turn around and ask, or go home.

She was already halfway back and in God's honest truth, she

wasn't prepared for more of anything. She was tired and so many things were on her mind already, darting around like tadpoles in a pond. If she crammed anything else in there, she feared she'd go mad.

Verity picked up her feet, pushed off the tree, and headed home.

The rest of the walk was filled with so many thoughts and fears that Verity hardly noticed she'd set foot back in the village. Her feet had carried her on familiar paths without her mind being present, and she was grateful for it. She just had so much to think about.

It was getting dark when she returned. Candlelight filtered out through the windows of her family home. She walked up the path to the front door, the laughter of her family inside luring her in, but as she reached for the door handle, she stopped.

Though her pain had lessened and her bleeding had slowed to a crawl, she *was* still bleeding. It went against the ways of God and the ways of her village for her to go inside and be near others.

Frozen in place, Verity breathed in the scent of a fresh supper that wafted through the cracks in the door. It would be warm inside, and the chill of the autumn wind had started to cut through her clothing once more. She turned to look at the barn. The cold, dark loft waited for her.

She had done so many things as of late that she would have been ashamed of only a few months ago. Her visits to the witch. The visions that sprang up when someone lied. Drinking tea to addle her body. Shirking her responsibilities. They weren't the things a person devoted to God and family and service should have done. She *should* be ashamed.

And yet, as she stood there, caught between the warm house and the cold barn, she felt this was a long time coming.

For years, she had done what was asked of her, and for years she had built up resentment, one shallow cut at a time. She had given and given, which she had assumed—wrongly—would buy her compassion for the moments when she slipped up. Now, when she was suffering in her body and in her mind, scared of the pain and the visions, she had no one to turn to for help.

How many of the people who had burned as witches had been like her? Scared and alone and tired, looking for help?

Had her mother been like her? Had she once searched for help, only to be killed for it?

Verity was tired of being left to suffer alone.

She felt so weak, and yet something in her wanted to turn that handle and walk in.

Tomorrow. There would be time for bravery tomorrow.

First, she needed to lie down.

Verity slept long and deep. Perhaps it had had something to do with that tea, or perhaps it was the overflowing of her mind, but when she woke close to noon the following day, she was grateful. Her breakfast had been left on the loft floor, though she hadn't heard anyone arrive, and she ate it as quickly as her stomach allowed.

For the first time in a week, she felt rested.

She spent the afternoon lying in a patch of sun in the loft, thinking about all she'd learned from Arden and dreaming up her plan. The hours of discussion the previous day left Verity with an uncharacteristic wish to do something to spite everyone else. Not to get caught, of course, but to do something imperceptibly deviant. To take back a bit of her pride, when she was now so sure this village had stolen it all.

As the afternoon faded to dusk, she heard her family come home. Heard the familiar voices of each of them, and, through the knotholes of the barn loft, saw the candlelight flicker to life in the house. She would wait. She knew how long a supper took to make.

And for once, she would return, bleeding and unclean, and let them cook for her.

It felt so far from crimes like murder and theft, but so large a crime in her heart.

Knowing they would expect her to come back to them freshly bathed and clean of evil again, Verity took a detour to the back of the shed where she kept her bowl and soap. She washed every inch of her body, rubbing the goat's milk soap over her until she smelled like lies and cream. While she scrubbed, the voice of fear in her mind told her she could still stop. She could end this deviance and go back to the barn, and no one would know she almost committed a litany of sins. Twice, she put the soap down. Twice, she got angry and picked it back up.

And why shouldn't she be angry? She'd spent her whole life in Arrothburg, and no one listened to her, and she'd known the witch for a scant handful of days, but the woman had cut Verity's pain in half with *a cup of tea.*

This is how people are tempted into the arms of demons, Verity, her pious, worried mind told her.

Yes, she agreed. *And I'm starting to wonder if demons aren't kinder than people.*

Once she was scrubbed and dry, she went to the front of the shed. As usual, a fresh dress had been hung inside the shed for when her bleeding was over. Verity tossed her dirty one into the already-filthy bucket of sudsy water. She pulled on the clean dress, padded her underclothes with rags for safety, and went back to the house.

When she opened the door, her breath caught and her heart was in her throat. Her family stopped and looked up, startled. They stared at her like she was a ghost. It was likely they hadn't expected her back yet, and they were right not to. But since no one would be brave enough to ask how her bleeding was, Verity simply smiled at them. "Is there a plate for me?"

Asher smiled back. "Always. Come sit." He made room next to him at the table, and gave her seat a pat.

As Verity went to the table, their father's brow was furrowed. Perhaps he suspected her lie. But the only way to confirm it was to ask questions she'd never once heard uttered from his lips, and she prayed he would not start that day.

He did not.

They ate in companionable chatter, and Verity was thankful for the company and the warmth. In her tired mind, she said a little prayer. *Thank you, God, for the food you have given me this day, and for a family that loves me. And thank you for the gift of tea to heal my pain. My life is made better by them, and I am grateful.*

It felt wrong, and yet also right.

As her siblings slowly ate and left to do other things, and the duties of cleaning up wordlessly shifted back to Verity, she was left alone in silence with her father.

All the changes, all the things she had learned and unlearned and challenged, they were like a boulder rolling downhill. After days of pain and broken sleep, and all those lessons, she found herself still enthralled by it. Her mind felt full to the point of breaking, and yet she thirsted for more. She felt the question forming, and though she was afraid to ask, she knew she might not be so brave tomorrow.

"Father? Would you tell me about Mother?"

Verity's father stood stock-still, his plate hovering above the counter where he'd been about to set it down. She saw more emotion on his face than she had seen on him in a long time. "We do not talk about witches."

"I understand that, but how am I to avoid her fate if I don't know how she failed to see the devil in her own life?" Verity marvelled at herself a moment, wondering if she'd always been a manipulative liar at heart. "I never had a chance to ask her about our history. I don't even know what she did to deserve the pyre, and it seems unfair to ask me to avoid the same fate if I don't know what was done."

Jona looked up at her, staring. He seemed to be searching her eyes for something.

"Father, I don't even know why she's dead."

Jona inhaled, long and deep, and when he let the breath out, his shoulders fell. "Fine. Sit, and we'll talk."

Verity pulled two of the chairs closer to the hearth and watched as her father pulled open a drawer in the kitchen. She opened her mouth to ask what he was looking for, only to stop in shock as he pulled the back of the drawer away. A false back. And inside was a pipe.

"Father!"

Jona hushed her. "Quiet now. If I'm going to ask for penance later for speaking of a witch, I may as well sin twice." He sat down in the chair next to hers and set to work stuffing and lighting the pipe. "Life is hard, Verity. We are all sinners, though we pray our children will be stronger than we are." He took a drag and exhaled the smoke.

All of the words had fallen out of Verity's head. She'd never seen her father sinning so openly before. She had no idea why he was letting her see it.

"You want to know about your mother," Jona said, changing the subject. "When they came for her, Pastor Woolfe told me she'd been accused of cursing the woman she worked for. You remember she used to wash clothes for the Adler household, yes?"

Verity nodded.

"Well, Mrs Adler said your mother became enraged, threw the clean wash across the yard, and spat curses at the woman. Curses against God. Summons to invite harm on Mrs Adler."

"Did she?" Verity had a lump in her throat.

A wicked grin appeared on Jona's face. "It may be that she did. I doubt it was a true curse, not the magic kind. Your mother told me often that Mrs Adler would ask for unreasonable things, or demand something be washed multiple times. I think your mother just had enough."

Verity hardly knew what to say. She had expected a crime greater than that. True magic. Evidence her mother had withered crops or worked with demons. Not an angry outburst of curses. That was not godly behaviour, certainly, but was it something to die over?

Jona was staring into the fire, smoking, elbows on his knees. The corners of his lips turned up slightly, as if remembering something good. "Your mother had always been high-spirited. We both grew up here, and we'd always known each other. Your grandparents on both sides were close—God rest all their souls—and Daphne and I grew up in each other's houses. When we were old enough to know such things, your mother started to leave flowers at my window. I was slower to romance than she was, and it was two years before I began to feel for her in return." He took another drag and let it out. "She was always remarkable. She had a mind as sharp as an axe and a tongue too wild for her own good. I was too busy with frogs and games and chores to notice for a long while, but I did, eventually, and it was the end of me."

Father nudged forward in his chair, grabbed a piece of split wood from the pile next to the hearth, and tossed it into the fire.

"We married when she was 16 and I was 15. Our parents felt we'd waited too long already, but we wanted to be sure. These days a wedded couple will have a baby at 18 years old, but a generation ago you'd have been expected to be married with *two* children by 18. But Daphne's parents weren't a happy couple, and she was afraid we'd be just like them, arguing loudly into the night." He sighed contentedly. "Best day of my life, that was. Our wedding day."

The bittersweet smile on his face broke Verity's heart.

He had kept all of this in for years. It was a rare thing to see her father slow down long enough to tell a story, let alone share a moment of raw emotion. She had wondered more than once if he had cared so little about his wife that he never spoke of her, or if it was because he was so distraught he couldn't bear to. Verity still wasn't sure she knew.

"And me?" Verity had held on to questions like these all her life, never daring to ask. "Was she...happy to have me?"

Father looked at her a moment, a pitying frown on his face. "Child, of course she was. You were the light of her life, especially when you were her only baby. I could hardly get a moment of her time when you were born, because she was so in love with you. I never held that against her, though. It took so much to get you."

"What do you mean?" Verity asked. She'd never heard anything of the sort before. Every word of this was new to her, because when she'd had the chance to ask, none of it had mattered. She'd been a child when her mother was alive. If her parents had been telling these stories as she was growing up, she hadn't been listening. It had already been hard enough to memorise the rules of the family and of God, and to learn her numbers and letters and all the other things school taught. She hadn't had a care in the world for her family's history, and now that she did, half those stories were gone forever. No one would speak of her mother again, not outside her four walls.

The sigh that came out of her father was laced with pain. "We never told anyone, least of all you, but we waited a long time on a baby. Your mother and I wanted children badly, and we did everything we were supposed to. And we begged God every night. The town was watching and talking and everyone would ask us, *Daphne and Jona, when are you going to give us a baby?* And we had no answer for them, because it seemed God didn't want us to have one. The longer it went on, the more melancholic your mother became. She would leave the house and all the chores untouched and go for long walks in the woods. Sometimes she'd return with food, but I think she just wanted to be alone with God. Then, one day, she put my hand on her belly and told me you were with us. That God had rewarded our patience."

Without warning, Verity's vision shifted. A sharp ache in her head burst forth, and she saw a familiar place. A cabin in the woods. Arden's cabin. Verity's mother, young and beautiful, and speaking with a woman whom Verity had never met. The woman in the cabin had a young, silver-haired girl at her side, and somehow Verity knew it was Arden and her mother. The vision shifted, and Daphne was in a clearing, surrounded by flowers. She was lying in the tall grass, a halo of daisies around her hair, and something came to lie beside her. Not quite a person. Something more than human. Daphne seemed nervous, but determined. It kissed Verity's mother with a hunger Verity found unfamiliar, and as they entwined, the vision changed again. Her mother, her hand on her belly, speaking to Jona.

The vision fell away.

"Are you all right, Verity?" Her father was staring at her.

Verity nodded, blinking tears from her eyes. "Apologies. A small headache, I think. It is a lot to imagine."

And though she didn't mean his stories, he nodded along. "I see. Make sure you rest tonight. We can't have you falling ill."

"I will, Father."

"Good." He got up and gave Verity a hard pat on the shoulder. "I love you, child. Don't walk the same paths your mother did."

"I won't," she whispered.

Jona turned and went to climb the stairs.

Collapsing forward, Verity sobbed quietly into her hands. At best, Doctor Raam would completely dismiss everything she said. At worst, he might detect her sins. And the vision—it was all too much.

After her father had said what had gotten her mother killed, she had hoped her mother was innocent. But she *had* sinned; she just hadn't been caught over the *worst* sin. Her mother had lain with someone who was not her husband and who had not been human, and what did that make Verity?

Jona was not her father.

Her father was not her father.

Her father—

Her true father was some spirit or demon in the woods, and no wonder she had magics in her. She was made of something inhuman. She was not a person, not fully.

Verity dug her nails into the flesh of her face just deep enough to feel the pain of it.

She had wanted to know things, because learning it had felt like freedom. She hadn't realised things could be learned that could never be erased.

These visions, these truths, they were a burden. They were better left alone and buried. She hadn't been given a choice. They'd simply been thrust upon her and now she was forced to carry them for the rest of her days.

It was too much.

It was all too much.

CHAPTER ELEVEN

Arden

Arden spent a week tending to herself and the needs of the spirits after Verity left. The rage that had built up under her skin had needed to go *somewhere*, and so it had gone into her work.

By design, Arden had spent years in isolation from the people in closest proximity. She let them come to her, trickling in with their problems and leaving again. She liked it that way. She had let a few people into her life in the past, only for them to disappear or be burnt as a witch by association. She refused to even think of their names anymore, and wasn't about to add any new names to the list.

Verity was a problem. Despite her best efforts, Arden was beginning to like the girl. She was smart, and she had potential. Damaged, yes, but weren't they all? And yet, having someone come back and forth into her space unsettled Arden. She needed time away from it. To recover from it, away from the various horrors of Verity's life.

If Arden kept herself at a distance, she could find balance. Safety. Her duty to help others was fulfilled, and yet she also had all the time she wanted to live between the trees and breathe in the life of things, which was what she really craved. It seemed everyone else had forgotten how to live that way, in peace with things. Perhaps had never known at all.

Sometimes, when she was sitting alone by the fire and thinking, Arden wondered if the problem with Arrothburg was ambition. She had some, yes, but not in the way the leaders of that town had it. Her small ambitions had never led her to wipe a forest off the map to build a village. They had not led her to lie, cheat, and steal to gain power for herself. She took only what she needed to survive. To her, it was impossible to take more than a person needed and still live in balance with the world. Balance was using no more than was needed, and to have excess was to be unbalanced.

She was deeply, sadly aware that she could not control the will of others. She typically kept to herself until someone brought trouble to her.

She couldn't force them to change, and so she stayed away.

When trouble did arrive that day—as it inevitably always did—it arrived at dusk in the form of a woman old enough for smile lines and young enough to run through the trees at a steady clip. Arden noticed her when she began calling out, and set her embroidery down.

The woman reached the edge of the trees and stopped, leaning on one trunk to catch her breath. "My daughter—" she wheezed and gasped for air. "My daughter needs help. She—" Her voice broke and Arden realised she had been crying as she ran, tears and mucus wetting her face. "She gave birth yesterday and the doctor says she's well, but she's not. She pales and the bleeding hasn't stopped yet and I think it's infected but he won't help us. He says God will do the rest, but I cannot leave this to God. Please!"

Arden leapt up. The rush of someone's need dampened everything else. She thrived in the crisis of it. Throwing open the door to her cabin, she grabbed her bag of supplies.

With no time to spare, she followed the woman through the forest, letting her guide the way. They made it to the edge of the village with the urgency often brought on by impending death, but Arden brought the woman to a stop before they went any further.

"A moment, please." Arden reached into her bag and pulled out a white bonnet, which she swiftly tucked her long tresses into. Following that was a simple cloak in the same fashion as the average woman about town. While it was late enough that most people would be inside, it would do neither her nor the woman's family any good if she were spotted. "Lead the way."

The woman took her swiftly between several homesteads at the back of town. The streets were mostly empty due to the time of day, and those who did pass didn't pay them much mind. When they walked up to a quaint home with shuttered windows, the sound of sobbing came from inside.

The woman let Arden in and closed the door behind them. Immediately the metallic smell of blood hit Arden's nose. The home was made of a single large room. The curtains were drawn and a few candles gave light to the bed in the corner. It was large enough for a couple to share, and the new mother was tucked inside it, but the husband was nowhere to be seen. A pale, sweat-sheened woman lay in the bed. She was curled around a baby, crying. Arden drew closer. The woman's black hair was wet and tangled. Blankets were pulled up over her, and yet she still shivered as if she were out in the cold.

Arden put her bag down, took off her disguise, and put on her best bedside manner. A snide bitch she may have sometimes been, but only when the situation called for it. "Hello, darling. My name is Arden and I'm here to do what your doctor will not."

The girl nodded, shaking under her blankets.

"Your name?"

"Hope," the trembling woman answered.

"And yours?" Arden asked, turning back to the older woman.

"Flora."

Arden pulled the covers down from Hope's neck and felt her skin. She had obviously been fevered but she was cooler to the touch than Arden would've liked. "Flora, get water and a clean cloth, two sets."

Arden focused on the new mother as the sound of rummaging came from behind her. The front door opened and shut. "Hope, I'm going to need you to lie on your back. Yes, that's perfect. Now pull your legs up, feet on the bed. Good. I'm going to take a look at your parts and see what this doctor has done."

Hope said nothing, but her crying became more desperate, more lonesome.

Arden whipped the sheets up over Hope's knees and moved her thin dress to the side. A faint smell lingered, one that could possibly be an infection, but she'd treated infections much sourer than Hope's, and that was a relief. The skin of her genitals was red and inflamed. She didn't dare touch anything, not yet, but it gave her an idea of the battle ahead. Hearing the sound of boots outside, Arden quickly pulled the covers down. No use in her mother seeing more than she needed to.

Flora rushed back through the door with a pail of water and poured out two bowls.

As Flora worked, Arden instructed her. "One bowl at the bedside table. That'll be for you. Another here, next to me." A moment later, it was done.

Arden could tell the woman to sit and to mind her daughter, as was normally the way she liked to do things, but she found herself with a unique opportunity to get to the truth of things.

"I need one more thing from you, ma'am. Do you know the young woman Verity?" Arden waited for Flora to nod. "Fetch her and bring her here."

Flora's mouth gaped open. "But—if she tells anyone that you've been here, we'll all be burned for it."

"I understand it's normally so, yes, but Verity is already tangled up with me far more than she'd like to be. You can trust her." Arden stared at Flora until the woman grew uncomfortable.

"As you say. I'll bring her." And the woman was off.

Anything to save her child, even disobeying their god.

While Flora was fetching Verity, Arden took some of the water and a bar of soap from the counter and washed her hands into a dish basin. She scrubbed under her nails, like her mother had shown her a long time ago, rinsed everything off, and touched nothing between the basin and the patient. Once the blanket was out of the way again, Arden could begin her work.

"Listen to me, Hope. I'm going to touch your genitals and it may be embarrassing, but I need you to let me. If I hurt you, you must tell me. If something is wrong, you must tell me. Understood?"

Hope squeaked out a yes.

It only took a moment for Arden to determine what had happened. The birth had split Hope's skin between one opening and the next, and she had needed stitching up. The doctor had done this, but the stitches were crude and the wound was inflamed. Anger had started simmering in Arden's veins the moment she'd entered the house, and seeing the pain that had been inflicted on this poor girl, she was ready to put her fist through a wall.

She swallowed it down.

She was getting too good at swallowing her rage.

"I'm going to clean you," she told Hope. "It'll be uncomfortable, and I'm sorry for that."

With Hope's crying breaking the silence of the room, Arden used the fresh water and cloth to dab at the red, swollen skin. The girl was brave. Though it clearly hurt, she didn't ask Arden to stop, nor did she try to move or get up, or kick Arden in the face like others had done in the past. Soon the bowl was a murky pink. Despite the bad care, Arden had hope. The wound wasn't nearly as bad as others she'd seen in the past.

The door opened as Arden was finishing up her work, and a moment later came the sound of someone gagging. Arden glared up at Verity, standing in the doorway with Flora. It hadn't occurred to her that the young woman might find the situation more than she could handle.

Oh well.

"Close the door. Both of you, sit by Hope's head. Flora, you are to wash your daughter's face and her hair and give her comfort. Verity, you are to listen and tell me about anything that's false."

Blessedly, the women followed instructions with no hint of willfulness. Flora took to her task heartily, whispering kindnesses to her daughter as she started to wash the sweat from the woman's brow. Hope and Verity were not so different in age, and it was clear the daughter and mother were close. The adoration in the girl's eyes said as much.

Verity stood to the side, her eyes wide and scared, but she had not run, and that was something.

Arden pulled the blanket back down, covering Hope once again. She dumped the dirty water outside, and began to rummage in her bag for the correct supplies. As she worked with her herbs and ointments, she got down to the centre of things.

"Tell me about the birth," she said.

Hope groaned and made an attempt to speak, but it was clear that it was too much of a hardship. Her eyes were fluttering closed.

Flora spoke instead. "We called the doctor from his home in the middle of the night." She dabbed the skin around Hope's temple. "He was cross with us, but we'd waited as long as we could. He doesn't like to be with the women through the hours of suffering, just for the birth. I knew she was getting close, and she was screaming, and I thought to myself, *I'll not wait any longer,* so I went."

Hope looked at her, pain and fear on her face.

"I know that he's a learned man, and that God's will is above all else, but Doctor Raam wasn't patient. He complained about being tired and told her to push when maybe she should have waited, or he should have done something differently—I don't know. I'm not a doctor, but I am a woman who's borne children, and I felt he was wrong. In my bones, I felt it." Flora wiped her eyes with the back of her hand. "Doctor Raam was angry as he stitched her up. I didn't like his manner, but what was I to do? He wouldn't listen."

"Did you see what he used to stitch?" Arden began putting together a tiny fire in their hearth, enough to boil water by.

"I saw," said Flora. "A needle and catgut, like I've always seen."

"And did you see him clean his needle or his hands at any point?" Arden brought her tools to the bed, unrolling a leather strip of instruments.

Flora stared into the distance as she thought. Finally, she looked at Arden. "Perhaps?"

Verity's hand shot up to her head, grasping her face as if someone had slapped her.

Arden waited for the answer to come. It took longer than she would've liked, but there was no rushing whatever latent ability this girl was kindling.

"No," Verity whispered. She cleared her throat and massaged her temple with her fingers. "He didn't clean his tools, or his hands. Even as he left, he just wiped his hands off on his dirty apron."

"As I thought." The water in the kettle was steaming and she poured it into a cup, where she then soaked her needle and her slim knife. She brought it with her, sat down, and lifted the blanket back up over Hope's legs. "Hope, darling. I'm going to remove these stitches, apply medicine, and sew you up cleaner—and not so damned close to the opening of your nethers. Some men think it fun

109

to add an extra stitch."

Arden couldn't see if the girl nodded, but she proceeded anyway. As she worked, the baby grew upset, and that started the mother and grandmother crying. It was more emotion than Arden was comfortable with, and she felt compelled to fill the room with something other than tears.

"Verity, tell me what you think happened here."

The young woman cleared her throat. "I—I don't know."

"What about your vision told you the doctor hadn't performed a clean surgery?"

"I saw it in my head, clear as day. It's the way I see all the lies."

Flora spoke up. "Visions? That's—that's witchcraft!"

"So is this," Arden replied, her fingers busy. "According to your god, all of this is, and you are complicit, and because of it, your daughter won't die of infection. Don't go losing your nerve on me now."

Flora shut her mouth and remained blessedly silent.

"And is there anything else you can glean from that vision, Verity?"

Hope cried out as Arden touched something quite swollen, and Verity paled again. "I don't think so."

"What happened," Arden started, "was the same thing that has happened time and time again. The doctor does his work and I'm summoned in secret to fix it, and because I do, Doctor Raam assumes himself capable. In this case, that doctor felt his sleep was more important than the health of this good woman. Because she was at his mercy, and no one else in this village is trained to do his work in his absence, she suffered. He used dirty tools—even if they were clean to the eye does not mean they are clean—and did not mind his procedure. Carelessness will kill. Apathy will kill. Those things have taken many lives in this town already. Lives that my grandmother and my mother and I could not save."

"Is—?" Flora choked on emotion for a moment. "Is my Hope going to die?"

"No, she shouldn't." Arden had removed all the stitches and set to work dabbing an ointment on the skin that would repel the infection and numb the pain. "She is both lucky and unlucky. Unlucky to have a careless doctor in her life, and lucky that you came to me when you did. If you had waited another day or two, there may have been little I could do to help her."

The room fell silent after that. Arden had nothing left to teach, and the others seemed strapped for words.

Arden began to sew catgut sutures, which set Hope to sobbing. Even with the ointment, the wound was too sore, too delicate. Tears misted Arden's eyes and she blinked them away, lest she make a mistake.

Flora hummed a low, slow song to fill the desperate air of the home. The words lilted off her tongue in a soft, untrained melody.

If ever I saw you
Down by the river
A maid from the valley
No heart would I have
If I shan't say hello

If ever I gave you
A kiss by the river
A maid from the valley
My heart all aflutter
With one small hello

If ever I willed you
Down by the river
Away from the valley
Our hearts all a-tangled
All from this one hello

On and on she sang, one verse after the other, as the man from the river fell in love with and lured the maid away from her home. They tumbled together in the grass, and snuck out together many days after. Before the end, the maid's mother had given chase, and promised to throttle him if ever she caught up.

No godliness was to be found in that song, and Arden knew without a doubt it was a ditty brought over from across the sea, or from another town. It had stayed here, secreted away by these women, and many more before them, waiting for the right time to be taken out and polished up.

No matter the piety in the church, tiny pleasures—tiny sins— could be found in everyone's lives.

CHAPTER TWELVE

Verity

Arden was firm in her instructions to poor old Flora Harkness. "Hope is not to get out of bed for anything, not for at least two nights. She's not even to go out to the latrine; just have her use the chamber pot. If she rips her stitches or gets the wound dirty, it could kill her. I've shown you how to clean her wounds, and I expect you to keep to that. I'll be back tomorrow night to check on her after the sun goes down. Use that poultice like I taught you and everything will turn out just fine."

Flora nodded. Shadows had settled under her eyes and she was shaking like a leaf. The woman probably hadn't slept in days, and Verity couldn't blame her. "Thank you, both of you. I don't like sneaking around and trying to get things past God, but it's not right to lose a daughter either, is it? If it were God's plan, I could maybe live with that, but not if it's a man's laziness, no." Flora was getting angry again, her fists clenching at her sides.

The words Flora spoke were sharp, and they hooked on the jagged pieces of Verity's understanding of the world. It hurt to know how careless their doctor had been, not only with Hope. Verity wanted to reject the idea. She had been taught all her life, by the church and by her parents, to do good. To help others and treat her neighbours with kindness. Helping was a core tenet of God's will. And yet Doctor Raam hadn't helped Verity and, if she were to believe Arden, hadn't helped a lot of other people either.

Had he been careless with anyone else she knew?

Who else had come to him and been turned away? Who else had he not just neglected, but actively harmed?

All of this in the face of Arden, who Verity had been told all her life was evil. Arden had been disdained and hunted. She had more cause than anyone else to let the people of the village die. And yet she cared about them more than their own doctor.

Verity reached out and put a hand on Flora's shoulder. "I understand. I'm learning that God's will and what people *think* is God's will...well, those may be two different things."

Flora's face softened as she looked Verity in the eyes, like a small weight had been lifted from her. "You're a good girl, Verity. I won't tell no one about your ways."

"I appreciate that. I barely understand it myself..." Verity trailed off, not sure what else to say.

Arden filled the silence. "Who are we to say that a gift like Verity's isn't a gift from your god, hmm?"

"Aye." Flora nodded. "Aye, that could be, couldn't it? She used it today to protect a life, and isn't that what God wants for us all?"

Arden reached for the door handle and peeked out. Night had fully fallen. Opening it wide, she gestured for Verity to step out in front of her, and they bid Flora a good evening.

Out in the street, Verity was suddenly wary of herself. She was more than guilty of anything the town could accuse her of, and she hadn't thought to cover herself with clothing that would hide who she was. Arden had pulled a cloak around her shoulders, as well as her bonnet.

Arden led the way to the edge of town, walking at a calm but steady pace. Verity had to work to keep up with her.

"Do you feel good about your actions today, Dandelion?" Arden whispered as they walked.

"I'm not sure." Verity paused a moment, thinking. "I would feel good if so much of it weren't against the teachings of the church. It's confusing, to be honest. Helping Hope feels right, but the pastor would certainly tell me it was wrong."

"There's no glory in suffering, Verity." Arden took them around the corner of a house, the trees growing closer with each step. "Many people will have you believe that you have to suffer to earn happiness or food or a place in the afterlife. Some people will *demand* that you hurt in the same way they were hurt, and those people are jealous cowards. It's a lie fed to you by people who benefit from your pain." She looked at Verity, intensity burning in her eyes. "That new mother doesn't need to suffer to prove her worthiness, and neither do you."

Verity's mouth hung open, her feet stumbling under her. Arden's words were always blasphemous, but these were like a knife to the heart. *Another* knife to the heart. The wounds came quickly these days, threatening to tear down every piece of the foundation she'd built her life on.

Before Verity could form a response, shouting rose up nearby. Two men dressed in dirty field clothes were ambling toward them, sharp grins on their faces.

Arden cursed under her breath. "Leave," she commanded, and when Verity didn't move, the witch threw up a hand and pushed Verity violently off her feet. She stumbled into the alley between two of the homes and crashed into a pile of wood.

Pain lanced up Verity's side. As soon as she could gather the

Cat Rector

presence of mind, she felt around her body, praying that there was no blood. She sighed in relief. Though she'd be bruised for a while, she hadn't been impaled by anything.

Raised voices came from the mouth of the alley, and Verity managed to get up to her hands and knees to crawl forward. Once Arden and the men came into her view, Verity sat down, pressing herself against the wall. She knew them, of course. She knew almost everyone in the village, at least a little. Billy Smith and his friend Jacob Friar.

Billy laughed, clearly too comfortable in Arden's presence. "Hello, darling. And who might you be?"

"I thought she was May, from all the way out in the field," Jacob said, stepping closer. "But you're not her at all. I don't know if I've ever seen you before."

Verity's skin prickled. It was bad that anyone had approached the witch, but she wasn't sure *how bad* it would be. Nighttime made young men brazen, even the godly ones.

"You don't know me, no." Arden was calm and collected, even as they inched closer, backing her against a wall.

Jacob looked her up and down, his face twisted into something almost feral. "I bet you're not anyone's wife, are you? You could be mine for today, if you like."

"If you don't step away from me, you may not live to regret it." Arden's voice was venomous.

Jacob laughed, looking at Billy as if the whole thing were a joke. "That's adorable. She thinks she's strong."

Jacob reached out to touch Arden's face, but before his fingers hit her cheek, Arden's fist collided with his nose.

Jacob reeled backwards, cupping his nose in both hands. "You stupid cunt!"

Verity shrank down as small as she could get without losing sight of them, her heart hammering in her chest. She had never seen Arden

116

do true magic, but she had a feeling the men were in more trouble than the witch.

"I guess we need to show you a thing or two, bitch." Billy grabbed Arden by the arm.

But all Arden did was laugh.

"To the dark places, I offer this sacrifice." The witch's voice was low and cold, barely above a mutter. "To fear and be feared in equal measure, to be still and quiet and foreboding—"

"What?" Billy's eyes were wide with alarm. "What the fuck are you doing?"

"To be an agent of death and revenge when it's asked of me."

Billy released her arm and backed away, his attention roving back and forth from Arden to Jacob. "She's a fucking witch, Jacob."

"The pastor, he can help." Jacob let go of his nose. Blood had spilled down over his lip, down the curve of his chin.

But Arden was still talking, pressing her back into the house until she was almost entirely out of sight. Her voice...Verity had never heard anyone sound so monstrous. "To occupy the unpredictable night and respect its power. When the time comes, I will be *unforgiving.*"

A sharp breeze startled them all, and Verity covered her mouth with her hands, trying not to scream. It was suddenly so cold, and—

Something hit the roof of the house hard. Before Verity could even look up, someone screamed. She had blinked and Billy was gone. *Gone.* He had been there a second ago, and simply no longer was.

"What the fuck!" Jacob fell back, landing on his bottom and trying to crawl away. "God protect me from this monster, this witch!"

Arden only laughed. "There's no one here to protect you now."

The wind shifted again. With a thump, a shape landed in front of Jacob, blocking Verity's view. It was black, like a shadow, made of strange, flowing lines. Its shape moved, and in the dark, it was hard to tell what it was. Looking at it brought dread to Verity's soul, and she bit down on her hand to keep the scream in. The tears were unstoppable, cascading down her cheeks.

The thing let out an ungodly growl before snapping Jacob up in its maw and bounding away, Jacob's screams disappearing into the night.

Verity was frozen in place, even as Arden came into the alley and knelt in front of her.

Arden peered around the corner of the alley. "Are you all right?"

"No." Verity could barely choke out the word. "What...what happened to them? What was that?"

"Come. You have to get up. People are coming and we need to hide." Arden hauled on Verity's arm until she climbed to her feet.

They ran together into the woods, away from the clamour of voices. Arden led them back, into the brush, and they dove behind a wall of pine trees. Verity sobbed into her hand, trying to stay in control but swiftly losing the battle.

"Hush," Arden whispered. "It's all right."

"It's not!" Verity hissed. She knew to keep her voice low, but she was terrified. "What happened to Jacob and Billy?"

"Jacob an—oh." Arden's voice dropped off for a moment. They couldn't see each other in the pitch darkness, but huddled as closely as they were, it didn't matter. "The Gloam took them."

"The Gloam?"

"A spirit of darkness that I work with. It's not pretty, Dandelion, but this is part of how I protect myself."

Verity wiped her face on her sleeve. "What will happen to them?"

Arden sighed. "They're already dead."

Voices rose from somewhere nearby, and Verity had to choke back the grief and the questions. She had so much to say, and she felt like running, but if they caught her, it wouldn't matter what she felt. She'd be killed as well, and she had a little more sense than that.

Verity all but held her breath, waiting for the shouting and the footsteps to fade away.

Waiting...

Waiting.

And at last, all was quiet. All except Verity and Arden's shallow breathing.

Arden let out a long sigh of relief and collapsed onto her bottom. "And we live to tell another tale."

"But Jacob and Billy do not," Verity snapped. "Why did you kill them? They were only—"

"Only what, Dandelion?" Arden was a faint shape in the dark, but the hiss on her breath told her everything Verity needed to know. "Only harassing me? Only about to touch my body? Only about to take what they wanted? Or maybe once they realised who I was, they'd only make sure I burned."

"You didn't have to kill them." Verity's tears were coming fast again. Those men weren't even people she loved, but she felt dirtier for knowing this. Aiding in a murder, allowing it to happen under her nose—she couldn't be that kind of person. "When your magic helps people, that I can understand. I cannot sit by while you kill people."

"It's easy to say that now, isn't it?" Arden leaned in, her voice growing closer. "It's easy to protect yourself when no one knows your secret. But someday, Verity, they'll come for you. Then you'll learn how desperate you are to live."

Though Verity heard the words, they slipped off her immediately, barely piercing her consciousness. To her, the witch seemed to be comprised of two different moral codes. She spoke of healing and justice with fervour, and had taught Verity so much already about her own body. It was also true, however, that Arden thought very little of taking a life. The difference seemed to be as simple as whether or not someone was on the witch's good side.

This was not something Verity would ever be able to live by.

Verity shifted away from the witch, trying to decide what to do next.

Arden stood, staring down at Verity. "Don't forget, you and I aren't so different. I chose this, and you did not, and that's all that

119

stands between us. You have a power these people won't abide and one day you'll have to choose: protect them or protect yourself. Perhaps then you'll understand what it takes to survive *against* your god's will."

Verity looked away. She couldn't stomach any of this. Though she hadn't watched Billy and Jacob die exactly, she had watched it unfold. They would disappear from the lives of everyone around him, and no one would ever know what had happened to them. Being witness and accomplice to it was more than she could bear.

Verity stood and began to stride away, back to her village.

"There's magic in your blood, Dandelion." Arden's voice carried low. "They *will* find out."

Verity's breath caught, but she kept walking. There *was* magic in her. Did Arden know about her father? A part of her wanted to turn back and beg Arden to tell her, but she couldn't trust the witch. She was a murderer. She couldn't be trusted.

Without so much as a glance behind her, Verity left the woods and started home. It took every bit of self-control to push her feelings down and keep a straight face as she passed people in the streets. An air of frantic panic had fallen over the town as people searched for whatever had caused the screaming, but Verity knew they'd find nothing. She doubted they'd even find any blood where the men had been taken.

She hurried on, knowing it was better to be home. If anyone read guilt on her face, she'd be questioned and she wasn't sure how long she could keep her emotions contained.

When she opened the door to her home, she was greeted by a burst of voices, all talking over each other. The noise stopped as her family's attention turned to her.

"Where have you been?" Her father was *angry*.

"Mrs Baker came to the door to tell us about the screams, and you weren't here." Asher's face was pale and he was leaning on the back of a kitchen chair. "I thought you were dead."

Clarabel approached timidly, her cheeks red from crying. She said nothing, only clamped her arms around Verity's waist and hugged her tight.

Verity held her in return. "I'm not dead. I just went for a walk."

Jona gestured to her dishevelled state. "You're a mess. What kind of walk leaves you with dirt all over your dress?"

"I fell." She offered nothing more than that.

Her father threw the drying cloth onto the table. "You're filthy. I came home and there was a half-finished bowl of bread dough on a chair, no supper cooking, no floors swept, and the hare I'd gotten from the market yesterday hadn't even been so much as skinned. And you just went for a *walk*?"

The wealth of emotion under Verity's skin was quickly turning to rage. Forget that she had been with Hope Harkness trying to save her life. Forget that she had just witnessed two men disappear, never to be seen again. Forget that she had been thrown around like a child's doll and gotten hurt. All her father saw when she arrived were all the things she had *not* done for the household.

"Answer me."

Verity couldn't tell him the truth and she hadn't been swift enough to come up with a lie before she came home. She had too much on her mind already to be adding deception into the mix. She wanted to lash out, to make him regret what he was saying, but telling him any fraction of the truth would only lead to more death. Maybe hers. "I went to gather some things in the woods and I fell. I hit my head and only just woke up a bit ago."

"You went to the woods in the middle of making bread?"

"Yes. I thought seeds or nuts would be nice in it. It's a good time of year for that kind of thing."

Jona's face contorted into a seething rage. "Verity, you lie! Why will you not tell me what is the matter with you?"

Because you would have me killed, she thought.

Verity said nothing, and her father's patience disappeared.

"You've been given too much freedom; that much is clear. You're a daughter but you act like a disobedient wife, doing as you please at all hours of the day. Don't think I haven't noticed. You're always off in the woods, always roaming in the dark. And I might think that to be some simple restlessness but now you can't even take care of your family? They need you, Verity! Your siblings need you."

Guilt swam in Verity's gut. She *had* been slipping up since she'd met Arden in the woods. Not just in her faith, but in her duties to those she loved. Her siblings depended on her to keep things in order while they prepared themselves for lives outside their four walls. She knew that. And no matter what she'd learned about herself, the cost was quickly becoming too high. What had these questions brought her? She'd become an accomplice to murder, become involved in magic and devilry, and come within paces of a monster, and it was stealing the trust of her family.

It had told her that her father was not her father, and what peace had she gained from that?

"I don't understand you," her father continued. "You can take days at a time and lie in that barn, pretending to be so sick you can't move, and then go traipsing off into the woods like a wild animal. Are you truly in any pain at all?"

Verity's compliant thoughts melted away. "How dare you? Those days are agony for me. You wouldn't question it if you were forced to be in the same room as me, watching what happens. Mother knew. Mother would never have asked me if it was *real.*"

"This!" Her father gestured to her, and then slammed both his palms onto the table. "This insolence! Where has this come from? You were a good, pious girl, and now I feel that I don't know you. I've tried to protect you, but if the town were to see what I see, they would name you a witch. Do you want to burn like your mother?"

And there it was, at last. The threat that had always been hiding under the surface of her life. The thing she couldn't fight. She was kept under the thumb of the threat of burning, as she always had been. No matter what Arden said, no matter what it awoke in her, it changed nothing. If she pushed back against the things that were alive and crawling in that village, they would kill her.

She wished she had never met Arden. Had never learned about the visions, or her mother, or the horrors she'd been living inside her whole life. It would be easier to be deceived by it. To live inside it and never know.

Bowing her head, Verity whispered, "I know, Father. I'm sorry."

The words took a moment to sink in, and then her father's body sagged in relief. "I believe you." He composed himself, throwing another piece of wood on the fire as the room sank under the weight of the silence. "Tomorrow you'll go to church and ask the pastor for forgiveness for your sins. He will be able to guide you back to the light."

A mix of relief and horror churned in her. Relief at a chance to redeem herself. To go back to the way things had been. And horror because she wasn't sure going back was possible. How did one unlearn the things they had seen?

He will be able to guide you back to the light.

Perhaps, thought Verity. *But the pyre was also a light, wasn't it?*

CHAPTER THIRTEEN

Arden

As Arden walked home through the darkness of the forest, the weariness slid over her like an old, familiar cloak.

She was used to the people of the village. It was never a surprise when someone tried to take something from her or use her, but every once in a while, they still managed to hurt her. The men had behaved exactly the way her mother had warned her about; it was Verity who had cut her so deeply.

Despite her best efforts, Arden had begun to trust the girl.

The disdain came from a place of ignorance, she knew. Verity hadn't yet had to fight for her right to exist. She didn't know. Arden truly hoped she'd never find out the toll it took. That fight wore a person down, bone by bone. But Arden refused to cower, refused to pretend. Those were the only options she had: shrink or fight.

And so, once again, Arden was left scorned and without a friend in the world—without a human friend, that was—dragging herself through the forest at night, longing for her bed.

It wasn't long before a shiver crept up her spine. She stopped, familiar with that particular sensation of dread. At first, she saw nothing. Then, in the distance, two glowing white orbs caught her eyes. They were suspended in the air, up in the branches somewhere.

"Good evening," she said to the forest.

It was impossible to follow those lights as they moved remarkably fast through the treetops. The primal parts of her mind wanted to scream and run, but a tiny bit of logic held her fast. If the Gloam ever wanted her dead, there was no conceivable way she would live to see the dawn.

Trust. She would have to trust.

The swirling shadow fell to the ground not with a thunk but with a hiss. In the dark, Arden could imagine the grass around its feet shrivelling up and dying, all the life seeping out of it. Without a lantern, the only thing she could see was those two eerie eyes glowing a few feet from her.

Arden snapped her fingers and a tiny flicker of flame lit on her fingertip. The light just barely helped to distinguish the difference between the dark and the monster. It sat like an enormous dog, its eyes fixed on her, its tongue lolling out of its open mouth, and black smoke drifting from its maw.

"Thank you for your help tonight," Arden said. "I hope the sacrifices were sufficient."

The Gloam hopped in place twice, its jaw stretching in a horrific, toothy grin.

"Then you're satisfied?" Arden hoped it was. She didn't have much left to offer.

The beast let out a hissing whine, the kind of thing people heard in their nightmares, and that always meant it was pitiably displeased.

Arden bristled. She'd given the Gloam two fully grown men and it was still hungry. These moods waxed and waned. Sometimes it was gluttonous and other times it left half a meal in the grass. It seemed a bottomless pit that night. "I can offer you an animal tonight. A deer perhaps, if that is what the forest will offer me."

Those enormous eyes blinked once, twice. Arden couldn't look into them for too long without the feeling of being pulled into the white voids. The god-fearing people talked about purgatory, and Arden thought purgatory was what she would find in those eyes if she kept looking.

The blackness of the Gloam shifted until it was more or less the shape of a deer. Then, as quickly as it had changed shape, it was itself again, bounding into the canopy, in the general direction of Arden's home.

She sighed. She was far too tired for this.

Arden dragged herself back to her cabin. Her muscles were begging her to sit and rest, but she wouldn't be allowed to. She didn't dare disrespect the Gloam; being eaten was always a large possibility. Some days she looked back at her past with the clarity of her mistakes and wished that, when she was choosing which demons and spirits she wanted to work with, she hadn't chosen the Gloam.

Her mother had warned her not to make the choice lightly. That there were other ways to protect herself. But she'd been young and stupid and had thought things would be different for her than for her mother.

They had not been.

It gave her no real pleasure to kill for the creature, especially when it asked for people, but she had wanted the ability to defend herself, and the Gloam could give her that. She killed for it, and if needed, it would kill for her. She rarely asked for its help, but the way she saw it, she was saving up a lot of favours for a big, terrible day.

Maybe someday she would have the courage to end the arrangement, but that day wasn't coming soon.

Once she was back in front of her burned-out firepit, Arden put her things down and lit the fire to stave off the cold. Once that was done, she sat cross-legged in the grass, her back to the fire and her eyes on the nearby brush. She recited the same old words, letting them flow off her tongue with sincerity and gratitude, and at length, the rustle of brush sounded nearby.

A large buck stepped out. His antlers were large and intimidating, made worse by the flesh that hung from them in dripping strands that glistened wetly in the firelight. It was velvet season. Each year male deer shed the soft coating of their antlers while competing for mates, and while fascinating, it made for a deeply disturbing sight.

Arden stood and went to the buck. It was docile, like all the animals she called, and it let her approach. She ran her fingers along the soft antler where the velvet was still intact, and avoided the pink wet places where it hung. Appreciating the moment of tranquillity, she slid her fingers down the nose of the deer and gave it a smile.

A second later her hand was touching thin air. The buck had been thrown across the clearing. The Gloam crouched over it, its paws pinning the deer to the ground. Blood flew, splattering into the grass, across tree trunks, and spilling into pools in the dirt. The beast tore into the flesh of the animal and the only word for it was *monstrous*.

Arden backed away, swallowing the shock and fear that threatened to overtake her. Gore didn't bother her, but the utter bloodthirstiness with which the Gloam was devouring that deer made her very, very determined to be nowhere in its sights when it was finished eating.

Arden grabbed her bag and went inside the cabin. She closed the door as quietly as she could. A door and four walls wouldn't stop the Gloam if it decided to eat her, but it made her feel marginally safer to be out of sight. With a shaking hand, she lit a fire and put on a kettle for tea. The brew she mixed for herself was made of every calming herb she had access to.

Often Arden prided herself on her lack of fear and her

hardheadedness, but she was still shakeable. She hated that she was. It was especially bad when she was tired and worn out and full of betrayal.

The Gloam wasn't the only spirit who needed things, and guilt welled up in Arden's throat as she realised how little time she'd made for Dalic and Ilyana in the past several weeks. In the morning, she would start making things right, no matter what Verity or anyone else of that village threw in her path. She couldn't afford to take risks when it came to her responsibilities to her patron spirits and to the woods.

Arden stared at the kettle, waiting for it to boil. She thought so hard, willing the things in her mind to block out the sound of ripping, wet death outside her four walls.

It was hardly on purpose when Arden woke far after sunup. She'd had a fitful night of wakefulness and bad dreams, and it had taken hours to fall into a deep sleep.

After she'd risen, dressed, and eaten, Arden packed a day's worth of food into her bag and started walking in the opposite direction of the village. She'd promised Dalic that if she couldn't stop people from taking trees, she would help the spirit plant new ones. As she walked, rain fell on the leaves of the canopy, the sound surrounding her completely. Not much rain made it to her, but the air was full of the smell of petrichor, and in some places, Arden needed to watch her step. Her boots were finely made, but they didn't always keep her feet dry when she stepped into too deep a mud hole. She made her way through the trees slowly, gathering acorns and pinecones and maple seeds and piling them into the large pocket on the front of her apron.

By the time she came to the edge of the trees, her pocket was full to bursting. The rain hadn't let up. Arden carefully removed her apron, then the rest of her clothes, and put the apron back on.

Everything that she wanted to keep dry, she rolled back into her bag and hung it from a sturdy tree branch.

Arden stepped out into the rain and squealed in delight as the cold, rich sensation of dozens of thick raindrops rolled across her bare skin. It was somewhere between a drizzle and a downpour, and the thrill of it brought Arden to life. After her horrible night, it was sorely needed.

Dancing through the grass, mud in her toes and her hair matted to her cheeks, Arden stopped every few paces to poke a hole in the ground and plant a seed. A few saplings had already sprung up here and there, so she avoided those. Trees needed space to grow, no matter how thin and tall they might start out. She made her way further into the field, planting one seed after the other, and stopping to take in the beauty of grass and rock and sky.

Arden wanted validation from very few people in the world, but as she planted seeds, she hoped Dalic would be pleased. Growing trees would take a long time, but Arden was nothing if not persistent, and she looked forward to watching the forest grow and age as she did. If she was lucky, these trees would be as tall and beautiful as the others before she someday died.

Arden rummaged around in her apron pocket and found only a handful of acorns left. When she looked up, her palm full, a bobcat caught her eye. It stood in the distance, watching her over the long grass.

Ilyana always had a way of sneaking up on her.

Arden waved and quickly set to work on the last of the acorns. By the time she rose, Ilyana was walking toward her, her pelt slung over her human shoulder. Her forearms and hands were covered in a tawny brown fur and speckled with black. The tall grass rubbed against the spirit's knees as she took long, languid steps toward the witch.

"You're a strange human, dancing in the rain," Ilyana said. "You're almost more deer than person."

"That's a compliment I'll readily accept." Arden brushed her dirty hands on her wet apron and stepped forward to meet her.

Ilyana reached out to take Arden's hand. "I was thinking about you all morning."

Arden turned Ilyana's hand so that she could kiss the spirit's knuckles. "Were you?"

Ilyana stepped in closer until the two were only a breath apart. "I would be grateful for some company, if you're finished frolicking."

Running her free hand up Ilyana's arm, Arden cupped the back of the spirit's neck with her hand. "Nothing would give me more joy," she whispered, and leaned in to kiss her.

As beautiful and moving as her time with Ilyana had been, Arden was freezing when she returned home. Between the cooling autumn air, her wet hair, and the sweat on her body, she was in deep need of a warm fire and a cup of tea.

The sun set as she warmed, and she dreaded going back out. But she had promised Hope and Flora she'd check in with them. Regardless of how dangerous it was, Arden felt obligated. It wasn't Hope's fault Arden had gotten herself into trouble, and she certainly didn't want the young woman to pay for someone else's actions. She was hesitant, yes, but she left under the cover of night all the same.

Arden kept to the shadows in the woods and took the long way around. She would enter the village as close to Flora's home as she was able and hope for the best. Her sense of self-preservation fought with her sense of duty the entire way. She nearly turned back twice. Apprehension coiled in her gut as she left the shelter of the trees to wade through a tall field of wheat. Travelling through it was somewhat claustrophobic; it seemed to push in on her, stalks clustered together and endless. Something about it was deeply unsettling to Arden, in a way that was based on neither logic nor experience.

She simply didn't fucking like it.

As she pressed forward, her mind alert and on edge, a shadow appeared in the dark. A shape. A person.

Arden stopped in her tracks, waiting for the shape to move. To leave. It stayed perfectly still, towering above her in the distance. One breath. Two breaths. After ten long breaths, nothing had changed. Suddenly, Arden felt very foolish.

She crept forward, and sure enough. When she reached it, the shadow was propped up on a tall wooden pole. She snapped her fingers to summon the smallest flicker of light.

A scarecrow.

Arden let out a long, relieved breath.

To her credit, even in the light, the scarecrow looked somewhat alive: its torso was a long tunic made of scraps of browning fabric, stuffed with hay, and its burlap head had eyes and a mouth of black paint. Likely, it was put together by children, and things that children made tended to be scarier than anything else in the world.

She let the flame go out, chiding herself for being far too tightly wound. Yes, she had to be careful. Yes, she had made a problem for herself upon her last visit into Arrothburg. And if she wasn't smarter, she would get herself caught just for being too jumpy or too alert to the wrong things.

Arden needed to be smart, not fearful.

She drew long, steady breaths and let them out slowly. In short order, her heartbeat calmed and her muscles unwound, her body falling into a calm rhythm. Feeling more herself, Arden pressed on, toward Flora and Hope.

As she entered the village, she kept her head low, her bonnet helping to hide her face. She had learned to mimic contrition from the women she helped in the village, though she had rarely felt it herself. She must have learned well, because it had served her in most of her journeys through the streets of Arrothburg, and that night was no exception. Not a soul paid her any mind, though she only passed three others. Still, she was relieved to arrive at Flora and Hope's home, so she could take off her disguise, if even for a moment.

As she raised her fist to knock on their door, the voice of a man came from inside the home. Immediately, Arden scurried away from the door and around to the back of the house, keeping herself pressed up against the walls. A man was almost always trouble. The ways of the church often served them too well for them to have any understanding of the suffering of a woman, the birth of a child, or the queer ways of folk.

A window let dim light out into the darkness. Arden crept up to it and took a peek inside. She saw nothing at first, just the candle-lit inside of their one-room home. Then a face appeared at the edge of the window. One she loathed and wished she didn't know.

Doctor Raam had a countenance that reflected his insides. His skin was leathery and he bore thick scowl lines between his eyebrows and around his chin. He had wispy brown hair that he kept long and unkempt. Arden's mother had told her Doctor Raam had been a beautiful young man, but none of that had lingered. It wouldn't have surprised Arden if the man had always lacked the ability to smile.

Though the voice was muffled by the wall between herself and the doctor, Arden could still hear him speak. "—fretting was for nothing. As you can see yourself, the girl is healing well. No sign of infection, and even I must commend my own work with the stitching. Clean and masterful hand. They can be removed in short order, once the healing is done."

"Yes," said Flora, her voice laced with ire. "Hope will be well soon. That is certain."

Arden rolled her eyes. It was a good thing pride was not one of her larger *sins*, or she might have been tempted to break down the door to claim her own good work.

"And the babe?" Doctor Raam's boots were loud on the

floorboards. "It eats and cries and defecates as it should?"

The question brought tension into Arden's jaw, her teeth grinding together. Even she, who did not wish to be a mother and had no deep affinity for children, knew how to speak of them with more kindness than that. If the man held a baby upside down by the foot, it wouldn't surprise her in the least.

That was enough. Arden had come to the house to see the woman's progress, but she had heard confirmation of it. She didn't have the patience to wait the doctor out, and she hadn't the desire to get caught either. At some point, it was likely someone would notice the woman eavesdropping at the window in the dark of night.

Arden left through the yard, backtracking toward the field and the scarecrow again. Annoyance ran through her, at the inconvenience of the trek and at the misattribution of her fine work. And above all else, she was still fucking exhausted.

Once she reached the landmark of the scarecrow, Arden stopped, crouched down, and sat. She needed a break. It was still a long walk home and she hadn't even had the satisfaction of a job well done to motivate her onward. If it weren't deeply dangerous to do so, she probably would have lain down to sleep right there, under the looming shadow of her new scarecrow friend.

She stayed there a while, listening to the breeze toss the wheat around. Insects chirped around her, and the sky was a sea of stars interrupted by clouds. Little by little, the calm outside her crept under her skin and into her heart.

Arden sensed Dalic's arrival before she heard her. Sometimes the tree spirit seemed to appear from thin air. But the witch knew the arrival of her presence: the smell of petrichor she brought with her, and the energy she brought to any space.

"Good evening, friend." Arden stayed put, waiting for Dalic to come to her.

With a rustle and a thump, Dalic lowered herself to the ground next to Arden. "Good evening. I had a feeling you could use some company."

Arden smiled. "You have a keen sense for my moods, don't you?"

"Of course. We are bonded, after all. In both ephemeral and practical manners."

As Dalic spoke, a tiny glimmer of white light rose in her hair. Arden watched as Mouse appeared from between the woody locks, carrying a tiny sphere of cool energy, giving them something to see by.

When Arden left the conversation hanging, Dalic spoke once more. "What's bothering you, friend?"

Arden sighed. "What isn't?"

"Would you like to tell me about it?"

With that invitation, the words came tumbling out of her in a hurry. "How is a person supposed to trust anyone, Dalic? You're an exception of course, but humans! They can't ever seem to be trusted. Every time I let one into my life for more than a moment, they're gone again as soon as they learn the troubles that come with my life. You remember Agatha—"

"I do," Dalic confirmed. "Your friend that they burned."

"Yes." Arden's heart soured at the memory. "After that, I swore off friends. You know that. It's like I can't *help* it. I get stupid and it makes me want to tear my own eyes out. Verity is young and foolish and I know that, and *I* feel young and foolish for believing in her. She seemed smart underneath all that piety, and I was getting to like her, and—" Arden slowed herself as the tears welled in her eyes. "I know she's little more than a child, but I can't help that a piece of me longs for companionship beyond Ilyana and you. I don't want it to be true, but it is. It was *nice*, teaching her things. She seemed to care what I had to say. It doesn't happen very often."

Dalic gave her space, waiting to see if Arden would continue on. When she didn't, the spirit wrapped an arm around the witch and pulled her in. Arden settled against Dalic's torso, not dissimilar to the way her mother used to hold her. The familiarity and comfort of it loosened something in Arden's chest, and she began to sob.

The crying went on for a while. Dalic held her and didn't say a word. She simply let the woman empty the vault of grief she'd built up since the last time. Those moments of pure emotion, of unfettered vulnerability, were few and far between.

Eventually, the grief subsided and Arden was able to speak again. "Thank you, friend. Sometimes I'm not sure how a person can be as committed to solitude as I am and still weep over the callousness of others."

"I think you're alone because you must be," Dalic said into Arden's hair. "If the village were open to your ways, I believe you'd be a friend to so many. You've done everything in the name of survival, including closing yourself off to the world and pretending it was your choice."

Mouse crawled onto Arden's shoulder and curled into a sleepy ball on her collarbone. A kind gesture from a small creature.

"Perhaps," admitted Arden. "We'll never know, because these people will never change." With the grief emptied from her heart, the anger rolled back into place. "They'll take and they'll hurt and they'll do wrong by their people, and I'll be here to repair the damage, over and over. Thankless work indeed."

"I'll be here to help you, whenever I can." Dalic took Mouse gently back from the place where it had made its bed. "Is it time to go home?"

"Yes." Arden yawned and rose from Dalic's embrace. A moment later she was being lifted into the air, Dalic's form twice as large as it had been while they were sitting. Dalic swung Arden around, gently setting the witch on her back. Arden didn't argue; it would be nice for someone else to carry her weight for once.

"Then home is where we'll go." Towering over the field of wheat, Dalic strode back to the forest, Arden's arms wrapped around her neck.

CHAPTER FOURTEEN

Verity

Verity waited to go to the church until most of the village was busy with work or homemaking. Whatever sins she had to confess that day, she didn't want them overheard by the village gossips. They were good at what they did, the gossips. If she was overheard, news would reach every ear before sundown.

The heavy church door groaned as she pushed it open, and the sound made her grimace. She'd hoped she'd have a moment to compose herself, but Pastor Woolfe was already turning to face her.

"Verity, how lovely to see you today." Pastor Woolfe was lighting tall votive candles on a stand at the front of the room. "I wasn't expecting a visitor."

Trying to think of something to say that was both honest and not, Verity managed to squeak out, "I've been a little out of sorts lately, and Father thought it best that I visit with you."

Something strange flashed across the pastor's face, but it was gone so quickly that Verity had no choice but to dismiss it.

"Of course, child. You know you can always come to the church with your woes." He swung his arm out, gesturing to the front pew. "Please, sit."

Verity hurried to the front of the room. A small war was waging inside her. She wanted to be respectful and obedient as she'd always been taught to be, and she *wanted* to return to the ease of those teachings. Her time with the witch, however, had sown so much doubt. This building, this institution—even if it was not as bad as the witch claimed—it wasn't as pure as it let on. It was imperfect.

Still, it was best to show none of that in front of the leaders of the town, lest she be burned for asking the wrong questions.

She sat, and the pastor sat as well. He left space between them, enough for at least one other body. He was dressed somewhat less ornately than the last time she'd been in the church, what with it not being a service day. He wore a robe of deep purple, a beautiful colour of dye that was too expensive for someone like Verity to own. There were no intricate embroideries, only a white gown beneath, and a red pastor's collar peeking out from the fabric that encircled his neck.

"Please, tell me what you need this day." Pastor Woolfe placed his hands on his lap, everything about him displaying his intent to listen.

Verity looked into her own lap, wringing her fingers. "Father and I quarrel often these days. I think…I think I am restless, sir." Father's word, not hers.

His look grew inquisitive. "Restless? How do you mean?"

"Since my mother died, I have taken on much of the household responsibility. I take care of my siblings and my father, and do many of the chores."

Pastor Woolfe nodded. "As is the way of women."

"Yes. And I accept this. And yet I feel uneasy of spirit these days. It sometimes feels…stifling." Verity was careful to choose her words well. She needed to appear earnest but her earnestness could not lead her to the pyre. Truth be told, part of her longed to confess and connect with someone, to spill her new world out to them. She wanted to understand and be understood.

If only she could trust him.

"I see. And how old are you again?"

"Seventeen, sir."

He nodded knowingly and looked toward the dais, as if lost in thought. "You should have been married by now. In a kinder world, you would be. In fact, if your father hadn't been insistent that he'd not be remarrying, you might have. Does it bother you that you are not yet wed?"

Verity had thought about that plenty over the years. That her father had *selfishly* not found a new wife to have new babies with, and had kept her bound to her family. The injustice of it felt like a calloused wound, but not because she felt *she* wanted children. It was her duty to, but not her will. "Perhaps," she answered. "I think it should bother me more if I loved someone and was not allowed to marry them. I've had very little chance to find someone to grow fond of, by arrangement or by love. Father needs my help too much to consider leaving him."

"That is a great burden to carry. Do you often think of your mother?"

The question felt like a trap. She didn't want to be too closely associated with her mother. She also couldn't risk Pastor Woolfe discovering what she now knew. Verity had more to hide than she would like, and the fear of it hummed inside her.

"Mother is best forgotten," she said simply. "I do not wish to follow in her footsteps, and when I think of her, I am often angry with her. She stole much of my life from me when she was burned."

Pastor Woolfe adjusted himself in the pew, perhaps feeling somewhat uncomfortable. "I believe I've heard enough to give you advice. Is there anything else you need to share?"

Verity shook her head, relieved to be done with at least some of the deception.

"It seems to me that you'd be best served by finding a husband who would agree to move into your family's home. I'm sure someone could be found for you, if need be. Your restlessness will surely be calmed by the addition of a man, and perhaps a child of your own." He put a hand on Verity's shoulder. "Your days may feel limited, but there is always time for a small conversation between neighbours, and many marriages are built on the backs of small conversation."

If Verity had actually been seeking his advice, this would have frustrated her deeply. He clearly had no idea what she needed to accomplish in the span of a day, and it spoke volumes about what he understood of her life and what it meant to be of service.

"I understand," she said instead. "I will make better efforts to do so."

The pastor kept his hand casually on her shoulder. "I know it can seem like a simple answer—overly simple perhaps—but many of the women of this village find their complaints are lessened when their homes and hearts are full."

A dull murmur of pain rippled over Verity's mind. The flash of a woman crying in the dark obscured her vision for a moment, then passed.

"Yes," she struggled to say. "I imagine that to be so."

"The people of this village bind us together."

As the pastor spoke, visions of unhappy, lonely, overburdened people flitted in and out of Verity's mind, searing themselves into her sight.

"God asks women to be of service because there is strength in it."

—the image of a woman who toiled into the late hours while her family slept—

"There must be support for the men and the children."

—a man who stood in the doorway, towering over his wife,

shouting at her—

"Someone to show humility and beauty as God wills it."

—a woman dressed in expensive furs who dumped her plate of food on the floor for her servant to clean—

"And in this way we keep our community together, healthy and happy and free of sin."

By the time he was finished, Verity's head was throbbing. Tears ran down her face. She felt compelled to scream out, to tear open her own skin to make it stop. It was only fear of discovery keeping her from acting out against the pain writhing under her skin.

"What's the matter, girl?" Pastor Woolfe seemed mildly concerned.

"Sorry, pastor. It—it's only very moving; that's all. I hope to someday find the same beauty in my life." Verity dried her tears and rose from the pew. Her vision swam, and she felt unsteady on her feet. "I should return home. There's much to do and you've given me a lot to think on. Thank you."

"Anytime. Go with God, child."

Verity rushed out, only stopping to look back a moment in the doorway. When she did, the pastor's face was not the one she recognized. Something sinister had settled into his expression, and he looked at her as if she were a meal, not a person.

She left and did not look back again.

Not all of what Verity had said in the church was false, including having a lot to do. As she tried to release the fear from every inch of her body, to gain back her steadiness, she ambled toward the market. She longed to lie down and rest, but she hadn't been diligent enough with buying food in the days prior, and the family stores were running low. Though she was tired and afraid, she knew better than to try her father's patience further by shirking her duties again. So into the market she went.

Her head throbbed with every heartbeat. As she went from stall to stall, trying to think of the things she would need, she gave her neighbours as short and polite a greeting as she could manage. When no one was speaking to her, her mind raced with all the lies the pastor had spun. She knew they were lies because that seemed to be the way of this curse of hers, but she didn't readily understand the context of them. She only knew that as she looked from face to face, the people around her hid themselves behind smiles and closed doors. Her village contained more sadness than she'd ever thought possible.

As she bought a dozen carrots from Bethany Tanner, she stared into the older woman's eyes, trying to see the truth of her. The lines in her skin were deep, deeper than they should have been at her age. A yellowish tinge pigmented her face. Not so much that Verity would've noticed if she hadn't been paying attention. Bethany was smiling, but she didn't look…well.

How long had Verity been walking the streets of her village and not truly *seeing* anyone?

If her visions were to be believed, people in her village—people of God—acted in terrifyingly ungodly ways.

A door burst open on the other side of the square. Two of the town watchmen were dragging Lindsay Ramsey out of her house by her arms. She was in tears, trying to fight them, but she was a slight woman in her forties and couldn't possibly match her strong young captors.

Fueled by a rage that felt sudden and foreign and long overdue, Verity rushed across the square toward them. "What's the meaning of this? Let her go!"

David Farrier glared daggers at her, but he stopped anyhow. "Ain't none of your business. Church's orders."

Mrs Ramsey drew a haggard breath. "I'm not a witch!"

Verity snapped her gaze back to David. "Come now. What did

Mrs Ramsey ever do that was witchly? She's a woman of God. She takes care of children and bakes extra bread for the families who need it. How can you accuse her like this?"

People were gathering, coming out of houses to watch the commotion.

"Pastor says she's a witch. Someone came forward last night and said she spoiled all the food in their pantry and was running around in her knickers like that one in the woods."

Verity had just been with the pastor. Had he ordered this before she had even left the church?

"It wasn't me!" Mrs Ramsey sobbed. "I was home all night, in bed. Charlie can tell you. I—"

Her gaze strayed into the distance. Pastor Woolfe approached.

"Mrs Ramsey." His voice was silken and compelling. "Isn't it best to endure the tests and determine you are certainly not a witch?"

Another burst of pain rose in Verity's mind. A lie.

The expression of fear and contempt was sliding from Mrs Ramsey's face. "I'm not sure."

Pastor Woolfe reached out to stroke the woman's cheek. "If we don't complete these trials, everyone here—all your neighbours—will know you refused. And what will they think of you then? What do you have to hide? A true woman of God will certainly pass His trials."

The humming in Verity's mind was ceaseless. Each word came from the pastor's mouth dripping with something Verity couldn't place. It was wrong. His voice was *wrong*. It was a crawling itch at the rear of her mind. Like it was grabbing at her and couldn't quite reach.

Verity gave her head a shake and the grip of the voice was gone.

Mrs Ramsey had become very quiet, an eerie, serene smile spreading across her lips. She stopped struggling, and the two watchmen let her go. "I'm so sorry. I didn't mean to cause a scene." She looked up at David. "Would you take me to the church? The pastor is right. I'd like to prove I'm a woman of God."

"Really?" Verity stepped in front of her. "You just said you weren't a witch! Is that not enough?"

Mrs Ramsey shook her head sadly. "I was mistaken. The pastor has made an excellent argument. I must prove myself innocent for all to see; otherwise, people will judge my integrity. Thank you for caring, Verity, but this is the will of God. Go with God, Verity."

Verity's eyes darted around the square, looking for someone to help, but most of them had already gone back to their business. The ruckus had died down and Verity seemed to be the only person still paying attention.

"What is wrong with everyone?" Verity spoke under her breath, disbelief washing over her.

The watchmen sidestepped Verity, leading Mrs Ramsey to the church. She waved as she passed, and when Verity turned to look at Mrs Ramsey's house, the woman's husband was waving goodbye, eyes bright and hopeful.

What in God's name was going on?

Verity ran.

She sprinted through the forest as fast as she could as the sun fell in the west. By that point, she knew the way to the cabin by heart. A previous version of herself would have baulked at that. Instead, she was grateful. The world was falling down around her, and she had nowhere else to turn.

Her feet carried her forward even as her mind argued that she should turn around. Verity had fought with Arden. Had watched the witch kill two men. And yet who else in the entire world would believe what Verity had just seen with her own eyes? Who else would know what to do? Verity's pride was bruised, yes, but a woman's life hung in the balance. Mrs Ramsey was surely not a witch, but something devilish was happening.

Arden would know what it was.

A tree root nearly sent Verity sprawling into the underbrush, but she caught herself and kept going. Nearly there. A few moments later, she was bursting out into the little clearing and almost ran directly into the witch's firepit. Arden was nowhere to be seen.

Verity slammed her fist onto the front door, knocking so hard she could feel the vibration in her bones. Someone was going to die, Arden had to get up, she had to be there, had to help her, Verity didn't know what to do, not by herself—

The door flew open. Arden was squinting, her blankets wrapped around her shoulders like a travelling cloak, barely concealing her nightdress at the bottom. Relief rushed over Verity and she pushed her way inside.

"What are you doing here? Didn't you disown me? Or are you here to use me for my magic like everyone else?" Arden slammed the door shut.

With all the running, Verity found it difficult to speak. She had to take a few deep breaths before she could start. "There's something wrong. In the town."

Arden sighed and lit a candle on the table. "And you're just gathering this now? Congratulations."

Verity glared at the witch, still working to catch her breath. She collapsed into one of the chairs. "The town watch just dragged a woman off to be burned as a witch."

Arden nodded, lips pursed. She was on her guard. "As you people periodically do."

"You don't understand. Mrs Ramsey can't be a witch. She can't be. And whatever happened, it's not normal. It was like—" Verity searched for the right words. "—like witchcraft."

Sighing and rolling her eyes, Arden sat down across from her.

"From the start."

Verity told her. She struggled to put the words in the right order, to get them to make sense. Starting with the trip to the pastor, she relayed everything as best she could, right up until the end. "And she just changed her mind, just like that. People went from staring to just accepting that to be true. If she endures the trials, she may be killed!"

"People change their minds all the time, Verity." Arden was growing more impatient by the minute.

"It was a lie. All of it was." Verity tapped her skull. "I know it. The pastor lied to her and she just...believed it. Like he made sense to her all of a sudden."

Arden leaned her head into her palm, propped up on the table as if she was very tired. "Being compelling is not a crime."

Anger rose in Verity's gut. "Why are you doubting me?"

"Because you're a girl learning for the first time that people have been lying to you all your life. You're starting to see that people lie to people, and—"

"But I'm not *people*, am I?" Verity spat. "I'm part demon or spirit or witch, aren't I? So if I'm made of magic, why won't you believe I feel it?"

Arden sat straighter, staring into Verity's eyes, searching for something. "Then you know, do you?"

"Yes, I know. I saw it in a vision." Verity swallowed her shame and denial. "My real father is a river spirit or something."

Arden gave a faint nod. "That would explain why you reacted to my blood when I tried to heal you."

"Would it?" Verity didn't bother taking the bite out of her voice.

"It would." Arden looked down, her finger absently moving along the wood knots in the table. "A latent ability, woken up by the introduction of other magic. It's likely."

"So you believe me?" Verity pushed. "You'll help me save Mrs Ramsey."

145

Arden looked up at Verity, her gaze intense. "Not before we sort out this nonsense between us."

Verity's jaw dropped. "Someone's life is in the balance!"

"Someone's life is always in the balance, Dandelion." Arden crossed her arms on top of the table, as if creating the position she would refuse to move from. "If I stopped living every time someone needed my help, I would never get anything done. We can spare the few moments it takes to address the conflict between us."

Verity disagreed, but it would take more time to argue that than it would to simply discuss it. "What is there to address?"

"Don't be coy, Verity." The corner of Arden's mouth curled into a little snarl. "You can't come back to me every time you have a problem and expect I'll help you, not if you can't respect my way of life. You don't get to bring me trouble and give me nothing in return."

"What do you mean?"

"The people of the village pay me." Arden's voice was matter of fact. "They bring vegetables or coin or dishware. Some pay in kindnesses. *You* haven't paid me anything. I *thought* we were reaching a companionship, which would have been payment enough, but based on our last conversation, perhaps we haven't. If you insist on only bringing me things to fix, I'm going to have to start demanding reciprocity in one manner or another. My peace is not free to take."

Verity paused at that. She had never considered before that her actions had consequences for the witch, outside of the possibility of being caught. What *had* Verity brought to Arden aside from things to fix? She couldn't recall anything.

"I don't want to be an accomplice to murder," Verity whispered, properly chastised.

"And I understand that. But when it is my life or another person's, I will choose mine. You'll need to accept this if you can't understand it. My choice to do so might someday save your own life. Are we at an accord?"

Verity took a long breath and nodded. She didn't have much choice. "If I find a way to pay you back, will you help me save Mrs Ramsey?"

Arden let out a frustrated groan. "I don't want payment from you. I simply do not want to be the tool with which you solve your life when it's convenient for you."

Verity looked away. "You aren't. You've given me so much. I promise I won't take that for granted."

Arden stared at the wall, saying nothing for a long moment. "Good. Be sure you don't." Another moment passed in the quiet cabin, the sound of the wind outside the only thing to be heard. "This woman. Have they put her through the trials yet?"

"I don't think so. Normally they wait until the next day and call the town to witness them. They're taken to the church and left to pray for their souls overnight."

The witch got up, fetched a bottle and two cups, and poured a bit of amber liquid into both cups. She set one down in front of Verity. "Drink up. We have work to do."

Verity picked up the cup and sniffed. She recoiled at the scent of the near-poisonous strength of the whiskey. Trying to seem brave, she took a sip and regretted it immediately. "What are we doing?"

Arden tossed back her whiskey, corked the bottle, and put it away. "We're going to save a witch."

CHAPTER FIFTEEN

Arden

Arden had demanded she and Verity wait until later in the evening to attempt their rescue of Mrs Ramsey. Verity had protested, since it would certainly put her at odds again with her father, but they could hardly sneak a grown woman from a church in broad daylight. After some fretting and a threat of backing out entirely, Verity had agreed to wait.

Now, with dark fully fallen and most of the village packed away in their homes, the entire town felt quiet and deserted. The only sounds came from a few creaking boards and the scrape and scrabble of night creatures trying to break into hen houses and waste bins.

Arden found herself marvelling bitterly at how she continued to find herself skulking through Arrothburg at night. She wasn't at all happy to be back in the village, not in such quick succession. That was the trouble with her, she knew; when she got attached to people, she began to make stupid choices. It was easy to be practical and

148

distant when she was alone in the world.

Verity had seen them take Mrs Ramsey into the church, but the woman could have been taken elsewhere. The town dealt with most crime through burnings, fear of burnings, and redemption through the church. It was customary for a witch to spend their possible last night of life inside the church in penance. It was seen as a chance to repent during their final hours. To beg their god to rid them of any evil, so they might pass the trials. It never seemed to work, however, because once a witch was named, Verity said they always burned.

After making their way through the outskirts of town and into the centre, the two women tiptoed around to the back of the church, looking for the rear entrance. Arden had only ever been inside the church once, but Verity had grown up in it, leaving the witch to follow the timid woman's lead. They made their way quietly, wary of anyone who might be hiding around corners.

Verity tried the handle, but the door didn't budge. She quickly turned to Arden in desperation, as if a locked door was the end of the rescue entirely. Arden rolled her eyes and nudged Verity out of the way. She had plenty of experiences with barriers such as these and she had come prepared. Pulling a chisel and a small hammer out of the inside pocket of her cloak, Arden pried the chisel between the wood of the door and the base of the handle. Once the chisel was deep enough to start, she covered the end of the chisel with the material of her cloak and hammered it the rest of the way. The material concealed the heavy clunk of the impact of each hit. After a moment, the outside handle popped away from the door, hanging on by its inner workings, and the door squeaked open.

Slowly inching her way in, Arden peeked around the edge of the door. It was hard to tell with only the moonlight to guide them, but the church seemed the same as it had when she was young. Her mother had wanted to teach her about why the villagers were so dangerous to them. The pastor had stood at his lectern and had—in very different words—essentially told his congregation that every single one of them was a sinner and would be until they died, and if they did not work to be good in the eyes of their god, they would suffer for eternity.

Arden had learned her lesson quickly. She'd never felt the need to replicate that particular visit.

Seeing as they were entering from the back, Arden and Verity found themselves immediately on the dais. The lectern was front and centre, little more than a shadow in the night. The only light came from the large glass windows, which had been crafted in tiny scrap-like pieces and set together with strands of thin metal. The bright moonlight from outside the windows cast a strange pattern over the church, like the floor had shattered into thousands of pieces.

Verity's breathing was heavy as she followed Arden to the edge of the dais. Everything smelled of pine needles, covering some odd smell that reminded her of a swamp. Verity and Arden were looking out over the pews, a dozen on each side of the room. And there in the middle was the shape of someone on their knees.

Arden held out a hand to stop Verity from rushing forward. She leaned toward her ear to whisper. "I'm going to light a flame and we're going to try to get her out of here quietly, yes?"

Verity nodded.

Keeping her eyes on the woman, Arden crept to the stairs. They were quiet, certainly, but they were hardly ghosts. Boards creaked under their weight, and Verity was breathing like she'd just run from one edge of town to the other. Whoever was kneeling there should have been aware of them already. If it was the accused witch, why hadn't she gotten up? Was she asleep?

Arden snapped her fingers and a tiny flame caught. The person in front of them was indeed a woman, and by the look on Verity's face, it was her Mrs Ramsey. Arden knelt down, gesturing for Verity to do the same. In the years she'd been healing these people, Arden had never met the kneeling woman.

"Mrs Ramsey?" Verity pulled her hood tighter around her face, making an attempt at anonymity. "Are you all right?"

Mrs Ramsey blinked and looked up, as if just noticing them for the first time. "I'm well. Are you here to take me to the trials? My prayers aren't finished."

Arden and Verity exchanged a look.

"Who do you worship?" Arden adjusted her hand so she could see Mrs Ramsey's face more clearly.

"God."

"Do you commune with the spirits of the forest?"

"No, certainly not."

"How do you practise your magic?"

"I'm not sure. I don't think I practise at all."

"If you don't practise magic, how are you a witch?"

Mrs Ramsey's brow furrowed. "One can never be sure *who* is a witch. The pastor said the trials will clear my name if I'm not one. I could be a witch and not even know."

Arden took a moment to push down the rage and irritation bubbling to the surface. "You would know, believe me. Mrs Ramsey, are you a witch?"

The woman's expression hardly changed, everything docile and unmoved. "Maybe, yes."

A hiss rose up from Verity. When Arden turned her head, the young woman had her fingers pressed to her temples, pain written on her face. Her eyes closed and she tilted her head like she was focused on hearing something in the distance. A moment later, she looked up.

"There were flashes of a pious life. It showed me the moment the pastor spoke to her. Mrs Ramsay changed her mind so quickly... Everything after is muddled."

Arden let out a long breath. Something unsettled her and she couldn't say what it was. "We need to go." She turned her attention to

Mrs Ramsey, who was staring blankly at them. "Darling, you're going to stand up and come with us, all right? We're going to leave."

Verity reached out a hand. "I can help you."

Mrs Ramsey shook her head, brow furrowing again. "I can't leave. The pastor needs me here. Tomorrow I'll be tested."

"And do you know what those trials consist of?" Arden prodded. She certainly knew.

"They'll search my body for witch marks and lie me in water to see if I float."

"So—" Arden spoke slowly and deliberately. "If you have a single brown mark on your body, or if you try not to drown, you'll be a witch. They'll burn you for that. Do you know how to swim?"

Mrs Ramsey looked around the dark room as if searching for something. "Yes."

"Does that mean you're a witch?"

"I—" The look on the woman's face was growing increasingly confused. "I don't know. Pastor Woolfe said I could prove my innocence. He's so good with words, isn't he? He says things and they make sense and—" Mrs Ramsey began to cry, her hands flying up to cover her eyes. "My head hurts. He speaks truth and so do you, and I—"

"It's time to go." Arden didn't like where this was going. The woman could be old and confused, her mind failing her, or...Arden took Mrs Ramsey's hand and urged her up. "We're going to go somewhere special, where you can offer your repentance to your god before you die."

Verity let out another hiss, and Arden gave her an apologetic look for having lied.

Mrs Ramsey stood, but there was a reluctance to it, like something weighed her down. She began to shake her head. "No. No, that's not right. That's not what the pastor said to do. Please leave."

"We're not going to leave you." Verity reached out and hooked her hand around the woman's shoulder. "You aren't going to be harmed."

"Shut up," Arden hissed. "She needs to—"

"I can't leave!" Mrs Ramsey squealed. She bucked her shoulders, trying to get the two of them to let go of her. "Leave me alone. I need to face the trials and be judged. How else will I prove I'm not a witch? Sinners. Sinners! *Sinners!*"

"Shit." Arden knew they were out of time and fighting something neither of them understood. It wouldn't be long before Mrs Ramsey's screaming alerted the whole town.

Arden wound her fist back and punched Mrs Ramsey in the face.

The woman slouched over. Luckily for her, Verity was quick enough to catch her before she hit the ground.

"Why did you do that?" Verity snapped.

"We can discuss this later when we're not about to be discovered. Pick her up, come on—"

"Mrs Ramsey?" a voice called out from outside the front doors of the church. "Are you all right?" Something jingled, like the rustle of keys.

"Fuck fuck fuck." Arden shook her finger, snuffing out the flame, and rushed up the dais stairs to the back door. Verity was struggling to drag Mrs Ramsey's unconscious body up the stairs, so Arden darted back and grabbed the woman's legs. The two of them fumbled the woman's body in the dark, uncoordinated and desperate.

The jingling stopped and the front doors creaked open. The moonlight illuminated the face of the one and only pastor. He was only a shadow in the dark, but his garb gave him away, all long raiments and cloaks. Besides, he had the posture of a man who thought he had his god on his side.

"Who's there? Unhand that woman." The pastor stepped forward and let the door close behind him.

"Stay back! Don't come any closer!" Arden couldn't exactly drop the woman to turn and threaten him.

"And what will happen if I do?" The pastor inched forward. "She's a witch. Anything you could do to her would only be God's will. Step out of the shadows so I can see your face."

"You are a disgrace—" Verity started.

Arden cut her off. If the pastor knew Verity's voice—"She's not a witch. I've been the only witch here all these years, and you know it."

"Ah, it's you. I should have known." The pastor put a hand on his chest, his voice full of mock sadness. "You insult me, witch. You crawl out of your woods and come into *my* church as if there's anything you can do to stop me? As if you're the only one with power?"

"You don't have power—"

"Of course I do."

Verity twitched, drawing Arden's gaze. "Something's happening. It feels like it did in the market. Like something isn't right."

Arden whipped her gaze back to the pastor. He'd stepped closer.

"Aren't you tired of running?" His voice had taken on a softer quality. "Hasn't this gone on long enough?"

Arden stared at the shape of the pastor in the dark. It *had* gone on too long. She *was* tired of running. But how had he known that?

"It must be so difficult, living the way you do." The pastor kept inching toward the dais. "Alone in the woods. Hunted."

His voice was so compelling, but Arden couldn't say why. He just kept saying true things. She couldn't deny how true they were.

"Arden!" Verity still had ahold of Mrs Ramsey's unconscious body. "What are you doing?"

"Listening," Arden whispered. "He makes a good point."

"What?" Verity set the woman down and strode in front of Arden. "No, he doesn't. What's going on in your head?"

"It's compelling." Arden looked at the girl, confused. "I hate running and being alone." She knew the truth was more complicated than that, and it warred with his words, but she wanted to hear more of what he had to say. Maybe, if he kept talking, she would discover the depth of his truth, in time.

Verity grabbed Arden's face between her fingers and backhanded the witch. The contact of their skin sparked electricity in Arden's muscles and burned her cheek. The impact alone was enough to rattle her skull, but the rest—

Pain bloomed across her skin, moving through the bones of her skull. "What *the fuck,* Dandelion?!" Her mind righted itself and Arden's scowl fell off her face. "Oh. Oh no."

"Don't squabble, ladies." The pastor was almost to the steps of the dais, taking his time, as if nothing mattered in the whole world. "All you need to do is submit to the word of God."

"You're not God," Verity spat. She moved to pick up Mrs Ramsey's shoulders once more.

Arden smacked her hand away. "Leave her. We can't risk staying."

"I—"

"If he pulls me under his influence, you're all dead."

A groan rose up from the floor. Mrs Ramsey was stirring.

"New witch, girl whose voice I can't place." The pastor's silken words floated through the air. "Kill Mrs Ramsey."

Verity hauled the dizzy woman onto her feet. "I will not. I know what you are, demon. Spirit. Hypocrite."

Pastor Woolfe laughed. "How did you get out of my grasp, little one? An interesting trick. Mrs Ramsey?"

The woman in Verity's grasp answered with a dull murmur of the affirmative.

"Use the knife I gave you."

Before Arden could act, before either of them knew what was happening, Mrs Ramsey had fished a small knife from her pocket, the blade gleaming in the moonlight.

"Put it down!" Arden screamed.

The woman pressed the blade to her own throat. "A living witch only poisons the flock." And before anyone could reach her, the blade was deep in Mrs Ramsey's throat.

"No!" Verity rushed forward, too late to catch Mrs Ramsey before she collapsed to her knees, choking. The girl pulled her into her arms, blood splashing down onto them both.

"You're a monster!" Arden cried out. "Where did you get this power? Who gave it to you?"

"God, of course." The pastor sounded so delighted with himself. "A version of God. Mrs Ramsey was in the flock for so long. She was so malleable. Such a pity I don't yet have that power over you."

If it was a matter of time or exposure, Arden wasn't going to give him either.

"Get up." Arden hauled on Verity's shoulders, forcing the sobbing girl to let go of the body in her arms. Verity resisted, but she was slight compared to the witch, and Arden hauled her to her feet.

She didn't wait for Verity to consent. She pulled the distraught girl by the arm and the two of them took off toward the back door. The pastor spoke as they ran, and Arden tried so hard not to hear him.

"God is mighty," he called into the echoing space. "He gives the tools of success to the truly righteous. Your power is so much smaller, isn't it, witch? You lead this girl to evil through your sin."

That much was true, even as her head spun and the lingering pain of the slap hummed under her skin.

Arden pushed the door and pushed Verity out first.

"Go on." The pastor's voice grew dimmer as they ran toward the woods. "I know you're here now, new witch, and the hunt is always better than the catch!"

Just as Arden thought they were far enough, one last loud, dark bellow followed them into the night.

"See you in church!"

CHAPTER SIXTEEN

Verity

Mindless terror had enveloped Verity as Arden dragged her through the streets of Arrothburg. Her hands were warm and wet and *blood* was on her fingers and she knew that if she looked down—bile rose in Verity's throat. She swallowed her feelings far enough to keep running, following Arden through the dark paths of the village without question.

Arden veered into a small space between a home and a barn, squeezing into the shadows and squatting down into a ball, a bit like an animal hiding from danger. Verity squeezed in after her. They were shoulder to shoulder, panting and afraid.

Heart beating fast and body thrumming from the run, Verity waited to be found. Waited for the night watch to reach into the space and grab her by the neck. Surely *someone* had seen them hide and knew what they had witnessed. Had heard the screaming. Had felt someone *die*. But as her heart slowed and her breath returned, no one came.

It was Arden who broke the silence. "We need somewhere to go," she whispered.

Verity thought about responding, but her cheeks were still wet. She tried to wipe the wetness from her face, the tears, but without light to see by, she was certain she was smearing it all over her instead. It was thicker than tears, smelled metallic, whatever it—

Blood.

She had blood on her face.

Mrs Ramsey's blood.

Verity began to shake. Great gasping sobs rose in her. She tried to choke them down but she couldn't stop hearing the moment over and over. Though it had happened in the dark, her mind had conjured the scene in broad daylight, forcing Verity to imagine the woman's death in full, living colour.

Arden shook her. "Verity. Verity, you need to breathe. We don't want anyone to hear us."

Clapping a hand over her own mouth, Verity continued to cry in overwhelming waves of grief.

Arden sighed, mumbling something long under her breath. "Well, I can't leave you alone like this, can I? You said your family has a barn. Will you take us there?"

"Y-yes," Verity managed to choke out.

Arden forced her arm under Verity's and hauled her upward. Verity felt like a dead weight, everything in her wanting nothing more than to collapse to the ground and stay there. But at Arden's insistence, she picked herself up enough to guide them both between houses and common places until they were standing outside her family home.

Verity proceeded automatically, untangling herself from Arden's grip and following the worn footpath onto her family's tiny piece of land. Arden followed, and the two quietly went into the barn. The goats were sleeping and the air was pungent with all the earthy smells of animals. Verity climbed the ladder and went up to the loft, where she collapsed against the wall, trusting Arden to follow.

Although she'd cleaned the space since, the oil lamp was still there from her week of bleeding, and Verity picked it up, holding it aloft in the dark. "Can you make fire?" Her voice was raw and deflated.

In lieu of an answer came the snap of fingers and a pinpoint of light. Arden opened the oil lantern up and lit the wick. A moment later, the loft was significantly brighter.

"Better." Arden settled down along the wall with Verity, sighing as she slumped down.

In the light, Verity could see how red her skin was.

The sobs came back. Her mind circled one looping set of thoughts, unable to break from the horror of Mrs Ramsey's words, of the things Pastor Woolfe had said to them. Arden was speaking, but Verity couldn't hear her, not in any way that counted.

It wasn't until Arden returned that Verity realised she'd been gone at all. She must've been gone for a while, because she came back with a bucket of water, a cloth, and a bundle of fabric. Arden sat down again, but this time in front of Verity.

"Let me see your hands." Arden's voice was kind, and Verity realised something had shifted between them. She was using the voice she had used with Hope and Flora: assertive but calming. Verity had become her patient again, if only for this moment.

Numbly, with neither objection nor care, Verity put her hands on her own lap.

Arden reached out to take one, and the moment their skin touched, both women recoiled. A burst of lightning ran through Verity. She shook her hand, trying to dispel the feeling. When she looked up, Arden was nursing a burn, the skin scorched. She let out a litany of curses.

"I forgot, somehow. Shouldn't have." Arden gestured to the burn that Verity's slap had left on her cheek. She put her hand in the bucket of cool water, letting it soak. "I suppose we'll need to be creative."

Taking the cloth out of the water, Arden tore it down the middle and wrapped each large piece around her hands, as if she were bandaged. That done, she picked up Verity's hand again. The cloth was wet and cold, but she gave off no further sparks of pain.

Gently, Arden washed the blood from Verity's skin. The two said nothing, sitting in the quiet of the night. The goats rustled below. Crickets chirped beyond the walls of the barn. It could have almost been serene, if it weren't for the thrum of dread under Verity's skin.

Removing the cloth from around her hands, Arden washed the material, wrung it out, and wrapped her hands again. "Hold back your hair."

Verity did as she was told. Arden touched the cloth to her face and the kindness of it melted something in Verity. Tears rolled down her cheeks, soft and quiet, unlike the uncontrollable weeping from earlier.

"Verity."

She looked up. Arden was staring at her, but she knew if she opened her mouth, her heart would pour out.

"Being that close to death is difficult." Arden cleaned off Verity's forehead. "But you know you didn't kill her, right?"

Verity said nothing.

"The pastor killed her. You did your best."

"He needs to pay for this." The words were out of Verity's mouth before she could think about them. She felt as if she were crashing into waves of emotion: first grief and helplessness, and then rage. Deep, seething rage. "I don't know what's real, what was ever real. How much of what he's told us is a lie? How many people died for nothing? Was I in his power before? I don't know."

Tongue rolling over her teeth, Arden bobbed her head. "It's likely you were. But you weren't tonight, hmm?"

"No," Verity admitted. "Maybe that has something to do with my ability. If I can see the truth of a lie, perhaps his pretty words don't work on me anymore."

"That's logical." Arden found a new line of blood to wash away. "I wish I could say I was immune. I know myself so well, and yet it only took a few of his words to begin stripping that away."

"Some people are just compelling..." Verity offered.

"No." Arden shook her head. "You and I both know better than that. Do you know how many of your kin have tried to convince me toward the ways of the church? I've hardly ever faltered, but a few moments with this man made me want to attend a sermon. He's too good. I'd bet everything I own that he's working with a spirit of some kind."

Anger rose in Verity's gut. "Hypocrite. Burning us for doing nothing, while he works magic to influence our minds. All these years and my faith has come to nothing."

Arden guided Verity's neck with one covered hand and worked to clean the blood from the girl's collarbone and neck. "What you believe in is your choice. You can still have your god even if you have no pastor and no church. He can't take that from you."

"Can't he?" she snapped. "There's nothing about faith in this village that he doesn't have his hands in." Verity wiped away some of the stray tears.

"Do you believe I have faith?" Arden asked.

"I—Not in God, no."

"Not in your god. But faith is belief, and mine is for the spirits that are my patrons. I've travelled a little. Not much, but enough to meet people who reserve their faith for nature or for other people. Who live good lives without a church, some with your god and some without. Anything is possible, Verity. You'll know that after you live long enough."

"That's all well and good," Verity said, dismissing every word of it without a second thought. "But the pastor deserves to die for what he's done."

"He probably does," Arden admitted. "Everything he's done, well, it's probably worse than what we know. But it's important to be smart about this. If I get caught, there's a good chance I can kill anyone who tries to stop me. And I will do that to save my own life. But if you get caught, you'll burn."

"If I can stop him, maybe no one else will burn again." Verity had struggled back and forth with her faith and her obedience, but this was as damning as anything could be. If she turned away from it, if she let it continue, she was willingly handing over the lives and minds of everyone in that town.

How far, she wondered, had they all fallen? The pastor had said Mrs Ramsey had been devout. She'd been in church often, but some people never went to church, or chose work or rest above their faith. Were they as poisoned as the others?

Verity's own family. How far gone were *they*?

"I want revenge as much as you do, Verity." Arden's expression was a struggle between composure and anger as she removed the cloth from her hands. "This town has murdered so many people over magic they don't possess, and likely one or two who did. I understand your rage; I do. It's horrific—oh, please don't keep crying. I don't do well with crying."

But Verity couldn't help it. Tears streamed down her face. She'd lost her whole world so quickly, like the shattering of glass in slow motion. Even at that moment, her father was probably in the house, sitting up waiting for her, furious that she had betrayed him. How many of their fights had been about things the church had spoon-fed them both? How much had she held back from her dear father because she was afraid to be honest with him?

The door to her own truths creaked open, and a few tumbled to the front of her mind.

That she wished for a different life.

That her body hungered for touch.

That she felt giddy and inappropriate at the sight of pretty women.

That her own family had held her in a prison and taken away her future.

She slammed the door shut. Already those truths were more than she could bear to contend with. The things she'd been told, been raised to believe, they were all under question. If God was there, watching and listening, which of His words were real? Which had been the pastor's poison?

She might never truly know.

Arden was still watching Verity when the tears finally subsided. The witch looked at her with a tenderness on her face that Verity hadn't seen before, like a mother would look at her child. Arden reached out slowly and brushed her fingers against Verity's cheek.

The touch sparked through Verity's skin and they both recoiled, the stench of burnt skin on the air.

"Goddamnit!" Arden shook her hand violently, hissing.

Verity rubbed her cheek to take the sting out of it, the contact rippling through her bone and muscle. It hurt, but so too did the loss of that moment of tenderness.

It would have been nice to be soothed by a mother again.

She reached for the abandoned bundle of fabric and found that it was one of her dresses. How Arden had gotten it was a mystery to her, but she was thankful for it either way. Rising and turning away from Arden, she pulled off her bloodied dress and slid on the new one. It smelled of river water and soap, and it brought a bit of peace back to her mind.

"You should sleep, if you can." Arden took off her cloak and bundled it up to use as a pillow. "It won't be long until dawn and I suspect you'll have a lot of explaining to do in the morning."

The thought sent a shiver down Verity's spine. She was exhausted, all the energy disappearing from her like a candle burning from both ends. She'd run through so many emotions, had felt so many things, and at that moment all she knew was how tired she was. How dry and ineffective her mind felt.

By the time Verity made a little pillow of her old clothing, strategically tucking the soiled parts away, Arden was already gently snoring. Verity laid down her head, and a moment later, she was overtaken by ghoulish dreams.

CHAPTER SEVENTEEN

Verity

The ringing of bells woke Verity.

The noise was familiar but unwelcome, combining itself with the pounding inside her skull. The importance of it eluded her as she struggled toward consciousness. She hadn't slept enough. The world felt foggy and her limbs ached.

"What is *that*?" Arden groaned.

Verity had mostly forgotten where she was and whom she was with. The terrible sleep left her irritable and unhappy to be speaking to *anyone*. Then the night before came back to her in syrupy slowness. The running. The death. The blood on her hands.

Her chest clenched and emotion threatened to overtake her.

She wished she could forget again.

It took a moment to pull herself together enough to answer. "It's the bell in the market. Someone is calling the town together."

"It's a horrific noise." Arden pressed her thumbs into the skin near

165

her ears, opening and closing her jaw. She pulled her cloak around her more tightly, exhaling a cloud of misty breath. "Seven hells, it's cold. They make you sleep out here, even in the winter?"

Verity nodded. She was shivering as well, but it was nothing novel to her. "In the winter, it's best to sneak down with the goats. They're warm."

Arden let out an exasperated growl. "I fucking hate these people."

After the last few weeks, Verity was beginning to understand why.

Blinking, she willed her mind to wake, but only the pieces that didn't threaten to overwhelm her with grief. She needed them to stay dormant. "Probably…probably the bells have to do with us. What we did."

"That's likely," Arden agreed.

Sounds rose from nearby. Verity slunk closer to the barn wall and peered through one of the knotholes. They hadn't yet come around to her side of the barn, but she could hear her family speaking in low voices as they stepped outside. Each of them walked into sight and left again, heading toward the sound of the still-ringing bell.

Verity watched until her family disappeared around a building, and then turned back to Arden. "Should we…should we go to the market? It seems important that we know what's being said."

"You should go." Arden rose from her spot on the floor, stretching and cracking from an uncomfortable night sleeping on boards in the cold. "I shouldn't even be here, risking your family and yourself. I'll glean what I can from a distance and return home. At least there, I can stand my ground if someone comes after me."

Verity blanched. She felt woefully unprepared to go back out there, especially alone. She was still waking to the new nightmare of her life, the one where a woman's hot blood had spilt out onto her skin. A flash of darkness passed before her eyes and she could feel it again, feel the terror in her chest as the pastor spoke. Fearing the return of it, she slowly looked down.

Clean. Her hands were clean.

She wished very much that Arden would stay.

It seemed lately Arden was the only person who would understand any of the things that had happened to her. Her family hadn't understood her in the past, let alone now, as her whole world was collapsing around her. No matter how much she loved her family, she wouldn't be able to tell any of them about what she had seen and learned. She could never make them understand how her own body betrayed her every moon cycle. Couldn't make them understand the pain or loneliness she felt, living the way she had. If they couldn't understand that, how could she even begin to explain the stain Mrs Ramsey's blood had left under her skin?

Only Arden knew these things. The breadth and depth of them. And she was going to leave Verity to cope with it alone.

Verity wished she had the courage to ask her to stay.

She tried to summon it. Tried to get the words up her throat, but they stayed lodged in her stomach with the other feelings she was pushing down.

"Don't get caught," Verity sighed instead.

Arden nodded solemnly. "Be safe," she said and pulled her cloak back on. She climbed down the loft ladder. Verity watched as the witch pushed open the door of the barn and left, letting it slam behind her.

Fighting back the complicated feelings welling in her gut, Verity tried to turn her mind to something else. She stood and began to minimise the blood-soaked spoils of the previous night. She didn't think anyone would look in the loft, but if she folded things tightly around each other, she could maybe hide the red stains, for now. Just in case.

She needed to get to the market, but she struggled to right herself. She was tired and out of sorts. She hadn't felt rested in a long time, not since any of this witchery had started. It was a slog to pick herself up and go into the house, but she did. She kept up a steady pace as she checked herself for blood and made sure her clothing looked fresh enough. And then it was off to the market to face whatever came next.

By the time she arrived, the crowd was already quiet. It seemed like everyone from town was there, huddled together against the crisp wind surging through the square. Winter was coming fast, if that chill had anything to say about it.

In the middle of the crowd was the bell, secured on a tall stone platform. It had been built for just such occasions, and now Doctor Raam, Mayor Hart, and Pastor Woolfe were atop it like three of God's disciples from the Good Book. Behind them stood four tall metal bars surrounded by stacks of wood. It was Mayor Hart whose voice was booming over the crowd.

"We've lived in fear of this for long enough. God help me, I cannot fathom how we continue to weed out witches and yet they are *still here*. Still among us." Mayor Hart gazed over the crowd, his face stern and unimpressed. "I've asked both Doctor Raam and Pastor Woolfe to speak to you *again* about the signs of witchcraft, so that you may know a witch when you find one."

How were they still among them? Verity had a few ideas about that.

Mayor Hart stepped back, making room for Doctor Raam. Verity hadn't seen him face to face since she'd met Arden in the woods. Now, with her ability to see the truth of things, she found the doctor's appearance to be faltering and fluid, much like the pastor's had been. Until recently, she'd thought the doctor to be a good man, something that had shown through on his face. Now it seemed that the knowledge of his carelessness brought out each imperfection in him.

"A witch looks no different than any of your neighbours," Doctor Raam said. His voice was deep and gravelly. He smoked his pipe often, Verity remembered, and she wondered if that had anything to do with it. "It isn't until you get up close that things become obvious. A witch will have markings on their skin. Brown moles and strangely shaped birthmarks. Their breath may smell of rot, and you may notice in them a fear of water. A witch may walk abnormally, with a limp perhaps, or with an unnatural grace. They may resist burns, or burn too easily. And if you feel yourself drawn to someone, it may be their magic ensorcelling you to do their bidding."

The words stirred up so many images in Verity's already struggling mind. She was shown neighbours they had burned as witches, one after the other. She knew it was to refute the details the doctor was listing, though she couldn't tell which lie matched which face. As she listened, she recognized the silken voice the pastor had used, and it turned her blood cold. If the doctor could compel people just the same, could the mayor as well?

Between her visions, she worked hard to focus on the faces around her. Some of her neighbours nodded enthusiastically, enjoying the speech. Others seemed puzzled or unsure. Some of the faces of the unconvinced were strangers to her, people she knew kept to themselves more often than not.

And their scepticism was well warranted. Verity could so easily poke holes in what the doctor had said. How could a witch be either someone with a limp *or* someone who walked too prettily? Shouldn't it be one or the other? She knew many people with bad legs who had worked in the field or in the woods and had been injured. It was common. And yet so many of her neighbours seemed to believe it wholeheartedly.

"There are many other ways to know a witch," Doctor Raam said, holding his arm out to gesture to Pastor Woolfe. "But many of them are matters of the spirit, which only the pastor can truly speak to. Please, friend."

Pastor Woolfe stared across the crowd, unspeaking, his hands clasped in front of him. He drew in a long breath and sighed. "A witch will be disobedient." The pastor walked the small platform like a dais, dividing his attention across the crowd. "They will work in contention to your efforts. They will try to compel you against your will. A witch within the calling of service will be lazy, failing to meet the needs of the home. A witch within the calling of leadership will make choices that lead only to ruin. The sabotage may not be obvious; witches work carefully. They will convince you they deserve leniency, and turn you slowly from God's will."

The crowd nodded along. Verity's head shrieked with all the lies. At some point, she had stopped seeing the world with her eyes and her vision had become a blistering number of vivid images, people in their everyday lives, doing everyday things, and Verity couldn't sort them out.

"These are troubled times, I know. They are times in which we must choose the greater good over those we love. If witches are among us—and they surely are—then they must be people we care about."

Verity felt faint. The world bobbed around her and she was concerned she was swaying. It took concentration to press her feet into the ground and steady herself. The curse in her mind, this truth mechanism, it was going to be the death of her.

Why was everyone *always* lying?

Looking around, Verity needed to know if anyone else was questioning the things they were hearing. Surely it would be on *someone's* face. And it was. Here and there, people in the crowd wore incredulous or worried expressions. Some whispered to each other. And though she couldn't decipher exactly what they were thinking, *surely* they were as upset as she was.

But no one spoke.

No one was that foolish.

"Be vigilant, friends. There are witches in the crowd as we speak. Surely you know who they are. Tell us! Who among you is a witch?" Pastor Woolfe's voice rose over the mutterings of the people, commanding and calm.

The silent fear of the moment became a simmering pot as the pastor called his flock to action. The voices of her neighbours rang out around her, calling for justice and vengeance. *Burn the witch.*

"Amberlee Shepherd is a witch!" came a voice from the other side of the crowd. "She has a mole on her bottom shaped like an onion!"

"My wife is a witch! She wants me to help her in the home but that's an act of service!"

"My brother is a witch! He nearly cut off my finger with an axe the other day!"

Faster than Verity could comprehend, the mood of the meeting had turned to bloodlust. People cried out, tossing the sins of their loved ones toward the pulpit, waiting for judgement. As Verity watched, most of her neighbours pushed toward the platform, while some gathered their families and slunk away.

"Amberlee Shepherd!" Mayor Hart pointed into the crowd. "Bring her to us!"

The people around Verity moved, jostling to aid in her apprehension or to see the spectacle. Boxed in on all sides, Verity had no choice but to keep herself small. Everyone around her had turned to madness. One after the other, people were dragged toward the three figureheads of the town to face their fates.

All the while, the crowd screamed.

Burn the witch.

Burn the witch.

Burn the witch.

CHAPTER EIGHTEEN

Arden

Burn the witch.

Burn the witch.

From behind one of the homes, Arden peeked over a crate.
She was crouched, trying to keep out of sight. She'd never been in
Arrothburg at the precise moment when they'd called for a witch to
be burned. She kept herself in the woods for a reason, deep enough
not to hear the noise or smell the smoke. She'd never watched the
people wound up to a fever pitch. Never seen them betray the people
they claimed to love and admire.

Arden had refused to find a perch that was too close to things. If
she couldn't hear the pastor that well, she reasoned he couldn't have
so large an effect on her. Neither Arden nor Verity had any true idea
how it worked, and everything was a guess on their part. A risky
guess, at that. But Arden wanted to have *some* warning of what the
people would do next, and staying was the only way to do that.

That far away, it was also hard to *see* much of anything. Too many obstructions stood in front of her, too many people. From what she *could* see and hear, the speeches had pulled the crowd into a frenzy. Arden had little ability to know the magic from the hateful thinking, but it was safe to assume an amalgamation of both was in the works. If a person could create doubt and sow new thoughts in the minds of others, how easy would it be to amplify any hate that was already in a person's mind?

It should've also been disappointing to realise the doctor and the mayor were in league with the pastor, but it was certainly not surprising. *The fish rots from the head*, as the phrase went.

Still, knowing the likelihood of it did nothing to soothe Arden's heart. Names were being called out and people were being hauled bodily onto the unlit pyres. They would burn soon if no one intervened.

She could stop them. Arden knew that much. With the power she borrowed from the spirits, and the skills she'd gained to survive, she was a match for half the town at once. If she wanted them dead, if she wanted to save those accused witches, Arden would win. And the cost of saving those few would be countless. Once summoned, the Gloam would cut down whatever stepped into its path. Once those floodgates were opened, she wouldn't be able to turn back. Were the lives of four strangers worth the weight of so many deaths on her shoulders?

She didn't know.

It was evident those monsters wouldn't change their ways on their own. It would require an act of force. But her mother had warned her about that as well. About martyrs and vengeance. By her estimation, people couldn't be forced to change. They had to be led to it. To turn into a witch who killed people was to be exactly what they had accused her of all along. Yet, killing their leaders might lead them to understand what was being done to them.

It could also make things worse, and in turn, she would take them down with her.

Arden tried to breathe. Self-preservation compelled her to leave and go back to her cabin, where she'd be safe. She couldn't control these people's actions, certainly not when magic of some kind was involved. Her duty to them stopped at healing and midwifery. Whatever the fuck was going on in that town, she knew she couldn't heal it. Whatever magic it was, it was true evil; she didn't need Verity's abilities to see that.

Verity.

Cursing, Arden began to move with the intention of saving that girl from whatever would come next. She forced herself to still, to stay put. Rushing in would help no one, and though she could do little for the entire town, perhaps she could whisk Verity away before something happened to her. If the pastor recognized her voice, if he suspected her *at all*, they'd likely burn her just to be sure.

Was it possible to stop the magic? Could they remove the pastor's ability, or was it tied to him the way Arden's was tied to her? What spirit would have gifted these men such horrific power over others?

Staring out into the mess of the town centre, Arden caught the bright slash of a smile across the mayor's face. A wide, cruel grin that could have split his cheeks in half. It was a sick thing, to burn people, and knowing he was enjoying himself made it so much worse.

Arden had been pushing her fury down for *so many years*. She wanted him *dead*.

Her blood boiled, her breath coming fast and ragged. The people who had stayed to urge their leaders on, who wanted to witness their neighbours burning...she had no respect for them. No concern for their wellbeing.

They condoned it. They called for it, screaming to their heavens for justice. *Burn the witch.*

They were strapping the people to their pyres. If Arden was going to move, it had to be quick.

Martyrs be damned, she thought. *It's time for war.*

Arden stood, and as she did, a loud crack reverberated in her skull, and the world went black.

CHAPTER NINETEEN

Verity

The entire village had gone mad and Verity had no idea what to do.

"Bring more wood!" called Mayor Hart.

Her neighbours dispersed in droves, clamouring to help each other. The people left in the square were the ones helping to secure the four accused witches and to mind them as they waited obediently to be strung up. The podium's four iron rods stuck out of the ground, waiting for new bodies to be seared into them.

The chaos enveloped Verity, her mind a jumble of overwhelmed sensations that immobilised her. The sun was beginning to set and people ran past her in all directions as if she were a statue, paying her no mind. The leaders huddled together, speaking in voices she couldn't hear above the racket, as if all of this were normal. Business as usual. Nothing to worry about.

Too much was happening. Too many people, too much noise. Her neighbours worked together like bees in a hive, organising the

deaths of their friends and family. Justified. Righteous. Bundles
of wood were thrown onto the platform, stacked and piled, her
neighbours bound to the poles with grim determination on their
faces, as if God Himself had reached down and put them to their
purpose. And all the while, the hum of compelling voices wriggled in
her mind, the lies and truths of hundreds of people flickering across
her vision in quick succession.

It was enough to make a person mad.

Barely able to think, Verity seemed to shrink in on herself, getting
smaller and smaller until she was just a passenger in a body, watching
the impending doom as if it were a dream.

She no longer wished to exist. It would be preferable to simply
blink away, out of the square and to somewhere where no one was
about to die in front of her.

A peaceful, warm, white void.

When she became aware of herself again, the sun was just a sliver on
the horizon. Verity had moved, but she didn't remember doing it. She
was still in the crowd, but had drifted somehow. Floated off course
like a boat on the waves.

The wood had been piled high on the podium around her
neighbours, waiting to be killed. The accused witches were faces
she knew. Of course they were. People she wished to know better
or didn't care for or had heard plenty of rumours about. They were
strapped down, two of them unwilling and thrashing against their
bonds. The other two were devout members of the church, and
their fate didn't seem to bother them in the least. They were smiling,
looking down at the crowd like it was the best day of their lives. They
stood, ready to burn. Like it was all God's will, come to pass.

Perhaps the cursing was what had woken her from her stupor. It came to her then, calling her attention. A loud, angry string of slurred words came from the woman they were hauling up the platform.

"Quickly!" yelled the mayor. "Take that one down and let her go. We have a bigger threat in our midst! The witch of the woods is a much better prize."

The men did as they were told. They freed young Melissa Maison and she walked calmly back down from the dais and joined the crowd. A moment later she was cheering like the others, as if she hadn't almost been the fourth body herself.

Wait. Verity's mind was still catching up, so tired from all the lies and visions. *What had he said?*

The fourth.

Verity strained to see—why was it so hard to *focus*—and her breath caught in her chest.

Arden.

The witch's white hair whipped in the breeze, the skirts of her dress twisting around her legs. Blood seeped from her head, down her cheeks and neck. Arden seemed to be fighting for consciousness, her head lolling and her eyes fluttering open and closed.

An urgent thought pulled Verity into full consciousness. Arden was the only person strong enough to stop whatever was going on. The only people who suspected the evil of this had already run back to their homes. These people weren't *awake.* If the witch died, Verity would be powerless to end it. To *change* it. No matter how strong of will she was, she was not a fool; she had no magic and no physical prowess, only a strange moral compass that gave her blistering headaches.

"Stop." Verity's voice was a crack in her throat. She swallowed and licked her lips and tried again. "Stop!"

No one seemed to hear her.

The leaders on the podium were paying so little attention to the tasks at hand that they'd started smoking cigars and chatting between themselves. Their focus had been caught by Arden, who inspired nothing but raucous laughter. It kindled a rage in Verity that she hadn't known she was capable of.

Willing her body back under her control, Verity pushed through the crowd toward the podium. Several voices protested as she shouldered her way through, and the doctor, pastor, and mayor standing in front of the soon-to-be pyres stared at her. She didn't let their irritated gaze stop her from climbing up onto the podium with them.

"You must stop!" Verity held her hands in the air, trying to get everyone's attention. "You are good people, all of you. Most of you, at least. I don't believe you're so eager to kill the people you care about. You're under some sort of devilry and if you can just break loose of that and see what's happening, you'll know what to do. You'll know to set these people free!" She gestured to the people of the poles. "These are your friends, and they are not witches. And the one true witch, she has helped more of you on your sick beds than Doctor Raam ever has. These men compel you to do evil using their sly tongues, twisting the word of God! Please, come to your senses!"

Verity's speech ended and silence filled her ears. After a moment, the jeering began.

Get down from there, you stupid tart!

That one's a witch as well!

Her mother was a witch!

Burn the witch!

Mayor Hart and Doctor Raam were staring at her, amused. Only Pastor Woolfe seemed at all concerned with her behaviour.

Growing desperate, Verity searched the crowd until she found the familiar faces of her family. Father, Asher, Clarabel. She swung her arms wide. "Please! You're my family. You must know I speak the truth. You must trust me! You *must listen*!"

"Verity!" Her father moved forward through the crowd to lean against the platform, her siblings on either side of him. "You shame us. Get down here this instant."

Clarabel had climbed up the podium wall, her chin propped on the top of the platform. "Come down! We're going to burn witches! Don't you want to join us?"

The glee in her sister's voice made her stomach heave.

"Please!" Verity cried out. "Please stop this!"

Mayor Hart let out a deep, hearty laugh. "Naive girl, thinking you could *do* something. The effort was a good one, but you're a bit out of your element, child."

Pastor Woolfe was scowling at her. "I don't know how you released yourself from the spell. You should've been long under our influence. Would you care to enlighten us?"

"Go fuck yourself," Verity spat. She wasn't sure she'd ever spoken to anyone that way before.

Pastor Woolfe grew subtly more irritated with her. "What would God think of you, cursing a pastor like that?"

"I don't think God lives here."

"Maybe, maybe not. I assume you're the one who broke into the church to try and free poor Mrs Ramsey?" The pastor clicked his tongue. "Stupid girl, aligning yourself with a witch. Now we'll have to kill you too. We do *try* to warn them all, don't we?"

"We do indeed," Mayor Hart cackled.

Verity opened her mouth to admonish them, but her voice caught. They were so open, so blatant in their crimes. Didn't they even have the decency to deny it? She turned to the crowd again, calling out over the noise. "Do you not hear them?"

"Of course they don't, not really," Doctor Raam scoffed. "A little devilry, as you say."

Mayor Hart's face grew sour as he looked at the doctor. "Too little, if you ask me. Influence is all well and good, but half of these simpering idiots went to hide, didn't they? Can't compel people who stay at home."

"It was your job to rein in the minds of the ones who shirked church," Doctor Raam barked back.

"And yours!" The mayor wasn't impressed in the slightest.

"I hate listening to your fucking bickering—" the pastor began.

A groan came from behind them. Arden was regaining herself again.

"We'd best burn them before the witch wakes up. This one too." Pastor Woolfe gestured at Verity. "I've always found her to be grating, even when she was a doting little church mouse."

Mayor Hart and Doctor Raam sneered in agreement.

"No!" Verity pushed past them and ran to Arden, stumbling up over the logs that had been piled around her. She fumbled with the rope binding the witch's hands, but the knots were too tight.

"You there," Doctor Raam snapped at someone in the crowd. "Tie the girl to the pyre with the wood witch. Let them burn together."

Verity's eyes shot wide open. She ran to the opposite side of the podium and leapt from it. Instead of Verity landing between the onlookers, they reached up to snatch her mid-jump. Struggling against all of their dozen hands, she kicked and screamed. It made no difference. They pushed her back toward the platform and threw her onto the wood. Into the waiting hands of Hope and Flora, who began to bind her to the pyre.

Their glassy eyes told Verity everything she needed to know.

"Let her go." Arden's words were slurred.

The rope burned Verity's bare wrists, each yank on it ripping into her fragile skin. As tight as it was, she would likely stop feeling her fingers soon. Someone slammed her into the pole and tightened the rope around it, and nothing that Verity did to try to squirm away was of any use.

On the other side of the pole, Arden struggled to stay on her feet. Though Verity couldn't see her, she could feel the slip and fall of her back against hers, hear the clunk of the wood as Arden's feet hit the logs. Was she losing consciousness again? Nearly out of her mind with fear, Verity kicked Arden as hard as she could, but the impact only earned a groan from the witch.

Light flickered in the periphery of Verity's vision. Someone was approaching the pyres with an enormous torch, the fire burning fast and high against the dark of night. If she didn't soon find a way for them to get out of their bonds, they'd both be dead, and in a very unhappy manner.

"Arden! Arden, please!" she screamed.

Arden fell silent. Her body slumped down. The parts of the witch that were pressed against Verity weren't moving anymore.

Panic threatened to overtake her. Verity watched the torch being pressed into the kindling. If she couldn't wake Arden, they would both die, along with the three others bound to the enormous pyre. What could she possibly do? Verity had no power, no fire or magic, nothing that made her special except those stupid lies—

And one other thing.

Verity wiggled her fingers. She was tied tightly, but she could feel Arden's bound fists pressing into her back. If she could wiggle just a little farther—

The crowd began to chant.

Burn the witch!

Burn the witch!

Still working her wrists, Verity looked up. The torch had caught the kindling and had been tossed onto the wood between the two centre pyres. Soon it would spread out among the tinder and brush, catching the wood and burning them to bits.

Verity's wrists burned as she contorted her arms to give her leverage, trying to pull her bound hands closer to Arden's. And finally—finally!—her fingers pressed against the witch's.

The spark was instantaneous. Pain shot across Verity's body, splintering down her hands and into her arms and the core of her, the prolonged contact like a bolt of lightning.

Arden cried out like a wounded beast.

Wind burst from behind Verity, a powerful force that emanated out from them and swept over the crowd. People were tossed from their feet. The flames of the pyres went out. Verity couldn't see how, didn't understand when the burst of heat rose up near her hands or how Arden managed to free herself. The rope loosened and Verity fell to her knees.

Above her, Arden stood like a beast uncaged. Her hair was wild and tangled, her rage plain on every line of her face. Something feral had risen in her, and it chilled Verity to the bone.

Whatever came next, it would be bad.

The mayor took a step toward Arden and she braced herself for attack, her lips curled back over her teeth in a horrific grin.

"You wanted a fucking witch. *Here I am.*"

CHAPTER TWENTY

Arden

Bolts of pain lanced their way through Arden's body as she stared down the disgusting, simpering men in front of her. Her hands were a patchwork of charred, raw black over her skin, as if she'd dipped her hands in coal dust. Each breath she took was a hard, labouring jolt through her body.

Arden was seething.

Verity's touch had woken her up, all right. It had woken up parts of her she'd kept dormant with the guilt of duty. Each time she'd grown angry and weary with that town, she'd listened to the words her mother had fed her about responsibility and guiding the ignorant. Now her mother's voice had gone silent and all that was left was rage.

"Stay back." The pastor nearly tripped over himself to back away. "Come no closer."

"What are you going to do, Pastor? Kill me?" Arden took a step closer. Every excuse she'd made for these people, every sense of duty she'd had, it had all evaporated. The doubt, the back-and-forth debate she'd held with herself before they'd smashed her in the head and tried to burn her alive—it was over.

She was ready to bring a merciless reckoning down on them.

"Kill the witch!" the mayor cried out as he gingerly hopped down from the platform and threw himself into the crowd. The crowd split. Some lingered back, unsure, but the majority of them surged forward. Hundreds of people rushing toward her, creating an impossible wall between Arden and the people she needed to kill.

Verity grabbed Arden and pulled her back, but they had nowhere to go.

The crowd swarmed up and over the sides of the platform, hands reaching for them. Verity was pressed up against Arden's back, screaming, begging them to stop. Fists and palms and boots struck out from the crowd. A knife cut through the air, narrowly missing Arden, then again, slicing into her palm. She had no choice but to make herself small, pulling Verity down with her. They crouched, Verity draping her body over Arden's in a feeble attempt to shield the witch from the blows.

Grateful for the reprieve, Arden pressed her palms into the podium. The rage surged in her. The blows that struck Verity reverberated into Arden, as did the girl's screams. Each blow stuck, each fist and slap, each strike. Pain. Pain. Pain.

She would survive these murderers, no matter what it took, and she would take Verity with her.

Pushing the suffering from her mind, Arden spoke her intentions into the earth below her. She called for help.

For favours long saved.

For justice long past due.

She called them all.

When it was done, she forced herself out from under Verity. The girl's face was awash with tears. Bloody slices ran along the fabric of her dress, and boot prints on her back. Arden pushed her to the ground and curled up on top of her, waiting in the long, loud cacophony for help to come. She forced her mind away as the violence rained onto her, enduring every blow. To protect the girl. To build the rage. Destroy them all. Then it came.

A monstrous groan filled the air.

"Stop!"

The pastor's voice was muffled through the wall of bodies, but the assault stopped nonetheless. Arden had room to breathe again, but it was too late for them. Far too late. She picked herself up, pain bursting through every inch of her body, and helped Verity stand. The girl was a mess of blood and tears.

Arden stumbled, and Verity locked herself under the witch's arm, the two of them supporting each other to stand. They joined the rest of the town, watching the woods.

The black shapes of the trees swayed as if in a hurricane, even with no wind. Another long groan filled the air, deep and nearly deafening. Earth-shaking. The people clapped their hands over their ears as they watched. A thumping in the distance, growing closer with each repetition, gravel bouncing as the earth moved.

The treeline broke open and out stepped an enormous, towering tree. Thick, tendriled branches twisted out of its bark-covered body, the entirety of it as tall as the church spire. Its eyes were empty pits, its body seething with crawling critters of all shapes. Each step it took shook everything around them as it strode toward the village.

The pastor stepped back, fell from the platform, and scrambled to his feet. "Defend your homes!"

The congregation broke from their stupor and began to move, some running away from the threat and some toward it.

"Is that your tree spirit friend?" Verity's voice trembled. She let go of Arden and backed away.

It was Dalic, yes. At the tree's feet was a horde of deer, badgers, and wolves, all following the lead of a woman who bore the claws of a bear. Ilyana had come as well.

Arden had never seen either of them so angry.

Arden turned to Verity and took the girl by the shoulders. "Hide, Dandelion. Stay safe until this is over. This is no place for you." Arden strode away, down the steps of the platform.

She grasped onto her rage and let it consume her.

Reaching out, Arden grabbed the first person to run past her. A man. A complicit man. One of the people who had tried to hurt her. One of the fists that had tried to break her. Had it only been that once? Or had he lived his whole life with hate in his heart for her? It didn't matter anymore.

He was afraid, trying to pry her hands away from his clothing. When she sank her dagger into his gut, it slid in so easily. A satisfying itch deep in her mind was satiated. Some long-lived pain that had been waiting for a salve.

She let him drop.

He fell to his knees, clutching his gut. "Please, no," he begged. "Let me live. Please!"

Arden walked away, her heart singing as the man cried out for someone to help him.

"Please, where's the doctor?" he screamed.

Where was a doctor indeed? A healer? Someone who *cared*? Where had the good doctor been all those years when Arden was sewing up these people's wounds? Where had he been when the women were dying and the babies were crowning and the infections blazed through their bodies?

She was done with that life.

She was only rage.

Who would help them now?

The three leaders had disappeared into the village somewhere. She would find them; she was certain of it. But she had been waiting a long time for justice, and now that it had come, she would have her fun first. She would use the dark gifts she'd bartered so heavily for, all these years.

The hair on the back of her neck prickled.

Arden turned.

A shadow moved along the rooftops, one heavy thump after another. It seemed to have no rhyme or reason, at one point carving its way toward the edge of town. The Gloam was certainly taking its time helping her.

A large man lunged at her, swinging an axe back above his head to strike. Arden leapt out of the way, narrowly missing being sliced in half by the blade. She punched the man in the gut, and as he bent over to hold himself, she kneed him in the face.

It was her fault. She'd allowed herself to get distracted.

The sound of grinding metal rose up behind her.

Stepping out from between two homes was a scarecrow. *The* scarecrow, the one from the field with the fucked-up eyes. It stood taller than her, its ragged pieces swinging on its newly animated limbs. Black mist streamed from its edges, fading into the air like smoke. Its sharp angles and scraps of wood and steel and fabric, it all looked so much more horrific as it strode through the streets—and its face. Its face was a burlap sack with a drooling, fang-filled maw and two black, void-like eyes.

The Gloam leapt down from the roof beside the scarecrow. It had brought a friend.

Three villagers ran at Arden, farming tools brandished like weapons.

With a swoop of its hand, the scarecrow tossed the villagers across the stone. It followed after, picking up someone in a long, pretty fur coat and sticking their head in its mouth. Arden didn't look away as its teeth crunched down and the body fell limp.

They asked for it, she reminded herself.

Everyone in the village had *asked* for it. All those years of burning false witches and terrorising real ones. All the women she had sewn up and put back together, they'd been neglected by their friends. People who believed things that got them killed. Everything she had *done for them* and for *what*? So they could kill her for it?

No.

A tiny bit of reason niggled at the rage in her. Asked her to stop, to have more compassion for the people caught in the tangle of magic and hatred and fear. She pushed it aside. She refused to live in dutiful compliance anymore. She and her patrons would end *all of it*.

CHAPTER TWENTY-ONE

Verity

The screaming was too much for Verity. It ate at her as she watched her entire world fall to pieces. Arrothburg was everything she'd ever known, and now so many of the people she had grown up around were running for their lives. The tree spirit and the shadow spirit and an enraged witch and a murderous scarecrow, all of it straight out of her worst nightmares. Animals raced across the square, wreaking havoc. One man was covered in chipmunks and he rolled around in the dirt, trying to get them off as they bit every inch of his bare flesh. Once again, Verity was paralyzed, powerless to stop any of it. Her feet stuck in place. All she could do was watch in horror as the worst possibilities came to life.

Arden had killed someone, again. At *least* one person.

People were *dying* all around her.

And where were the men responsible?

As she looked, Verity caught sight of Clarabel. She was marching toward the monstrous scarecrow with a pitchfork more than twice her height—too big for the child to even wield properly.

Life sprang back into Verity and she pulled herself off the ground, hurtling toward her little sister. She didn't bother to call for her, knowing the girl wouldn't listen. She simply knocked the pitchfork from her hands, hauled her up over her shoulder, and carried her away like a sack of grain.

Clarabel kicked her, struggling to get out of Verity's grip. "Verity! I have to help defend the town! That's what the pastor said!"

"No, you don't." Verity wasn't that strong, but she was still strong enough to drag her sister away. "The pastor lies, darling."

"No, he doesn't!" Clarabel kept kicking, and each blow to Verity's gut was a swift, deep pain. Fortunately for Verity, she'd pushed on through much worse in the past. "The pastor speaks for God, and God thinks we need to kill the witch."

The hatred pouring out of Clarabel's mouth wounded Verity. To hear such a kind, generous girl saying those horrible things…the guilt of it settled in Verity's bones. *She* had been responsible for her siblings all those years, and *she* had continued to bring them into the church multiple times a week. It was by her hand that her sister's mind was so poisoned with hate. She had failed to protect the girl from the evils of the world.

If Verity could turn back time and do it differently, she would have.

Verity threw open the door of the first home she reached. No one was inside. Still hauling Clarabel bodily over her shoulder, she tossed the girl into the first room she saw, pulled the door shut, and secured it from the outside. Clarabel threw herself against the closed door from the other side, screaming.

The violent banging broke Verity's heart. Clarabel's voice took a pitch Verity had never heard from her before. "Let me out! This is God's will! Why are you turning your back on us?"

"No, darling. I don't think *any* of this was God's will." Tears welled in Verity's eyes. She checked the firmly secured door once more. It was a fine enough solution to keep a little girl out of trouble, but it was hardly going to solve anything. She wouldn't be able to overpower and lock her brother and father in a room—if she even found them—but she needed to do *something*.

She needed to find a way to end it before everyone was dead.

Walking back outside, Verity spotted a flutter of colour in the distance. The pastor in his gaudy robes. He had just run inside the church and was attempting to close the enormous doors by himself.

An idea began to reveal itself to her. If the pastor was compelling others with his words, perhaps he could reverse it somehow. Stop what he had done, or compel them to act in the opposite direction. He was a pastor, wasn't he? A slice of humanity *must* have been left in him. These were his people. His flock. He had to want to protect them from *this*.

He had to have a reason for doing what he'd done. Something she couldn't see, but still had the town's best interest at heart.

And if he wasn't worth redemption, she could make him stop. Somehow.

She had no magic, but she had to do something.

She barrelled across the square, weaving her way through her neighbours as they crowded themselves around the monstrous tree spirit's feet. The enormous tree kept picking them up by the shirt and putting them further away from its roots, enduring the small cuts they attempted to inflict on her.

Rather than attempt to go in the front, Verity hugged the side of the church, running around back. She prayed that the lock Arden had destroyed hadn't been replaced since the night before. It hadn't. Not stopping to allow for any loss of courage, Verity cracked the door open.

Candles and oil lanterns were lit, but she couldn't see the pastor.

Verity stepped inside and closed the door as gently as she could. While she intended to reason with the man, she didn't want anyone spotting her before she spotted them. She kept her guard high, but as she approached the lectern, looking out over the pews, she found that the church really was empty.

Where had he gone?

A scream and a burst of flames lit up the night outside the church window. Verity needed to be quick. Lives depended on it.

As she stepped away from the lectern, she spotted a crack in the floor in front of the pews. It had never been there before, not in all the years she'd been in that church.

Listening to the suspicious little voice of Arden that seemed to have taken up residence in Verity's mind, she stepped as lightly as she could and went to look at the piece of floor.

It was a square of flooring that, when slipped into place, would be practically invisible to anyone looking. A door.

Slipping her fingers underneath, Verity lifted the door and set it aside.

A pungent smell rose up from the hole in the floor, reminding Verity of a bog. That smell the town had been putting up with for years—it was coming from the door. With the hatch open, not even the candles and pine boughs could cover the stench.

Verity pinched her nose and ducked her head inside. Stairs led down into a secret basement, and familiar voices rose up, locked in a panicked disagreement.

Creeping down the stairs, her heart hammering in her chest, Verity pressed herself against the wall. The ceiling was barely high enough for most adults to stand straight, and it seemed more like a cave than a basement. The walls were made of dirt and support beams, and the floor was carelessly laid wooden boards.

Crouching at the bottom of the stairs, Verity peeked around the corner.

Pastor Woolfe, Doctor Raam, and Mayor Hart stood facing each other, arguing as they passed a bloodied knife from one to the other.

"And what do you think he's going to *do* about it?" Pastor Woolfe pulled the blade across his palm, then turned his hand to let the blood drip on the floor, just as Mayor Hart was doing.

Doctor Raam took it next. "Kill the witch. If we let this town die, it's going to be hard to get our hands on another. This is the legacy of our families for four generations! *Four*! It's not going to be simple to strut into Bloomsdale and reestablish ourselves in these positions."

"Won't it?" Mayor Hart asked. "With Elithiaz, we can build it back up. It will take time, but all we need is a few sermons on a public pulpit and they'll be ours to take."

The pastor stared at Mayor Hart for a moment. "Perhaps we've been thinking too small all this time. Bigger towns, bigger rewards."

"Perhaps." Doctor Raam slit open his palm.

The three leaders began to chant something Verity couldn't understand. For a long moment, nothing seemed to happen, aside from the drip-drip of blood onto the stained wooden floor and the odd humming of their words. Then a shadow began to form on the far wall, growing deeper and darker each moment. A shadow that looked eerily like the one Arden had thrown that poor man through when he'd tried to attack her.

A man stepped out, too tall for the room, and the room grew colder. His skin was purple, deep and rich like a plum. The peak of his brow was lined with scales that appeared to Verity like an evil crown around his long, black hair. His entire body looked sharp and dangerous, like a knife, and shadows emanated from him.

Fear shot through Verity, deep in her core, but she knew this moment was important. If she ran, it would do nothing to end the death and destruction outside the church walls.

"Are you not enjoying the chaos out there?" the demon asked. His teeth were daggers.

"You either need to kill that witch or get ready to move our business elsewhere," snapped Pastor Woolfe.

The laugh that came from the spirit sent a ripple of terror down Verity's spine. "You've misunderstood the agreement. I offered you power in exchange for blood. I didn't offer you my obedience. Your great-grandfathers bargained badly when they made the deal. If you want more than the ability to influence your people's minds, I'll need more than a few witches every few months."

Verity had heard enough.

The people she had trusted with her life and the lives of her community were so unconcerned with them that they'd abandon them to ply their magic somewhere else. And to deal with a demon! Wasn't that the very thing they accused all of those dead *witches* of? That they hated Arden for?

Verity snuck back up the stairs, venom in her heart.

Everything was a lie. *Everything.*

She had tried to give them grace. To let them prove their good intentions and repentance to her. Perhaps, she had thought, there had been more to the story than what she had seen. More than anything, she had wanted to know that the people who had governed her town were not evil, not truly. People could be so many different things all at once, like all her neighbours outside, who were complicit in the deaths of so many, but were still good people. They'd been compelled; that was all. They could change.

But no.

She had come into the church to reason with the pastor, but there he was, bargaining the lives of everyone she knew to a spirit who enabled their devious ways. How much of her life had been formed around the wants of those monsters? How much had she suffered for nothing? The church—how many lies had been woven into it? Was her religion real? Her god? Was *anything* in her life *real*?

Her mother had died at their hands, *and for what?*

Verity stood at the top of the stairs in the empty church and let her rage guide her hand. As shadows loomed outside the windows,

as homes burned and people died, Verity put the door back over
the hole to the basement. She walked to the lectern and opened the
compartment inside. She'd seen the pastor use it a thousand times.
Inside were all the tools of his trade, but she was looking for the glass
jars of rendered oil. She took both in her arms and brought them
back to the false floorboards. Unscrewing the first, Verity poured the
oil in an enormous puddle over the door, watching it spread.

Her mind numb and so full of screeching violence, Verity picked
up one of oil lanterns, climbed the dais, and threw the open flame at
the slick of oil.

The lies had to stop.

If she killed them, the lies *would stop.*

The lantern shattered and flame shot across the oil so rapidly
that Verity came back to herself for a moment. Guilt and shame
knocked at the doors of her mind, trying to pierce her consciousness.
She knew this was right, however. She knew she was doing the right
thing, maybe for the first time in her life. How many people had died
at the hands of those men? Their three deaths would save so many, in
this town or the next.

As flames shot up the walls of the church, Verity walked out of it
for the last time.

CHAPTER TWENTY-TWO

Arden

Arden felt a beautiful freedom in letting go of the restraint she had shown all these years. As she fought off the small mob of people around her, she found herself not thinking of the fighting as much as she should have. She wasn't revelling in it, not exactly. They were mice and she was a mountain lion. It wasn't a fair fight. At best, the town was made of blacksmiths and woodcutters with strong arms and angry dispositions. No one posed any threat to her magic, especially as Dalic stood sentinel and the Gloam and its scarecrow tore apart anyone it wanted.

She had warned them. She had warned those people for years, as her mother and grandmother had before her, that if they *ever* came for her, she would tear them to pieces.

It hadn't even been difficult.

And so her mind, during all that blood, was on the people who had been lost.

Her mother, who had died young from the lonely, strenuous life of midnight midwifery and tearing off pieces of her soul.

Her friend, whom the village had burned when they discovered whom the girl had been spending her time with.

The people who would be alive if they'd had a doctor who *listened*.

One life after another that hadn't needed to be sacrificed, but had been all the same. And for what? For a stupid god and a rigid way of life and ideals no one could live up to. For greed and dishonesty and apathy.

The night lit up in a vibrant, violent shade of orange. Arden turned to see the church enveloped by flame. The fire lit up the stained glass windows, shot up into the spire, and licked its way toward the clouds. It went up so fast, like a campfire doused in lamp oil.

It was peculiar enough that the building had spontaneously caught fire, but the people were more curious than even that. The fighting waged forward between the spirits and the town, until it didn't.

One moment the villagers were at war, and the next, they weren't. Those people, the ones who were most desperately under the thrall of their leaders, stopped in their tracks, their heads craned up to the sky. Each of their mouths opened and the night was overcome by their screams. Long, unending cries. A market square full of motionless people, bellowing a death howl toward the heavens.

It went on. And on.

Arden put her hands over her ears and pressed hard, trying to drown it out.

All at once, it stopped.

"What in the seven hells?" Arden whispered.

Individuality set in all across the square. Tears. Whimpering. Confusion. The people didn't know where they were, let alone why they had blood on their hands.

How could so much have changed so quickly? Who—?

"Please, listen!" a strained voice called out from the platform.

Arden turned to see Verity there once more, arms outstretched, pleading.

"I know you're confused, but please, end this madness! Pastor Woolfe, Mayor Hart, and Doctor Raam have held you under their power and made you do unholy things! They made deals with demons! It is not your fault. But they are dead and it's over for all of us. Friends, put down your weapons! Arden, call off your spirits!"

As confused as anyone else, Arden looked at Dalic. It was possible she hadn't actually harmed a soul yet, and she began to back away, giving the burning church a wide berth. The scarecrow stood stock-still, frozen with a deadly arm craned in the air. As for the Gloam, it was occupied; it gnawed on the fresh corpse of...someone. It would want another, she was sure, but it would buy her time.

Arden approached the platform. "What do you mean, *made deals with demons?*"

Verity opened her mouth to answer, but before she could get the words out, a shadow rippled behind her, suspended in the air.

A purple man stepped out from the black puddle and brushed off his shoulder. "One of you killed my devotees. I'm going to need to know who. They were extremely valuable to me, and I've invested decades into that arrangement. You can't just buy devotees like those at the market."

Arden approached the platform and held her hand out to Verity. The girl wrapped her hand in her sleeve and took Arden's, using the support to climb to the ground. Arden looked up at the spirit, assuming he must have been Verity's demon. "And who are you?"

"Elithiaz, good lady." He gave a dramatic bow. "You must be the wood witch I've heard so much about. You stink of spirit magic."

"I am she," Arden said, refusing to flinch under his gaze. "If you're a spirit, why haven't we met?"

Elithiaz picked something out from under his nails, unconcerned. "I come from the old world. So much greed and violence wrapped up in their religions. When their ancestors came to this new place, it was a perfect opportunity to create my own corner of the world. Worked out fantastically, in fact. Until now."

"And you gave them what? The ability to control minds?" Arden glanced about, taking stock of the square. The Gloam, no longer under attack, was still contenting itself on bodies—something Arden didn't have time to feel guilty about—and the villagers had stepped back to the edges of the square, most of them sobbing or in shock, leaving room for whatever came next.

"Oh no, nothing so complete. Simply the chance to persuade them." Elithiaz pushed his hair back over his shoulder, giving her a pitying smile. "Influence. Charisma. They could have used it to create a utopia, if they'd wanted. Persuade the town to work together in harmony." He gestured to the scene around them. "But humans so rarely take a righteous road."

"How generous of you, giving them the power to kill whoever they wanted. With someone else's hands, no less." Arden shuddered. "All the people who were burned, for nothing."

"For me, Arden. They burned them for me." Elithiaz rose and walked slowly toward the villagers who had remained bound to the witch-burning poles. He slipped a finger under one's chin, and the girl began to weep. "These men you hate so much, they kept me full of life. It's not so big a price to pay, is it? A few little witches, here and there."

"You monster!" Verity stepped out from behind Arden, her face flushed with rage. "You killed my mother. You killed everyone we loved!"

Elithiaz shrugged. "I didn't kill anyone. You did. All of you did."

"We did nothing!" Verity pressed toward him. "We were given no choice!"

"Hush." Arden put her hand on Verity's shoulder, but the girl continued.

"No, I will not hush! All this time! All these lies!" She turned around to look at her neighbours. "Are you not tired of this? Tired of losing the ones you love? I know you've just awoken to this, but we have lost *so much*. Will we all stand here and let this demon go unpunished for the suffering we carry?"

Arden had to give it to her: Verity was getting good at speeches. Perhaps the town already had its next pastor.

A murmur rose around them, the expressions of the people varying from confusion to rage to fear. One by one, the bravest came forward.

"My sister is dead," said one.

"My cousin was burned because of that demon," said another.

"I don't want to go back under a spell," said yet someone else.

Two men came to stand at Verity's side, and Arden saw the resemblance between Verity and her kin.

Elithiaz rolled his eyes. "You're threatening *me*? Your hands did the killing, not mine. And there's not a thing you can do to me. If I wished to leave, I could be gone in a cloud of smoke and none of you would have any power over it."

"I have power." Arden was the only one who did, in fact.

"You have what spirits gave you." Elithiaz moved back to Arden, raised a finger in the air, and gave it a twirl. "And what they give can be taken away."

Arden's stomach lurched. Something tore at her insides. It rose up from her stomach and into her throat, choking her. The taste of metal coated her tongue. As she gagged, the strange, sharp pain rose until it was nearly in her mouth. It wouldn't come any further.

She couldn't breathe.

Something forced her mouth open and black mist poured out of her throat. It was thick and tasted of death and ash. She tried to get it out, to pull at it with her fingers, but it wasn't something that could be touched. It seeped out of her, drifting off into the air and gathering above Elithiaz's palm. It circled there, an undulating ball of power that had come from her.

Elithiaz watched the smoke float in his hand, a satisfied grin on his face. "A witch without magic. I wonder how confident your threats will be now?"

He couldn't just take her magic, could he? Most of what she'd had belonged to the Gloam, and that mist—she tried to summon up a snap of flame on her fingers. Nothing. Something was missing in her chest, gone from the very core of her. She felt diminished. Weak. Each of the cuts and bruises along her body throbbed, and she wondered how much of her ebbing endurance had come from the bond between her and the Gloam.

"You filthy—"

"Ah ah," Elithiaz interrupted her. "You'd best watch your mouth. One of us has power here. And it isn't you." With a flick of his wrist, the spirit summoned up a burst of wind that hit Arden in the chest at full force.

Arden's knees wobbled. She teetered, her body giving out from under her. She fell. Before she hit the ground, Verity caught her by the middle and held the witch halfway up as if she were a ragdoll.

Arden had already been beaten and bruised unlike any other time before. She was missing all but a few magical tricks her other patrons had gifted her. Certainly, she had nothing powerful enough to defend herself. The world had come crashing down on her.

For the first time in her life, she *knew* she was powerless.

Dissent was rising behind her. Utterances that turned into cries.

I'm not going back to sleep!

No more lies!

Arden saved my daughter!

And mine!

Long live the witch!

"Lord above," Verity muttered. "Long live the witch. Look." Her hand tightened on Arden's shoulder.

Arden's dress was torn. Verity's fingers were pressed against the witch's skin.

And nothing had happened.

No shock. No burn.

What had changed?

Verity's expression went from one of confusion to one of pure clarity. She set Arden gently on the ground and approached the platform. "Perhaps I was wrong, lord."

"Wrong?" Elithiaz raised an eyebrow at the girl.

"Yes. I was angry about being used and controlled, but perhaps..." She moved toward the stairs up to the platform, making her way to him. "Perhaps the secret is to be the one in control." She stopped a few paces away from him as the crowd looked on. "What would it cost to have the power you gave the pastor?"

A raucous cry rose up among the people still stupid enough to have stayed in the town centre.

"No." Arden's throat was raw, and the word barely escaped her lips as she struggled to right herself.

Elithiaz was not impressed. "You're still a child. You won't have the prowess for it."

Arden pushed herself to her feet, her body screaming at her. "No, don't. Verity, you can't. You can't trust him, you—"

"Neither of you knows anything about me." Verity's voice had turned hard and angry. "I'm capable of so much more than anyone knows and I am sick to death of living in lies. I could build that utopia. I could turn this place into a town of generosity and pure morals. I could make them live in peace with each other."

"You would kill your neighbours in return for this peace you crave?" Elithiaz asked.

Verity nodded, staring him deeply in the eyes. "The cost would be so little to pay for a life free of lies and constraint."

The town clearly didn't agree, their voices of dissent fighting to be heard, one on top of the other. They were pressing in against the platform, pushing Arden into the base of it. She wasn't strong enough to fight back.

Holding his free hand out to Verity, Elithiaz smirked. "If you're willing to pay the price, come and claim your power."

Verity stepped forward. "I'm ready." She reached out a hand, tentatively hovering her palm over Elithiaz's. She took a breath, and her other hand shot out to grasp the ball of black mist in the spirit's other hand.

The world went white.

Arden was thrown onto her side, the explosion whipping her into the bodies of the people behind her. She was on the ground, mixed in with the other bodies. She tried to scramble up among the limbs, her vision swimming with light. Her eyes struggled to regain their sight, despite the burst of light having disappeared as quickly as it had come. The platform was charred and smouldering, and neither Verity nor Elithiaz were standing where they'd been a moment ago.

Frantic, Arden looked around. The world spun around her. Her vision returned slowly, white dots floating over everything. "Verity!" Arden called out, crawling across the rocks and gravel. "Verity!"

She couldn't see her—could hardly see *anything*—and the girl wasn't responding. Verity had known, somehow, had pieced it together so *quickly.* Arden had been too slow to realise that whatever existed inside Verity was opposed to the power the Gloam had given Arden. Since she'd gotten to know her, Arden had thought that small, pious, worried young woman had had promise. When the moment came to act, she had done so without a hint of apprehension.

And for all that, Arden couldn't even find her.

Dead, alive, or somewhere in between.

"Verity!" At some point, Arden had started crying.

The ground began to quake, emanating from behind her. As she turned, the smoking, blackened shape of Elithiaz rose from the ground behind the platform. His whole body heaved as he took one panting breath after the other. His shape was blotted in place by her slowly recovering vision, but she had a distinct feeling he was done pulling his punches.

With a crouch and grunt, Elithiaz leapt into the air, landing a few steps from where Arden was lying. Up close, she could see the blood pouring out his nose and the wide, cracking burn on his hand where Verity had touched the magic.

"You and your *fucking pet*—" Elithiaz took a strained, hissing breath. "—are *dead.*"

Elithiaz grabbed Arden by the neck and hoisted her off the ground. His claws dug into her skin, threatening any second to pierce her. She wanted to speak, to say something snide and distracting— something that might buy more time—but she could hardly breathe.

Instead, she strained to get purchase on his hand, struggling to pry his grip from her throat. She dug her nails into his skin and dragged, but it hardly seemed to bother him. Her gasping breaths were getting harder and harder to come by. She'd known she'd die someday—though she'd always thought it would be because of the Gloam—but it was suddenly imminent. A matter of moments.

She wished she'd had more time.

She wished she'd spent more time on her freedom and less time on hate.

Somewhere out there was Ilyana, who she wished she could hold, just one last time.

She didn't want to go.

For a moment, she thought she could hear her mother calling her home.

Blood trickled down her skin, pain sparking under her jaw, the world darkening at the edges—

Warmth sloshed over her in a thick wave and everything holding Arden aloft disappeared. She fell, crashing into the ground in a heap, a great, lancing pain running up her spine. One more pain among many. The square had erupted into screams. She was wet and bruised from the fall, and her throat was so raw she wasn't sure she could speak. When she wiped her eyes, her hands came away soaked in blood.

Towering above her was a pair of void-like black eyes attached to a scarecrow, chewing open-mouthed on the severed head of the spirit Elithiaz.

The rest of him was sprawled out next to her, blood pooling out beneath his body.

Arden had paid the price over and over, saving up favours for a day she had known would come. The Gloam and its minion had saved her life and the lives of everyone in the village. Everyone that was left, at least.

Too numb to be put off by the sight of the Gloam's feeding, Arden sat up and watched. She had no idea if the beast had eaten its fill that night, but none of them could afford for its hunger to grow any larger.

Arden took a breath and worked up the courage to speak. When she did so, it burned like no other pain she'd ever experienced. "Thank you for coming to my aid tonight. Even with our bond ripped away. You have done enough. You should take this last prize and rest. You have my eternal gratitude, old friend."

The scarecrow chewed, lazily side to side as a cow would, staring at her with those black pits. It swallowed, and after a moment, the shape of the scarecrow collapsed in a harmless pile to the ground. The Gloam stood over it, its form shifting like mist, wolf-like one moment, bear-like another. Then it grabbed what was left of Elithiaz by the gut and leapt into the night with its meal.

CHAPTER TWENTY-THREE

Verity

When Verity woke, she had a new definition of the greatest pain she'd ever felt.

Noise filled her world. People screaming, barking orders, boots on stone, the crackle of flames—so much noise. Her body, already bruised and cut open, felt numb compared to the burst of pain anchored in her leg. She had—yes, she'd been thrown by the light when she'd touched the ball of magic, and she'd been knocked unconscious by it, but—

Verity opened her eyes, terrified to see what had happened after.

People surrounded her. Were touching her. She couldn't see past them, could barely feel their hands through the screaming pain in her leg.

Lifted. She was being lifted up by the shoulders, her arms slung over the sides of two people, and in front of her...

Silver hair. Red, so much red. The face came into focus. Arden.

The witch's hand came up to touch Verity's face, to cup her cheek in her palm.

"It's going to be all right," the witch said, and Verity fell back into the black.

It was a week before Verity felt well enough to leave her bed. A week of fevered dreams and moments of consciousness. Someone had fed her soup. Her sister, she thought. Her brother had brushed her hair, and Arden had hovered over her, mending her wounds and washing her body. Or she had dreamed it all, perhaps. Between the moments she knew were real and the dreams she knew weren't, she remembered bits and pieces.

Conversations about her state of health, and of unrest in the town, and of time running out.

Her father was asleep at her bedside when she came to properly. Verity woke and her vision was clear for the first time since the town centre. The blur was gone from the edges of everything, and she wasn't immediately tempted back into sleep. She was still tired in her bones, yes, but this time she would fight to stay awake.

Verity opened her mouth to speak, but she did nothing but cough. Her throat was so dry. The sudden violent noise startled her father awake.

"Merciful God, Verity." He held his chest, bent over. "You scared the shit out of me." He grabbed a cup off the nightstand and held it out to her. "Drink."

She sat up against the headboard and did just that, and the water was the best thing she'd felt in ages. Her parched mouth soaked it up and begged for more, so she held the cup out to be filled. Jona poured out more from the pitcher and Verity drank it greedily.

When she'd drained the second cup, she stopped and held the cup in both hands, as if to anchor herself. "How long have I been in bed?"

"Six days. Almost seven." Jona took the cup from her and set it on the nightstand. "How do you feel?"

Verity took a moment, discovering it for the first time on her own. Underneath the blankets, one of her legs felt thick and abnormal. It throbbed, and Verity pulled back the blankets to see what lay underneath. Her leg was wrapped in thick material that was hard to the touch, and positioned between two slabs of wood. A splint.

"Is it broken?" she asked, fear catching in her throat.

"No, no. Thank God, no." Jona took her hand in his, squeezing tightly. "The witch—Arden…she says you've torn something. Badly, she says. It was blue and purple underneath, and she says you'll be fine but she wanted to keep you still, to be sure."

Verity blinked. So she hadn't dreamt up Arden's visits. "You let her in the house?"

Jona opened his mouth to speak, but couldn't seem to find the words.

"What?"

"She's been here each day, before she goes off to the next person who needs help." He let out a breath. "A lot has happened while you've been asleep, Verity."

At her insistence, Jona prepared the wooden crutches they'd borrowed for her eventual return to the world, dressed her, and helped Verity out into the wreckage of Arrothburg. She listened as he told her about what had happened in the time between.

"The people are divided," he began, walking slowly beside her as she got her bearings. "It was decided collectively that the town would take ten days to recover before attempting to move forward. It…there was too much to do. Injured to tend to and bodies to bury. Missing people to mourn. None of us were in any state to be making choices about who will govern this place. Especially not with the church gone and everyone's faith in shambles…"

Jona's voice faded at that, and he stared out ahead, lost inside himself. Verity took the reprieve to look deeply at the town around her. As they got further from their own home toward the edge of town, and closer to the place where everything had happened, the damage was more dire. Stains in the dirt. Broken wood in the streets and holes in the walls of homes. A lingering scent of smoke in the air.

"Who leads them now?"

Jona cleared his throat. "No one, not officially. One of the butchers rang the bell the day after, demanding someone organise things. And he was right, of course. We had no idea how many people were injured or where food was going to come from…People stepped up. Whoever wanted to, whoever could. It was decided we'd have a town hall in ten days. We could make sense of things then, together."

"In ten days?" Verity asked. "That's…three days from now?"

"Three days, yes."

Verity was forced to slow her gait even further as they approached the centre of town. The ground was littered with scraps, broken items, and pools of darkly stained dirt. Debris was scattered across the square, and the remnants of the would-be pyres were still piled up on the broken platform in the middle. A half-full cart sat nearby, heaping with scraps of homes, broken brick, and shattered pots. Three men ambled around, gathering what they could in an unhurried pace.

Why bother being in a rush? she thought. It would take weeks to clear everything out.

Longer for the blood to be washed from the streets.

In the distance, something creaked and groaned. Verity looked for the sound, and found it emanating out of the burnt husk of the church. "Have they found the bodies?"

Jonas turned to look in the same direction, as if puzzling out whom she was referring to. "Oh. No, they haven't. It's too dangerous to go inside, and even if it wasn't…I'm not sure anyone wants to. People are angry, Verity."

"At me?" Anxiety curled in her gut.

He put a hand on her shoulder. "Not all of them, no. Some people are hanging on to what they did as if it were the right thing to do all these years. I think it's easier to do that than admit what evils they were part of. Others, they're happy to be free." He pressed a kiss to the top of her head. "Grateful to have a chance to start over."

Verity looked up at her father. His face was lined with worry, the dark circles under his eyes deeper than ever. This affection from him felt misplaced. Not foreign, exactly. He'd had moments of gentleness with her over the years, especially before her mother had died—had been killed, she reminded herself—but it felt abrasive. It gnawed at her. She hadn't forgiven him yet for the things he'd put her through. For the nights in the cold and the disbelief and the years of holding her close to the threat of the pyre. She loved him, yes, and she would be a long time in forgiving all those sins.

But, in no position to fight or flee, she let him stay close. She would need the support in the coming weeks as she recovered, and in the days leading up to the town hall. If the town was going to decide its fate, she would be there to say her piece.

CHAPTER TWENTY-FOUR

Arden

Arden had never been inside Arrothburg's town hall before. On any normal day, the wooden building would have been a fine size for any gathering, but she doubted any meeting had been as popular as the one that night. From her seat on the stage, Arden looked down on the crowd of hundreds, all packed in as tightly as they could get. The seats had been given to the injured, the old, and the pregnant. The windows and doors had been thrown open to fight off the stifling heat of hundreds of bodies crammed into the space. Heads bobbed outside the windows as well, with dozens of people straining to hear what was going on inside.

She sat on stage with four men. Verity's brother, Asher, sat near her, and Samson the butcher stood at the podium. Those two had been reasonable people by any estimation, while the merchant and the wealthy churchgoer had held tightly to their fear of her. Plenty of people understood the complexity of the matter, and were ashamed of what they'd done over the years, but many still saw her as devil-spawn. Having killed some of their friends certainly didn't help. She'd done her best to make up for it, despite the cynical voice inside her that said not to bother. It didn't matter to her critics that she'd swallowed her pain and pride to heal as many of the hurt as she could. She'd worked herself raw for days, but it did nothing to tip the scales. Some refused to see the control their old mayor, pastor, and doctor had had over them, and how it had threatened her life.

Nuance was often too much to ask.

It hardly mattered to her. Even with her bond with the Gloam ripped out of her by Elithiaz, she instilled enough fear in them that no one had yet attempted to lay a hand on her.

Arden looked out over the crowd and found Verity. She sat toward the front, her crutches tucked between two chairs, staring back up at Arden. In the three days since she'd woken, the two women had discussed this moment at length. It was an opportunity for things to be different. A chance to start over. This was the moment to push for change. There might never be another.

The loud thwack of a mallet on wood rose over the noise in the room, startling more than half the attendees.

Samson the butcher stood behind the hall's wooden lectern and cracked the mallet again. His thick grey hair and beard obscured most of his face and neck, and his tattered, well-loved beige coat did the same for most of his body. "Order! Shut your fucking mouths, all of you!"

Arden grinned. She *really* liked that man.

The room quieted, and Samson cleared his throat. "You all know why we're here today, but first things first. If none of you can keep quiet, this isn't going to work. We've appointed representatives up here to speak for the majority of the concerns of Arrothburg. There'll be questions, aye, but save them until we ask for them. We need new leadership now, not in three weeks' time after you've all said your piece. If you understand me, raise your hand."

Hands shot up around the room in as much consensus as an assembly that big was ever going to get.

"This is going to be a fair procedure," Samson continued. "Everyone will have a chance to speak and to raise their concerns. Before we start, a round of applause for the people who've been doing what needs done in these last ten days. You're all tired, we know that, and we're grateful to you all."

The room clapped generously.

"Right, that's enough dillydallying." Samson put a hand on his chest. "I'll be making sure things keep moving today." He pointed at the representatives on the stage. "These are the people speaking for most of you today. I expect you've had words with them recently enough, but it bears repeating. Jimmy, who speaks for the church. Waldren, who speaks for the market businesses. Asher, who speaks for the labourers. And Arden, who speaks for herself."

A murmur of disdain and confusion was evident. Arden only gave them a disinterested wave.

"Jimmy, why don't you start."

Jimmy stood, wiping off the front of his finely tailored suit. He was well-kept, perhaps too much so. The majority of the room seemed to be tired, many of the onlookers covered in the dirt of a day's toil, and it was hardly even noon. In contrast, Jimmy seemed well-rested and full of unearned pride.

"After speaking with many of you, I'm certain that as a community, we can overcome what's happened in Arrothburg. There's an invested interest in rebuilding. Founding a new church with a new pastor. Someone the community trusts. I and others like me wish to establish this as soon as can be, including providing you with a makeshift place of worship for the time being." He took a breath and held his hands behind his back, looking out over the crowd with smug confidence. "A community without God will turn to sin, and we must maintain order. Put things back the way they were."

Someone in the crowd let out a long, jeering boo, and Arden snickered.

"Hush now," Samson warned. "We're going to hear them all out, and we'll decide on things once it's all out in the open. Waldren?"

Jimmy took his seat, and Waldren stayed where he was, looking out over the crowd with his elbows on his knees.

"The market's in shambles, and I think it's an opportune time to focus on growing this town into a place of commerce. Come spring, we could be ready to start producing some of the finest foods and goods around. Bring in more money. Be more self-sufficient. Anyone interested in that should see me when all these repairs are over and done with. Under my guidance, and with a small contribution to its construction, we could turn Arrothburg into a thriving market for anyone around. Money is king, after all, and—"

"Fuck off, Waldren!" someone outside cried out. "Fucking penny-pincher!"

The room burst into laughter, perhaps for the first time in a while. Waldren shook his head and didn't bother to keep talking. The man appeared to have a reputation.

Samson cracked the mallet again. "No interruptions, I said. Even if he *is* a penny-pinching money-grubber. Asher?"

"Yes, all right." Asher stood, worrying a brown hat in both hands. "I think things ought to change around here, and I'm proposing that we keep on as we are now, until spring at the very least. People have lost their homes or their family members, and we need to lean hard on each other. I think the exchange of money ought to be paused until after the cold season, and every family should get what they need without any obstacles to that. And some families are better off paired up to take care of each other and all the chores involved on the farms. Our people should always come first, no matter what impropriety or sin this would all lead to." Asher looked at the floor

215

a moment, catching his breath. "People are going to die if we don't work together this winter. The crops aren't half harvested yet and this has ruined some of our stores. No church or coin should be more important than that."

A smattering of applause sounded around the room as Asher sat back down.

"Good man, good man. And Arden, what have you got for us?" Samson asked.

Arden stood, eager to see what her words would bring to the crowd. "I propose something altogether new. Some of you know me and have known me for a long time. While you burned witches and threatened my life, your wives, daughters, mothers, sisters—and even a few of you men—came to me in secret. Your women are in pain. If you know at all, you haven't cared. Haven't believed them. Many of you—even the ones Doctor Raam treated—are alive because of me. Who here is brave enough to admit I healed you when no one else would help you?"

Arden waited, and one by one, dozens of hands went into the air. The crowd looked at their neighbours, shock written on their faces, as they came to terms with how many sinners sat among them.

"There are more than that. I know your faces. I see you sitting here, protecting yourselves. At least fifteen of you haven't put your hands up. If that many of you needed help, why would you all go on pretending it's otherwise? My dream for this town is to be rid of the church as it was. To give all of you access to the herbs that would treat your wounds. To train some of you to do what I do, so that there's always access to a healer, no matter if I am here or not. I propose a life where women are done sleeping in the cold during their monthly bleed, where you all are taken care of, and where no one else is burned."

The noise in the room cascaded into a hundred discussions at once. Some people were yelling toward the front of the room, while

216

others were talking with the people nearest to them. The noise was deafening.

"Quiet down!" Samson's mallet hit the lectern over and over, until the room eventually calmed. "The representatives have said their peace. *One at a time*, we'll be taking comments. Hands up if you've got something to say!'

Dozens of hands shot into the air.

"You."

A man in grass-stained field clothes spoke up. "I won't be staying anywhere that there's no church. It's not right to have a godless town." Voices rose up in support, but it hardly extended to the whole room.

The man sat and another stood to take his place. "My family and I did just fine without a pastor. We have our faith, but we didn't like what was going on around here, and we were right to be wary. I'd be just fine to burn fewer of my neighbours if it means bringing God into my home instead of my church."

Another round of scattered applause.

A woman stood, her face full of anger. "I don't want God in my home if it means no medicine for my daughters. One of mine will be a woman soon and I can't have her sleeping cold in the winter because of it. I did it all my life and that fate will *not* be for her."

The response to that was distinctly one-sided, many of the women standing as they clapped.

And on it went for a while, one voice raising a concern and another countering it. Some believed in Asher's idea to be liberal with the food stores and helping hands, while others countered that it would lead to financial ruin for the whole town. Some asked for medicine for their hurting families, while others reminded them that addling their bodies was a sin. The only consensus was that there *was* no consensus. And none of them were terribly keen on following a witch.

Arden wasn't worried, not in the slightest. Verity hadn't spoken yet, and they were letting the town get their emotions out before they put their plan in motion.

At long last, Verity picked up one of her crutches and stood. "I propose we follow Arden's lead."

The clamour rose again, and Samson called for order. "Let the woman speak!"

Verity waited patiently until the noise died down. "We clearly have a large difference of opinion here. Some of you wish to remain as fervently devout as you've been in the past, despite how red your hands are. I spoke with a fair many of you in the last three days, and plenty of you are carrying guilt and remorse in your hearts for what's happened. People died because our leaders led us astray, and *some* of you realise that. Many of you do not, and you stand here, willing to lead us back into the dark. Each of us must follow the path we feel is right, but I cannot knowingly live next to anyone who had a hand in burning my innocent mother on the pyre if you carry no regret. If you cannot repent, in my eyes, you cannot stay in Arrothburg."

Joy leapt in Arden's chest as the room burst into chaos. The voices tore through the air, attempting to be heard over every other, people screaming their throats raw. It was impossible to make out who felt what, but the rage on their faces was clear as day.

Arden stood, raised her arms above her head and clapped once. The motion pushed a wave of air through the room, silencing the crowd.

Jimmy had been content to observe until that point, but started to stammer. "You—you're not supposed to have magic anymore. The demon took it out of you!"

"The *spirit* did." She smirked at him, then looked out over the crowd. "The funny thing about deals with spirits is that you can always make new ones. Ones that better serve your current circumstances. If this town is no longer a threat to me, my deal with the spirit who cut all your people down is moot. It was taken out of me, and I feel no need to ask for it back. However, there are always spirits willing to act as a new patron for a capable witch."

She waited for her threat to settle over the crowd. No one interrupted her.

"So here is how this will work." Arden walked toward the edge of the stage. "You are free to do as you please. If you wish to stay and participate in the reformation of Arrothburg, you may." She gestured at Asher. "If Asher's proposal sounds appealing to you, you are welcome to stay. If you're content to live with witches and perhaps even learn to be one in order to serve your neighbours, you are welcome to stay. If you believe in a future where your women are warm and loved, where medicine is available, and your families are safer, you may stay. Even your god may stay. But the past goes. Anyone who can't root the pastor's words out of themselves, who can't tear the hate out of their hearts, must leave. I don't care where you go, but you won't be staying here."

Samson opened his mouth to speak several times, having a difficult time landing on his words. "But this—this is a vote. You can't just decide the future of the town for all of us!"

"You can't do this!" Jimmy bellowed.

Another clap of Arden's hands and a burst of wind, more forceful this time. The room stilled again. "I can, and I will. Arrothburg will vote when the culling is done. You're all being given a choice about your leaders and your future. Your first choice is simple. You must choose to do right by yourself and your neighbours, or you must leave. There will be no debate on this. I have no interest in leading this place, but I won't tolerate a return to the dangerous place this town once was. I have the power to break anyone who resists, and I will, if you force my hand."

Verity was staring up at Arden, a broad smile on her face.

"You have a week to decide. Two weeks to leave, if you're going. Don't let the door hit you on the way out."

EPILOGUE

Verity

Three Months Later

Some ground had the right to remain desecrated.

Winter had long since come to Arrothburg, but it never stopped Verity from holding vigil on her stump outside the lot of land that had once held the church. It remained a burned-out husk of its former self. The fire had lit up the night and much of the wood had crumbled to ash. What hadn't burned had been left there, jutting up into the sky in charred, snow-covered blackened pieces. No one had touched it since the fire, and if Verity had her way, no one ever would.

It was a symbol of the darkness that lay at the centre of their village. To erase it would be to forget the crimes that all of their hands had committed, even if they had not *all* committed them with their hearts.

The village, no matter how things seemed to be healing, would carry that night with them for a long time. Some of her neighbours carried it to the graves of their loved ones. Others carried it in their dreams. Some carried it on their shoulders everywhere they went, day and night. And while the town had devised moments and places to talk about such things, it would never truly be enough. How could someone unburden themselves of something that was seared into their minds like that?

It felt like a permanent wound to the heart to find oneself complicit.

Verity's family had told her many times that she didn't need to sit at the church each morning; it wasn't necessary to torture herself that way. But she felt it brought her clarity. When she stared into the distance, thinking with that wreckage in the view, she could tease apart the things that had brought them to their lowest and what must come next.

It didn't help that she had killed three people in that church. That was something her family couldn't truly grasp. No matter how right it was, no matter how free it had made their village, she had still killed people.

She had human blood on her hands and she was sure it would never come clean.

The village was starting to wake around her, signalling that it was time for her to stop pondering and get to work. Her neighbours had grown used to her sitting on her perch and knew better than to bother saying hello as they passed, not until she had finished and risen. But as she rose, she grabbed the wooden cane that rested next to her and used it to push her way to her feet.

Walking was easier than it had been only two months ago. Her leg had taken its time to heal, made worse by Verity's refusal to rest for any length of time. Even Arden had fretted over how it would heal. Verity was impatient with it, but the way she saw it, a temporary cane and some discomfort were a small price to change everything.

Besides, with her moon cycle, she'd been practising pain all her life.

The *good mornings* and *hellos* began as she made her way across the square. Life had always been quieter in the winter, but plenty of her neighbours were still around enjoying the crisp air and helping keep the streets clear of snow. Winter was hard work, after all, and it would take them all to get through it.

The platform in the centre of the square had been torn away. They would be burning no more witches and had no more need of it. As the sun rose that day, three young deer played in the snow, leaping in circles around an antlered woman in a deer pelt. Human children played there as well, some listening to Ilyana's stories before they ran off to school.

It was a beautiful sight, and one that Verity wasn't sure she'd ever get used to.

When Verity climbed the steps of the town hall, it occurred to her again that she'd spent her life outside of it. She'd had no business there before, especially as a woman. Even months after the burning, Verity had trouble reconciling that idea. She'd become a leader, something she had never set out to be, but a part of her soul was too tired to do anything but participate.

So much had changed in their village, and yet there was so much left to unravel.

The others were already inside the hall when she opened the door. Six in total. The air was warm, a fire crackling on the far side of the room, and Verity was glad for it. Though it was rare in recent days, the cold sometimes made her injured leg ache in the muscle, something she was advised would go away with time. That was well and good for her, since she had pain enough each month to contend with. Her moon cycle was roiling in her body at that very moment, and the growing pain in her gut reminded her that it was time for tea. The worst of it had come and gone, the stuff that kept her home and in bed. The tea did what it could, and worked some days better than others, but it made those weeks bearable.

As she hung her cloak from one of the hooks on the wall, she removed a small cheesecloth of herbs from one of its pockets and made her way to the fire.

"Good morning, friends. What have I missed?" Verity stole a cup and kettle from the top of the mantel, the kettle still steaming and half full. She poured water over the herbs and brought the concoction to the table with her, where her chair sat waiting.

Asher slid a piece of parchment in front of Verity. The chicken scratch all over it showed a muddled process of ideas and rejections, with more sections crossed out than left alone. "We're still working on the edicts."

Hector, a man Verity's father's age, sat back in his chair with a huff. "Clawing through the Good Book and deciding what to keep might be the most frustrating thing I've ever done."

"That you'll *ever* do, most likely." Verity skimmed the list. "Is there debate over *a crime against one is a crime against all* being kept as law?"

"Not entirely, but it does leave the definition of *crime* up for interpretation," said Asher. "If we keep that wording, shouldn't we be more specific about what crime means?"

Verity blew on her tea and took a sip. Her leg was beginning to protest. "Can you give me an example?"

"Well…" Asher took a moment to mull it over. "Killing someone is a crime, but what if it's in retaliation to being attacked? Or… Meredith Hudson was here earlier because her husband keeps trying to put her outside while she's on her moon cycle—"

"Still?" Verity's anger rose to the surface so quickly that it startled even her. "This has to be the last time. He can't keep trying to do this to her. It's torture, especially in the winter."

Hector gave a nod. "We sent a couple people over to deal with it. She'll be brought to the Red House until we can get her husband to come around to things."

The Red House had been designated under the consensus of a majority. By their lifelong training, some people felt too uncomfortable to stay at home while they bled. No matter how much Arden and Verity had discussed the lack of danger, some people held on to the story of being unclean. So a home had been converted into a warm, comfortable shelter for those on their moon cycles. Personally, Verity hoped to be rid of it in a few years. People deserved to sleep in their own beds, not be treated like exiles.

"Right," Verity conceded. Breathing deep was hard sometimes, but she did her best to come back to herself. "What else can I help with?"

"Well," started Asher, "Sally and Georgina wish to be recognized as married in the eyes of God."

"Excellent!" Verity leaned over the table, smiling. "How can we make this happen?"

The talking wrapped up at noon, as it always did. It could feel good to work all day on the future of their village, striving for hours to solve everything at once. Unfortunately, too many afternoons had ended with them talking in angry circles. A limit was instituted for their own good.

Besides, after a little lunch, it would be time for Verity to make the trek into the woods.

Verity opened the door of her home to a small commotion. Winter was a resting season for many people and it meant her father was home a lot more frequently. What she hadn't expected was to find Clarabel standing on a chair, directing their father's actions.

"See, if you add some of this sticky herb and some of the green stuff, it makes the bread nice." She pointed to each ingredient with her wooden spoon.

"How much of each?" he asked. Their father's face flushed as he looked up at Verity.

"Hmm. About this much." Clarabel stuck out her tongue and pinched her fingers together to show a tiny amount.

"I thought you already knew how to make bread, Father." Verity shook her cloak off outside, then shut the door and hung it up. The old scent of bacon and boiled potatoes lingered in the air. She must have been late for lunch.

Jona adjusted his apron. "I thought I did too, but Clarabel decided she had some things to teach me about being in the home."

Verity kissed her father's cheek. "I appreciate you trying."

"Happy to," her father muttered, and a vision fluttered over Verity's sight. Her father taking his frustrations out on a cracked wooden bucket out by the shed. A little lie, but a lie all the same.

Verity smiled through the buzz in her head. He *was* trying, which was better than some of their neighbours.

Two weeks after their town hall meeting, not long before the first snow, nearly a hundred people had packed up their things and made for the next town. Some had deemed Arrothburg too ungodly to remain in, while others couldn't stay without confronting their guilt at every turn. Even for those who had chosen to stay and to try, issues still arose. People who could abide one thing but not another. Many of them refused to live in a place that was training witches on purpose. At least five households were threatening to leave after the spring melt.

Good. Verity had no time to fight with people. Her duty was to make this life the best she could for those who wanted to abide by it.

Making a plate for herself, Verity sat down at the table, giving Clarabel and her father room to work. As she ate, she basked in the gratitude she felt. Things were changing, no matter how many growing pains she was forced to witness. Her family was healing their relationships, and her sister would never know what it was like to sleep in the loft alone.

The door opened behind her, shocking her out of her thoughts.

Asher took off his snow-covered boots, a grin on his face. "Any left for me?"

After weeks of being unable to travel far by foot, Verity deeply enjoyed walking to see Arden. The forest had a different brilliance to it in winter, and with so many making the journey back and forth to the cabin, there was often a path tramped down for her in the snow by those who went before her. The white powder around her bore the tracks of rabbits, and it made Verity smile, knowing that gentle creatures roamed nearby.

When at long last Verity came within sight of Arden's cabin, she found Arden and her students outside, gathered around the fire. The smell of wood smoke was in the air, as well as the faint scent of meat. As she neared, she could make out the lesson of the day.

"Can I choose a patron soon?" asked young Brandon Baker.

Arden shook her head. "We've been over this. Choosing your patrons should come after long, careful thought, and none of you have been learning long enough for that. When I was fifteen, I also felt impatient. I had been practising all my life and my mother still made me wait. In part, it's because what we want when we're fifteen is often very different from what we want when we're twenty-five. If you asked me now, I wouldn't have chosen the Gloam to work with. I'd have turned to someone else. But I made that choice, and most of your bonds will be for life. There are consequences to your choices. It's not fair to have you choose the rest of your life today."

"But Ilyana seems safe to have as a patron." Hope Harkness sat close to the fire, her baby bundled against her chest. "She seems to bear us no ill will."

"Ilyana is docile much of the time, but you forget she represents all beasts. She is as much deer as she is boar and bear." Arden reached behind her, picked up a quartered log and tossed it onto the fire. "She and I have an arrangement of love and physical passion. What do you plan to offer her, aside from pieces of your soul? What are you prepared to do for her until the day you die?"

Verity moved to the fire, catching the notice of three of the seven students. "If I were a witch, I would choose Dalic," she said, sitting down on the edge of the wooden bench.

"There are more patrons than mine, you know. Maybe you could start with your long-lost family." Arden's playful grin was contagious.

"I think I've solved enough mysteries for a long while, thank you." Verity said the words, in part to dismiss the conversation, but she didn't really mean them. Arden had spread the word that a woman was looking for her father among the spirits, but nothing had come of it. Verity was in no rush. She had plenty to contend with inside the town. Besides, while her neighbours were coming to a reckoning about their past, it had come to light that at least a dozen of the residents had children with questionable spirit parentage. She was hardly one of a kind.

Verity took in the circle. Each face was one she knew. Some were young, some a little older, like Hope. Some boys, some girls, and some who had started to waver in between the two—something Arden encouraged with fervour, but that Verity didn't yet understand. She hoped to, someday. What Verity did know, without a shadow of a doubt, was that there would be witches enough in Arrothburg for a long time to come.

It had been Arden who had proposed teaching apprentices. Verity had never thought her to be the type to like children, to which Arden said liking had little to do with it. Someday, Arden would die, and with her would die all the knowledge she'd gathered. She'd also like to retire someday, she'd said, and that wouldn't happen without someone to take her place. It was their hope that these people—some young, some Verity's age or older—would learn and pass on the knowledge to everyone they knew, including their own apprentices someday.

Arrothburg's people deserved to be cared for and kept healthy. Verity had faith that the people around the fire could do that better than Doctor Raam had ever dreamed.

"Will you tell us another story about your mum?" the youngest of the group asked.

"After herb study." Arden bent over to grab a bundle of herbs from the supplies in front of her. "It's more important than anything else you can learn. Our duty means needing to be prepared to help anyone, no matter their injury. If we're not prepared, people will be hurt. They'll die. So we do the hard work of anticipating *anything*, no matter what it—"

"Help!"

A voice came from the trees, catching the attention of everyone present. Arden stood, trying to get a better look.

Gladys Agnew was panting as she ran to the treeline and stopped for breath. "Robert burned himself halfway up his chest! Can you help?"

"Brandon, get my bag." Arden gestured toward the cabin. "Up, up, everyone! No herbs today, it seems. Lucky you. Follow Mrs Agnew back home and you can observe. I'll be right behind you."

Verity stood, intending to follow the excited bunch back to the village.

"Oh no, I don't think so." Arden spoke something long under her breath before Verity could argue. A moment later, an enormous stag wandered toward them, docile as could be.

It wasn't the first time Arden had summoned her a ride back to the village, so Verity didn't complain as Arden held out a hand and helped her mount the stag. Part of her hoped to be fully healed soon, but she still relished the excitement of the ride.

"Dandelion." Arden held on to the stag's antler, keeping it in place. "A sky spirit spoke with her kin, and she has an idea about your father. Someone we should speak to."

Excitement and fear blossomed in Verity's chest. This was hardly the first piece of information they'd gotten, and if it was a false turn, it would be one of many. Still, she allowed herself the joy of it. If this wasn't the spirit who would lead her to her past, then someone would be, someday.

"Arrange it," Verity said, grinning from ear to ear. "I want to know." She passed Arden her cane and hugged the stag's neck, having learned quickly she should hold on for her life.

"Are you ready?" Arden asked.

"Have I ever been?" Verity laughed.

And as Arden took off, running through the snow, the stag bolted into action behind her. Verity held on tight, bouncing to the rhythm of its hooves. The wind whipped her hair, throwing her hat from her head. She glanced back to look for it, but it was likely gone until spring, lost in the snow. It would be there waiting when the thaw came.

Maybe by then, everything they knew would be different.

Book reviews are key to supporting the work of indie authors. Please consider rating and reviewing This Too Shall Burn. Your honest reviews help books find their perfect audience.

If you want the latest news about upcoming books by Cat Rector, join the mailing list at catrector.com.

Thank you.

AFTERWARD

If you have gotten anything from this book, I hope you've learned to trust your gut about your health.

Verity is a fictional character inspired by a variety of women in my life. At the time of writing this, I'm nearly 35 and have already gathered a collection of women and queer friends and family who knew that their body was misbehaving, and no one would listen. It was a theme song playing in the background every year of my life. It wasn't until my late 20s that I started to hear it clearly and understand what it meant. People who had suffered from treatable diseases, mental and physical. People who hopped from doctor to doctor, begging for help.

People who died because that help came too little too late, or not at all.

We're brought up to believe that doctors will know. They will understand and they will help. And I do have faith in doctors. Many work tirelessly to give inhuman amounts of care, especially post-pandemic. They're tired, overworked, and understaffed. And sometimes you will also have to fight a doctor tooth and nail for the tests you need.

Women and queer people have been fighting for that help since long before the myth of hysteria, and we'll be fighting for it long after. If you're in pain, trust yourself. Advocate for yourself. Make them listen.

ACKNOWLEDGEMENTS

This is the book that grief wrote.

2022 was one of the hardest years of my life, and that wasn't the plan. I was prepared to return to the country I grew up in, see the people I loved, and begin thriving. Instead, I was challenged in ways that I didn't anticipate, starting almost the second we landed. I didn't get a chance to breathe.

This book was written between crises and is full of the rage and pain of the year. It was written while watching people suffer, especially those lacking the resources to relieve that suffering. I spent time thinking of the women and queer people in my life who can't access proper physical and mental healthcare. I poured myself into books about medicine and psychology, looking for solutions, because if I could just become as informed as a university-trained doctor, maybe I could fix it myself.

It shouldn't be like this.

All that said, I had a small team of people who kept me moving forward this year.

First and foremost, Jessica. More than anyone else, you were the person who held me tight or slapped my hand, whichever I needed at that moment. You braved things that should never have been asked of you. There are no words to express the gratitude I have for you and for the stability that you provided when I could hardly stand on my own.

Vincent. This wasn't what you signed up for, and you did your best to learn on your feet. We'd planned to use this move to grow together, and instead, I often left you to persevere on your own. Thank you for sticking it out, for understanding when I had to put my attention elsewhere, and for supporting me in the moments when you couldn't understand why I was still putting myself through the wringer. You've worked so hard this year to fit into this new life, and I hope that 2023 becomes our year of celebration.

Sheridan. What started as a random buddy read turned into a deep and fulfilling friendship. You met me at a very tumultuous time, and I'm so grateful for the patience you've had with my wild personal stories. You're such a kind and generous person, and I know you have amazing things ahead of you. The world needs more people like you, and I'm blessed to call you a friend. I'm so excited to see where life takes you.

To Dal, Erin, Tanni, and the dozens of early readers who helped make this book the best version of itself, thank you. During this book, I was in deep need of your help to guide the pieces into place and to see where I had gone astray. This story collects so much hardship between two covers, and it was only through your care and guidance that it has become what it is. Thank you.

And to you, the reader. If you resonate with this book, I'm sorry. I wish it was a set of stories that no one resonated with, ever. But trauma happens and demands to be felt. Healed. I hope that for some of you, this story has made you feel heard. I hope that you force people to listen. You deserve people who have the best interests of your mind and body at heart. There are enormous communities who believe you. Keep fighting. You matter.

FURTHER READING

Fiction

The Yellow Wallpaper - Charlotte Perkins Gilman
The Edge Of The Woods - Ceinwen Langley
Slewfoot: A Tale of Bewitchery - Brom

Witches in Western History

Malleus Maleficarum - Heinrich Kramer
Unobscured Podcast: Season One
Medicine Women: A Pictoral History of Women Healers - Elisabeth Brooke

The History of Women and Medicine

Unwell Women: A Journey Through Medicine and Myth in a Man-Made World - Elinor Cleghorn
Doing Harm: The Truth About How Bad Medicine and Lazy Science Leave Women Dismissed, Misdiagnosed, and Sick - Maya Dusenbery
Everything Below the Waist: Why Health Care Needs a Feminist Revolution - Jennifer Block
Witches, Midwives, and Nurses: A History of Women Healers - Barbara Ehrenreich and Deirdre English

Books on Health I Found Personally Useful This Year

The Wisdom of the Body - Hillary McBride
Being Seen: One Deafblind Woman's Fight to End Ableism - Elsa

Sjunneson

No Bad Parts - Richard C. Schwartz

Burnout: The Secret to Unlocking the Stress Cycle - Emily Nagoski and Amelia Nagoski

What Doesn't Kill You - Tessa Miller

Everything Isn't Terrible - Kathleen Smith

Come As You Are - Emily Nagoski

Maybe You Should Talk to Someone - Lori Gottlieb

Vagina Problems: Endometriosis, Painful Sex, and Other Taboo Topics - Lara Parker

Ask Me About My Uterus: A Quest to Make Doctors Believe in Women's Pain - Abby Norman

This Is Your Brain on Birth Control: The Surprising Science of Women, Hormones, and the Law of Unintended Consequences - Sarah Hill

CONTRIBUTORS

Edited and Proofread by Ivy L. James
authorivyljames.com
Twitter.com/AuthorIvyLJames
Instagram.com/authorivyljames

Cover Art by Grace Zhu
gracezhuart.com
twitter.com/gracezhuart
instagram.com/gracezhuart/

Scarecrow Art by Evangeline Gallagher
Evangelinegallagher.com
instagram.com/evangelinegallagher

Cover Text, Interior Formatting and Design by Cat Rector

MY SUPPORTERS

As an author, it's impossible to have a career without the support of amazing people. This list represents a collection of readers and colleagues who have gone above and beyond to champion my work in the last several years. Some have purchased ungodly amounts of books from me, while others have helped in the reading and creation process. Some of them simply listen to me gripe about never having enough time in the day.

To each and every one of you, thank you. Your support means the world to me, and without you, I wouldn't get to do this amazing job. Sorry I have to destroy your heart all the time, but if you didn't like it, you would read something cuter I guess *BIG SHRUG*

Rowan Liddell

Kaea Branch

LotteH

Carballo

Gabriela Florea

Jolien Nijns

Cheyenne Brammah

Allie B

Casey

A.J. Torres

Lisa H.

Aleksander E Petit

Alex Rae

Tanushka

Fem Lippens (loonieslibrary)

Erin Kinsella

Tanni

Amanda Diegan

DC Guevara

Michaela

Dina B.

Mireya

Vanessa R.

Brinley

Audrey

Matías Ruelas

Analiza

Becca Leigh

E. L. Pagès

fi

Suzanne Fraser-Martin

Nox T.

Lien drst

Esther

Elisabeth

Hannah Decock

Jules

Aiden

Cath

Alice

Rachel Kasparek

Alicia Ann

Tessa Hastjarjanto

Brea Helgard

Ash Helgard

ABOUT THE AUTHOR

Cat Rector grew up in a small Nova Scotian town and could often be found simultaneously reading a book and fighting off muskrats while walking home from school. She devours stories in all their forms, loves messy, morally grey characters, and writes about the horrors that we inflict on each other. After spending nearly a decade living abroad, she returned to Canada with her spouse to resume her war against the muskrats. When she's not writing, you can find her playing video games, spending time with loved ones, or staring at her To Be Read pile like it's going to read itself.

This Too Shall Burn is her fourth book.

Find her on Twitter, Tiktok, and Instagram at @Cat_Rector
Or visit her website, CatRector.com